Annabel Du Boulay has a BA degree in English from the University of York and an MSc degree in Socio_____ _____ of Economics, where her post-gradu_____ in which patriarchal religion has n_____ order to control women in societ_____ of her first novel *The Serpent's Tale*_____ therapist specialising in the use o_____ storytelling to facilitate healing and transformation. _____ workshops, talks and runs a private practice in Glastonbury, Somerset, where she lives with her husband and children.

To learn more about the writing of *The Serpent's Tale*, the issues the book explores and to join the discussion forum, please log-on to www.belashka.com.

Dearest Asth

but my love & blessings

from Avalon

lol & x.

The Serpent's Tale

Annabel Du Boulay

Belashka Books

First published in Great Britain 2009 by Belashka Books
trading name of Belashka Ltd
1 St John's Square, Glastonbury, Somerset BA6 9LJ
books@belashka.com
www.belashka.com

British Library Cataloguing in Publication Data
A catalogue record for this book is available from the British Library

ISBN 978-0-9562986-0-7

Typeset by www.theoldchapelivinghoe.com
Printed and bound in Great Britain by CPI Cox & Wyman

The cover is a photograph of a fourteenth-century mural in the Church of All Saints,
Little Kimble, depicting the hair torture of Saint Margaret. The photograph on the
spine is of Sapientia, or Wisdom, holding a serpent, from a stained-glass window
in Ogbourne St Andrew church, Wiltshire. All photographs © Nicholas Du Boulay,
except that of the author © Stefan Zabal.

Both biblical quotations have been taken from
The Revised Standard Version of the Bible

Mixed Sources
Product group from well-managed
forests and other controlled sources
www.fsc.org Cert no. TT-COC-002063
© 1996 Forest Stewardship Council
FSC

Author's Note

At least 60,000 wisewomen were tortured and killed during the European Witch Trials (1450–1750). The Roman Inquisition was a system of tribunals developed by the Roman Catholic Church (or Roman Church as it was then known) during the second half of the 16th century, responsible for prosecuting individuals accused of heresy, including sorcery and witchcraft, mainly in Italy and Malta.

Although *The Serpent's Tale* is set in the 16th century, the social issues it explores, such as the subjugation of women by patriarchal religious doctrines; violence against women, including abuse, rape and torture; and maternal mortality, remain endemic in our global society as the following statistics from www.womankind. org.uk (2009) reveal.

Domestic violence causes more death worldwide in women aged 15–44 than war, cancer or malaria

1 in 3 women worldwide are beaten, abused or raped

1 in 4 women worldwide are beaten while pregnant

1 in 7 married women worldwide are raped by their spouse

1 woman dies every minute from pregnancy related causes, most of which are preventable

5,000 women worldwide are killed in *honour killings* each year for 'crimes' such as trying to leave an abusive marriage

2 million girls worldwide are forced into marriage each year

6,000 girls worldwide are forced to undergo female circumcision each day

Acknowledgements

I would like to thank the following people: Moira 'Nora' Allen and Joseph Frederick Dunk for inspiring my love of storytelling; the Coiro family for their kind hospitality during four summers in southern Italy, where I first came to know the Madonna at her chapel; Professor Eileen Barker OBE for her academic supervision; Professor Melissa Hines for her support and guidance; Carolyn Proctor for her wisdom and teaching; the staff at Herts Mind Network, especially Carol Harris, for never judging; the inspirational survivors of abuse, domestic violence and mental health difficulties I have had the privilege of working with as a therapist; the late Zoe Schwartz, my raven; the many Goddess-loving people I have journeyed with, especially Elin Hejll-Guest, Koko Newport, Kathy Jones and my fellow priestesses in the Orchard of Avalon; the numerous medical professionals who treated my daughter Sophia, especially her surgeon Harry Ward; Kate Bowder and Kate Woodmansee for childminding; Keith Campbell, Helen Gumbleton, Joanna Perry, Rosie Thompson, Zoe Wigan and Lucy Willmore for their comments on preliminary drafts; literary agent Lucinda Cook of LAW for her comments on two drafts; Mary Sheaf for her extensive comments on the penultimate draft; Mary Breen at Womankind for help with statistics; Caroline and Roger Hillier for typesetting and cover design; my family and friends for their love and support, especially my parents Peter and Patricia Allen, who also commented on several early drafts; my husband Nicholas Du Boulay for being my soul-mate adventurer on the journey of life and always believing in me, and for the cover photographs; and my daughters Sophia and Jasmine, for shining their light into the dark corners of my soul and teaching me the true meaning of freedom.

Annabel Du Boulay, 2009

I am indebted to the following works, consulted during my research, which are recommended for further reading:

Ankarloo, Bengt & Henningsen, Gustav, eds., *Early Modern European Witchcraft: Centres & Peripheries*, OUP 1993

Armstrong, Karen, *The Gospel According to Woman*, Fount 1996

Ashe, Geoffrey, *The Virgin: Mary's Cult & the Re-emergence of the Goddess*, Arkana 1998

Bachofen, J J, *Myth, Religion & Mother Right*, Princeton 1992

Begg, Ean, *The Cult of the Black Virgin*, Arkana 1996

Baring, Anne & Cashford, Jules *The Myth of the Goddess*, Penguin 1993

Daly, Mary, *Beyond God the Father: Towards a Philosophy of Women's Liberation*, The Women's Press 1986

Eisler, Riane, *The Chalice & The Blade*, Pandora 1993

Engelsman, Joan C, *The Feminine Dimension of the Divine: A Study of Sophia & Feminine Images in Religion*, Chiron 1994

Gimbutas, Marija, *The Language of the Goddess*, Thames & Hudson, 2001

Gimbutas, Marija, *The Goddesses & Gods of Old Europe*, Thames & Hudson, 1996

Ferguson, Marianne, *Women & Religion*, Prentice Hall 1995

Grimassi, Raven, *Italian Witchcraft: The Old Religion of Southern Europe*, Llewellyn 2000

Hamington, Maurice, *Hail Mary? The Struggle for Ultimate Womanhood in Catholicism*, Routledge 1995

Haskins, Susan, *Mary Magdalen*, Harper Collins 1994

King, Ursula, ed., *Religion and Gender*, Blackwell 1995

Matthews, Caitlin, *Sophia Goddess of Wisdom: The Divine Feminine from Black Goddess to World-Soul*, Thorsons 1992

Powell, Robert, *The Sophia Teachings: The Emergence of the Divine Feminine in Our Time*, Lantern Books 2001

Roper, Lyndal, *Oedipus & The Devil: Witchcraft, sexuality & religion in early modern Europe*, Routledge 1994

Russell, Jeffrey, *A History of Witchcraft*, Thames & Hudson 1980

Schaup, Suzanne, *Sophia: Aspects of the Divine Feminine*, Nicolas-Hays 1997

Starr Sered, Susan, *Priestess, Mother, Sacred Sister: Religions Dominated by Women*, OUP 1994

Warner, Maria, *Alone of All Her Sex: The Myth & the Cult of the Virgin Mary*, Picador 1990

Sjoo, Monica & Mor, Barbara, *The Great Cosmic Mother: Rediscovering the Religion of the Earth*, Harper Collins 1991

For my daughter

Sophia Mary

whose courage in the darkness brought forth
the light of wisdom

The word
'philosophy'
comes from the Greek word
philosophia
meaning
'a love of Wisdom'

Family Trees in Santa Sofia

La Famiglia Galletti

Bernardo Galletti (1469–1531)
m. Lora Galletti nee Pancetti (1485–1521)

 Paolo Galletti (1506–1554)
 m. Francesca Galletti nee Croce (1509–1574)

  Enrico Galletti (1530–)
  m. Caterina Galletti nee Lorini (1554–)

   Paolo Galletti (1577–)

 2 children deceased

 Agnesa Gamba nee Galletti (1515–)
 m. Michele Gamba (1499–1545)

  Emilia Cesi nee Gamba (1535–)
  m. Luigi Cesi (1532–1573)

   Lora Cesi (1561–)

  Angela Gamba (1537–1576)
  & Piero Dini (1523–)

   Luca Dini (1563–)

La Famiglia Orsini

Roberto Orsini (1490–1558)
m. Cicilia Orsini nee Perosio (1494–1565)

——— Maria Colombe nee Orsini (1514–)
m. Bartolomeo Colombe (1512–)

——— Cicilia Lorini nee Colombe (1534–1554)
m. Guido Lorini (1527–1575)

——— Caterina Galletti nee Lorini (1554–)
m. Enrico Galletti (1530–)

——— Paolo Galletti (1577–)

——— Giorgio Colombe (1538–)

——— Dionisio Colombe (1541–)
m. Cristina Colombe nee Pitti (1548–)

——— 3 sons

——— I daughter Fiora (1577–)

——— Elena Colombe (1548–)

——— Lucia Orsini (1518–1579)

——— 2 children deceased

——— Donata Conti nee Orsini (1526–)
m. Zanobi Conti (1523–?)

——— Rafaello Conti (1550–)

——— Lorenza Dini nee Orsini (1530–1558)
m. Piero Dini (1523–)

——— Veronica Dini (1558–)

La Famiglia Lorini

Niccolo Lorini (1481–1537)
m. Caterina Lorini nee Grassi (1494–1552)

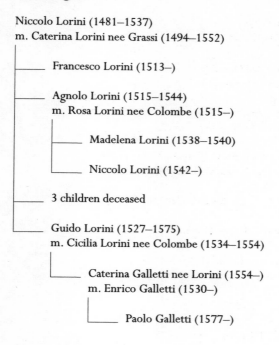

Francesco Lorini (1513–)

Agnolo Lorini (1515–1544)
m. Rosa Lorini nee Colombe (1515–)

Madelena Lorini (1538–1540)

Niccolo Lorini (1542–)

3 children deceased

Guido Lorini (1527–1575)
m. Cicilia Lorini nee Colombe (1534–1554)

Caterina Galletti nee Lorini (1554–)
m. Enrico Galletti (1530–)

Paolo Galletti (1577–)

The Mother's Tale

15 August 2008

The Festival of the Assumption

The Island of Gozo, Malta

I watch her now, skipping among the ancient stones of the temples, her eyes alight with the joy of the present, a smile of forgetting on her lips. It is tempting to join her abandon, but to remember is to transform the future. To dive deep into the shadows of the past and gather the wounded, fragmented parts of our story, is to reawaken to life.

Some say these temples on Gozo were built eight thousand years ago in the shape of a mother goddess and her daughter. They are the oldest free-standing temples in the world, the birthplace of the harvest myth, later written down by the Greeks in their myth of Demeter, Black Goddess of the Harvest, and her daughter Persephone, the Maiden Kernel.

I have come here this August to celebrate nine years of journeying with my own daughter Sophia. We have brought our harvest dolls, made from corn grown in the fields around Glastonbury, where the mystical Isle of Avalon is said to rise up out of the waters of the Summerlands.

I call to her and she comes to me, leaning her fragile body against my chest. I close my eyes, breathing in the familiar smell of her hair and skin, and allow my mind to wander back through the mists of time. I see myself stuck in a prison of depression and addiction, constantly seeking the high yet stumbling closer and closer towards death, trapped in a spiral of self-destruction.

Until, one day, she came to me. A babe nestling in my womb, bathing me in her healing light, with the hope of a life worth living. And in loving her, I began to nurture myself and to grow strong.

And then I see her birth and how blue she is, but the doctor says she'll be fine once I've fed her. So I offer her my breast and she starts to suckle, but then her head falls back and she stops breathing. I'm screaming for someone to help my baby, and they take her from me, running down the corridor to intensive care. But it's not until the next day, after I've watched her being resuscitated over and over, that they discover she has no oesophagus, no tube which my milk could flow down into her stomach. Instead, my milk filled her lungs and drowned her.

She needs life-saving surgery but it's Sunday and there are no surgeons available. Time is running out, she should be dead by now, her lungs clogged with her own saliva, but her tiny feet are still kicking. A warrior born from the light to save me from the dark. So they put her in a mobile incubator and we take the lift down to the waiting ambulance which will transfer her to another hospital. But just as we're pushing her incubator out of the lift, the doors slam shut and become jammed. An alarm starts to sound. For a moment, I don't understand what it's for. Then I hear the quiet, reserved consultant screaming for help. My babe's stopped breathing again, that's why the alarm is sounding, but the nurse can't open the incubator to resuscitate her because the lift doors are stuck. So now I'm screaming too. And three angels, three salt-of-the-earth London lads, stop and wrench the lift doors open, pulling her incubator into the entrance foyer. And there, amid the chaos of doctors, patients and visitors milling around, the nurse calmly opens the incubator and resuscitates my baby. I never knew their names and I never saw them again, but that day, some strangers came into our lives, saved my daughter's life and changed mine forever.

And now I see us waiting in my hospital room as the surgeons perform life-saving surgery on my daughter. Four hours of not knowing if I would see her alive again. Four hours of my mother recounting story after story to distract us from the waiting without knowing, a mother finding strength from deep within to support her daughter. A journey I was just embarking on, little knowing that ahead of us lay a further nine operations, countless hospitalisations and endless days of screaming pain. But that night, the only thing I cared about was that my baby lived. The call came to go down to neonatal intensive care. Our hands were shaking so much, we could barely press the lift button. We walked into the room where her incubator had been, but there was only an empty space. I felt my heart begin to close, a numbness spreading through my body, as I prepared to face her death.

But now her surgeon's walking down the corridor, tearing off his green surgical hat, and smiling. "She made it. She'd reached crisis point just as we made the first incision, but we managed to save her." My mother sobs into my father's arms, while I smile like I've never smiled before. My baby's alive. That's all that mattered. Life had never felt so good as it did in that one moment of time.

A few days later, I was sitting by my daughter's incubator, listening to the hiss of her ventilator and the rhythmic beeping of the machines, when a nurse came in. I hadn't seen her before. She was older than the others with Mediterranean skin. "Can't you sleep?" she asked, her eyes warm with compassion. I shook my head. "How are you?" I shrugged my shoulders and avoided her gaze, ashamed of the anger I now felt. As if able to read my mind, she put her hand on my shoulder. "You know, it's very normal to feel angry when your baby's ill." We both stared at the incubator.

"Is it?" I asked. "At least I have a child. I should be thankful."

"And you are, but she is suffering. It isn't easy to accept."

"No. It isn't," I said, watching my baby's chest rise and fall with each hiss of the ventilator keeping her alive, a bloody, stitched scar carved across the pale silk of her skin. Then I looked up at the nurse. She was so like someone I had once known in Italy. Short and plump, with strong, maternal arms used to carrying the weight of the family. The child in me wanted to collapse into those arms, to be held tightly and told that everything was going to be alright. That my baby was going to survive. That I would wake up and this would all be some terrible nightmare. "You remind me of an Italian lady I once knew," I said.

"Ah, Italia, my homeland," she replied, smiling with fondness. "Have you been there?"

"Yes. I spent many summers in a village just north of Naples."

The nurse's face lit up. "I too come from Southern Italy. The land of the Black Madonna."

"Yes," I said, looking at her with interest. "We used to sing chants to invoke her healing blessing."

"And dance so fast until our feet bled."

"Spinning around and around," I added, and we laughed until I caught sight of my daughter's limbs twitching in pain and my eyes filled with tears. "I just don't understand."

"Understand what?" the nurse asked.

"The Black Madonna. I thought she was supposed to be the divine Mother, healer and protector of children. If she really existed, why would she allow my baby to suffer?"

The nurse remained silent for a while, then settled herself into the chair next to mine. "Why don't I tell you a story while I'm on my break?" There was nothing else to do. "It is a story my grandmother told me when I was a child. 'Rosetta,' she used to say, 'never forget the old storyteller's words for they will serve you well.' And, you know, Nonna was right." I stared at her intrigued as she began to tell me her story.

The Nurse's Tale

15 August 1999

The Festival of the Assumption

London, England

As I mentioned, I am from Italy. I was brought up in San Lorenzo, a small village high up in the Apennine Mountains. I can still picture it now after all these years. The cluster of whitewashed houses clinging to the ridge above the valley; the snow-capped peaks glistening in the moonlight; the smell of wood smoke on a cold winter's night; and the sound of laughter carried on the breeze through the window of the *taverna*.

When my grandmother was a child, a *veglia* was still held each month. The villagers would gather around the fire in the *taverna* at the full moon to hear the retelling of their stories. You see, it was their way of keeping the memory of their customs and beliefs alive. First they would tell fairy tales to the younger children to teach them right from wrong. Then they would entertain the older children with heroic stories about their ancestors. And when the children had fallen asleep, they would take turns retelling the old folktales until the fire had all but died away.

There was one story, however, that overshadowed all others. It was a story that had been told to my ancestors in the year 1645. The villagers were gathered in the *taverna* to celebrate The Purification of the Blessed Mother, it being the second day of February. The priests now call it *Candelora* because they bless their congregations with candles and kindle new fires in their churches, but such rituals owe their existence to a much older tradition, as my ancestors were about to discover.

Seated on stools around the fire, the villagers were chatting to one another. Candlelight flickered all around them and on the hearth there were vases of snowdrops and libations of wine, ewe's milk and honey. Suddenly, the door flew open to reveal a strange, old man hunched over the threshold. The men tensed, for in those days the Kingdom of Naples was not a safe place to live. Gangs of robbers and murderers roamed the countryside and strangers were not welcome. "Who are you?" asked the innkeeper. "What do you want?"

The old man peered up at him from beneath heavy eyebrows and pointed to the guitar on his back. "I've come to offer you an evening of songs and storytelling. In payment, I ask only for some warm broth and a cup of wine to chase away the chill." The villagers continued to eye him with suspicion. Removing his fur hat, he patted down his long, white hair and placed the guitar strap about his neck. The room soon resonated with the notes of a well-known Neapolitan folksong. The women smiled and tapped their feet as the children clapped their hands. Confident the stranger posed no threat, the men resumed their discussions.

"Come, Storyteller," said the inkeeper's wife. "Sit by the hearth and I'll bring you something to eat." He bowed his head in gratitude and followed her to the rocking chair by the fire. Then the villagers watched with growing anticipation as he ate his soup while staring into the flames. When he at last looked up, they say his eyes glowed as if they held the very wisdom of the stars.

"Fire is the oldest form of divinity." His gentle voice filled the silence, startling the villagers. "The flame is one of the gateways through which we can enter the place of stillness that lies within, where we can speak to the spirits of our ancestors and come to know their ancient beliefs. It is the spark of wisdom that lives within each of us. Let me ask you, why do you light candles on this feast day?" The villagers were taken aback by the old man's question for it was not something they had ever asked themselves. Rather than be thought foolish for answering incorrectly, they remained silent.

"Allow me to explain," the storyteller continued. "When the Roman Church came to power, it desired to placate our pagan ancestors. By creating feast days on the same dates as their pagan festivals, the Church hoped to convert them with ease. It chose to celebrate the purification of the Virgin Mary on the second day of February because purification rites had been held on this date in honour of the wolf goddess Lupa and wolf god Lupercus. But the ritual lighting of candles and fires held a very different meaning for our ancestors. Instead of celebrating the cleansing of the divine Mother following childbirth, the *Festa di Lupercus* served to reawaken our ancestors' primal nature, which is at its most powerful when a woman gives birth. The filth that needs purging is not the blood of childbirth but the yoke of domestication. On this night, our peasant ancestors cast aside their fears and threw off their shackles of servitude. They ran with the wolves! They ran to freedom!" The children's eyes grew wide as the old man shook his hands in the air before continuing. "The Roman Church feared our ancestors' honouring of the wolf. Peasants with thoughts of power and freedom were not easy to control. Over time, it transformed the wolf into the savage werewolf, companion to the witch, and burnt them in the fires of its Inquisition. But the energy of the wolf continued in the hearts of those brave enough to keep our ancient beliefs alive. Some of whom were once friends of mine." The storyteller broke off and lowered his gaze to hide his sadness.

Then, shrugging off his melancholy, he picked up his guitar. "This is a song dedicated to Sofia. In the Bible she is known simply as Wisdom, but to the Greeks, she was the Goddess of Wisdom, fire of inspiration for philosophers and poets, to whom I give thanks at this time of year."

Sofia, sweet bride,
Maiden of mine,
I can hear your bells
Heralding springtime,
May your fires that burn brightly
Inspire my words,
Bringing forth your wisdom
Into this world.

Sofia, sweet bride,
Lady of springs,
I can feel your breath
Upon the swan's wings,
May your waters of healing
Purify my soul,
And your serpent and wolf
Protect us all.

Sofia, sweet bride
Of the sun and the moon,
I can see your white dawn
Shining through,
As the darkness of winter
Gives way to your light,
May your blessings be upon us
This day and this night.

As the old man sang, the villagers talked among themselves, enjoying the musical interlude, while the innkeeper and his wife went about filling empty cups until the song came to an end.

Then, when everyone was settled, the storyteller resumed speaking. "The story I am about to tell you is a true one. It is founded on events that happened in a village not dissimilar to this one, situated to the south of Rome in the westerly foothills of these same mountains. The year was 1583, when the elders of this village were but young men and women. It was a time when some still honoured the divine Mother. Not the Roman Church's Mother Mary, but an ancient Black Goddess of Wisdom whom they called Sofia. It was their belief in her teachings that gave them the courage of the wolf to stand up to the Church and to discover the true meaning of freedom. No doubt you still hear her whispered words in tales you tell your children and in prayers you dedicate to the Virgin. But these are just fragments of the great light that was doused by the Church Fathers, its embers scattered across the earth. Tonight, kind listeners, allow me to gather these sparks of wisdom and to rekindle the flames that burn a thousand times brighter than the Church will allow Mary's light to shine." The storyteller paused and looked around the *taverna* at the villagers, causing their feelings of trepidation to grow at the same time as their memories were filled with fleeting images of a forgotten past.

Then the old man broke the spell of his gaze and stared out through the open casement at the fullness of the laden moon. "It's time."

The Storyteller's Tale

Wednesday

11 August 1583

The Papal State of Benevento

Perched high upon a hill in the Papal State of Benevento, overlooking the warm waters of the Mediterranean, was the village of San Martino. Upstairs in the *taverna* lay a man called Alessandro. He too was a travelling storyteller but, unlike me, he was in the prime of his life with dark, noble features. As he slept, he moaned in distress. A spirit walked his dreams, blood dripping from the sodden dress that clung to her child's body.

A gust of wind slammed the shutter open, wakening Alessandro from his *siesta*. It was a welcome respite from the vision that haunted him. The sun had set and the air was cool against his feverish skin. Leaning his head against the casement lintel, Alessandro looked out over the mountains. Brushed by the dim light of the waxing moon, the high peaks unfolded before him, hiding the secrets of the valleys in their shadows. The contours of the land beckoned to be discovered and Alessandro knew it was only a matter of time before he left San Martino in search of some elusive fulfilment.

Lighting a candle, he picked up his journal, intent on recording the day's events in poetry or song. Instead, his thoughts drifted to the future and he sought comfort from prophecy. Donning his shirt, Alessandro climbed down the narrow staircase into the bar.

"Alessandro, join us! Matteo has come with news from Santa

Sofia," called the innkeeper Federico.

"In a moment," replied Alessandro, raising his hand to his friend. Instead, he made his way towards the back of the *taverna* and approached a table where an aged woman sat. "Sapia," he whispered. The old lady opened her eyes and stared at him. "I need your help," he continued. "Tell me what my future holds."

Waving a hand at the chair opposite by way of invitation, Sapia began to speak in a low voice, pausing now and again to cough into a rag. "The law of Free Will states that you must choose your own future. I can only warn you of things that may or may not lie ahead." Alessandro nodded and placed a coin in Sapia's outstretched palm. "Look into the flame." Sapia gestured to a candle on the table. As they both stared into the flame, their vision blurred, allowing Sapia's third, mystic eye to see into the wisdom of the void. From within this meditative state, Alessandro heard the wisewoman's words as if from a distant, unearthly land. "You'll travel again. There's a woman in danger. She needs your help. An outcast will also benefit from your friendship. A great evil has come to their village but you can help them. There's a fire and burnings. You must try to stop the burnings but keep the fire alight." Then Sapia blew out the flame, waving her hands through the smoke in a rhythmic pattern.

Alessandro's dulled senses awoke to the sound of laughter and the sweet smell of tobacco. "I don't understand," he said. "What burnings? What fire?"

"You'll know when the time comes."

"Where must I go?"

Sapia smiled at his impatience. "You'll know." With that, she settled back into her chair and closed her eyes.

Frustrated by his lack of answers, Alessandro left to join his friends. The young farmer Stefano, with his head of curls, poured him a cup of wine. "We were just saying how strange it is that the new Bishop hasn't visited San Martino yet."

"Has he been elsewhere?" asked Alessandro.

"He's been making his presence known everywhere," explained the fish-seller Matteo. "I'd imagine he's not yet found a way to haul his fat hide up here, what with San Martino being that much higher."

"I take it he's a large man?" asked Federico, who took pride in being a clear head taller than anyone else in the village.

"The man is a glutton. And that's not his only sin," replied Matteo with a knowing look.

"What do you mean?" asked Stefano.

Matteo looked around the *taverna* before continuing in a low voice. "When I was in Santa Sofia, the wisewoman Maria told me that the Bishop has forbidden the villagers to hold Sunday's festival at the Chapel of the Black Madonna. Instead, he's insisting that their priest Padre Francesco holds midnight Mass in the main church."

"Why?" asked Alessandro.

"Apparently he's heard rumours of a cave near the chapel where witches worship the goddess Diana," explained Matteo. "Padre Francesco told me that the Bishop has moved here from the north where our fellow country folk are being burned as devil-worshippers in their thousands. They say he's a fervent supporter of the Roman Inquisition and intent on ridding us of our heathen ways."

"And he's making an example of Santa Sofia," commented Federico.

"I'm afraid it's not just Santa Sofia," replied Matteo. "I've heard rumours that he's arrested four women and a man from other parishes in the diocese. The Inquisitor from the archdiocese of Benevento has already arrived at the Dominican convent in Arunca to hear the Bishop's evidence against them. If the Inquisitor finds them guilty of heresy, next week could see the first burnings to take place south of Rome."

The three friends stared at Matteo in shock. Federico's wife, Marta, who had been listening to their conversation, approached the table. "But the Inquisitor of Benevento has never found anyone guilty of witchcraft," she said. "He knows that the wise *strega* like Sapia are but healers and fortune-tellers, not devil-worshippers."

Federico drew his wife onto his lap. "Have no fear, Marta. If the burning fires ever made their way to the south, they'd be a revolt of such magnitude no other priest would dare attempt it. I'm sure the Inquisitor won't be swayed by Bishop..?" Federico looked to Matteo for guidance.

"Pazzini," Matteo said. "You can't mistake him. Not only does his girth rival that of a pregnant sow, he also has a long scar running down his right cheek."

Alessandro's chair clattered to the floor. "Pazzini?" The three men looked up at him in surprise.

"Do you know him?" asked Matteo. Alessandro ignored him, heading for the door, as Federico and Stefano followed.

"Where are you going, Alessandro?" asked Stefano.

"To Santa Sofia."

Federico grasped his arm. "Not at this late hour. The mountain paths are treacherous at night. Whatever it is can wait until morning."

"This can't," Alessandro spat through clenched teeth.

Matteo joined them. "Alessandro, you can ride with me at dawn. My journey back to the coast takes me through Santa Sofia." A long pause followed as Alessandro struggled with his urge to leave.

"What do you say?" asked Stefano.

At last, Alessandro turned back. "You're right for there's nothing I can achieve at this late hour."

"Then come, sit down, tell us what's wrong," urged Federico. The friends resumed their seats and waited for Alessandro to explain himself. Taking a gulp of wine, he steadied his hands on the table before telling them his story.

* * * * * *

I've never told anyone why I left my village twenty years ago to become a travelling storyteller. I thought my memories were better left buried, but at last the time has come for the guilty to be brought to justice. Friends, I will tell you my story, for one day I may need your help.

I grew up in a small Apennine village to the north. As a boy of sixteen, I found the routine of farming life monotonous. Daylight hours were spent in the fields, turning the soil or garnering the harvest, but at night I used to lie awake gazing at the mountains, wondering what mysteries awaited my discovery. I wrote down my dreams as poems and songs in a journal kept hidden beneath my mattress, lest my father should find it. A surly man, he hadn't time for artistic pursuits, believing a real man should only concern himself with farming and hunting. My mother agreed with him from fear of the consequences if she disagreed, but I wasn't alone. My grandfather used every opportunity when we were alone together to retell the myths of old and teach me his guitar. I would sit beside him, studying his fingers as he played, purple veins rigid beneath pale skin, nails yellowed with age.

Dearest of all to me was my little sister Isabetta. Four years younger than me, she was everything I wasn't. Working in the fields had turned my skin dark like my hair, whereas Isabetta had the fair colouring of the north, with green eyes that gazed up at me with the innocent trusting of a child. Where I was impulsive and fiery, she was calm and reserved. She would follow me everywhere, listening as I told her of the adventures we would have and the people we would meet on our travels. She believed in me and in my dreams, but such dreams were about to be shattered.

One summer's evening, I returned to the village in the cart that drove the labourers to and from the fields. Heading across the square to our stone house by the lake, I saw my father waiting for me, eyes glaring, jaw clenched. As I approached, he brandished my journal in the air, striking me across the face. My mother must have found it while making the beds and I glanced over at where she cowered, pained by her betrayal.

"How dare you disrespect me writing poetry! Call yourself a man? Hah! I'm ashamed to even call you my son." With another blow to my cheek, he marched inside and threw my journal into the hearth.

"No!" Isabetta lunged towards the fire, but my father seized her arm.

"You knew of his crime?" he bellowed.

"Leave her be!" I shouted and threw myself at him with all the anger and frustration of misunderstood youth, striking at his calloused hand.

"Alessandro, Isabetta, go! Now!" ordered my grandfather. I know that if he had been younger he would have joined us in our stand, but he was infirm and feared for our safety.

Seizing Isabetta's hand, I pulled her free and we ran out of the house and through the alleyways to the woodland beyond, where we sank to the ground beneath a hollow tree to catch our breath. Isabetta cradled my head, stroking my hair until I grew calm. "I know what will cheer you up. Why don't we go swimming in the river? Come on, Alessandro, it'll be fun." A cool dip seemed like an inviting prospect, so I followed my sister down to the edge of a dappled pool surrounded by low-hanging trees. I turned my back to allow her privacy to undress and, once I heard a splash, I too undressed and joined her.

We swam and dived, chasing the fish that darted beneath our feet, until memories of my burning dreams were all but forgotten. Then, in a moment of quiet meditation as I floated on the water, watching the birds soar across the darkening sky and settle on the trees, I caught sight of a figure lurking in the shadows. A head appeared sporting a black hat and a white collar. It was a Church Father hiding among the branches, watching Isabetta as she dried herself on the bank. Outraged, I climbed out of the water, calling to the village priest whom I now recognised. "Padre Rambaldo!"

But the priest hid his lechery beneath a cloak of false virtue. On being caught spying, Padre Rambaldo did not hang his head in shame like a true follower of Christ. Instead, he poured a torrent of accusations upon us. "Satan's bride, most wicked of women, clothe your lustful body and cast aside your devilish desires for your brother." Isabetta screamed as the priest approached, pulling on her dress while I tried to shield her with my still naked body.

"Son of Adam, you have committed the gravest of sins to be so tempted by this serpent. Clothe yourself so that I, God's holy messenger, may not be tainted by your debauchery." We had scarcely donned our clothes when he was upon us. Grabbing us by the hair, he dragged us back to the house, Isabetta sobbing in fear while I seethed with rage.

Pushing open the door, Padre Rambaldo hurled us onto the floor in front of our father. "Domenico, I have always thought you a devout son of Our Holy Mother Church, but now I see you have been nurturing Satan's spawn. I found these wicked children bathing naked in the river, fornicating like dogs!"

"He's lying, Father," I said. "We went for a swim. That's all."

"Now witness how the devil has hold of your son, forcing him to defend his sister so that the Lord of Darkness can continue to suck her paps by night."

"Enough!" exclaimed my grandfather, struggling to his feet, moustache quivering.

"Silence, old man!" shouted my father, pushing him back into his chair. Smothering a cry, my mother ran to comfort him as he struggled for breath, his hand pressed against his chest. Ignoring his distress, my father turned to Padre Rambaldo. "Pray, Padre, tell me what I should do."

"It is your daughter who must carry the blame. She is weak like all women and has succumbed to Satan's embrace. It is she who tempted your son and she who must be punished. From this day forth, she will wear the mark of the devil on her forehead, so that every man who sees it will know she has a serpent burrowing in her loins."

"No!" I pleaded. "Leave her alone! Punish me!"

My attempts to protect my sister went unheeded. Instead, my father and the priest dragged me kicking and bellowing upstairs. From behind the locked door of my parents' room, I heard Isabetta's screams as my father held her down and Padre Rambaldo pulled the iron poker from the fire. Then, with the slow deliberation of a torturer who takes delight in inflicting pain, he held it against my sister's forehead. A long silence followed, interspersed by sobs from my mother and grandfather. Isabetta had fainted from the pain of her burning flesh. Her body was carried upstairs and laid on her mattress, where my mother later tended to her burn.

A long time passed before Isabetta rose from her bed. Something died within her that day. Even when the wound had healed to leave a reddened scar, Isabetta's eyes never shone again nor did her lips curl up in a smile. No one spoke of what happened. My father barked out his usual orders but remained indifferent to his daughter's plight, while my mother wallowed in defeat.

Only my grandfather tried to lift our spirits with stories from a time when our ancestors knew the true meaning of freedom. "Hold fast to your dreams, children. Never let them die nor be destroyed by friend or foe. Find beauty, and where it does not exist, create beauty."

Despite his encouragement, the sight of Isabetta's scarred

forehead caused my chest to tighten with rage so at times I could scarcely breathe. The seeming hopelessness of our lives weighed on me, for the two people who should have protected us had ultimately betrayed us. I could not forgive my father for bowing to the priest's religious authority. Nor could I condone my mother's weakness in not challenging the men who branded her daughter a whore.

Matters were even worse outside the house. I continued to work in the fields, but was now subjected to crude taunts about my sister. Some days I returned to the house with a black eye or bruised cheek to find Isabetta sobbing. The other girls at the seamstress's house where she worked had been ordered to shun her. At morning prayers she was forced to stand before them a fallen woman when she was but a child.

One man in particular began to victimise Isabetta. Jacobo was the third son of a local lord, whose family owned a manor on the hillside above the village. Their wealth had secured Jacobo a priesthood without the necessary training at a seminary, for it had been easy to bribe Padre Rambaldo. Cut from the same cloth as his mentor, Jacobo accompanied Padre Rambaldo as he performed his duties, thereby gaining unquestioned access to the girls in the village.

One evening, Isabetta had been working late to finish a flower girl's dress for a wedding. As she walked home carrying the silk dress, a hard thump to her back sent her flying into the dirt road. Winded, she looked up to find Jacobo grinning down at her just before he kicked a cloud of dust in her face. "Eat dirt, you whore!"

Isabetta arrived at the house in tears holding out the dress, its pale blue embroidery streaked with mud. "What shall I do? The wedding is tomorrow and the dress is ruined."

"You stupid girl!" shouted our father.

"It wasn't my fault, Papa."

"Then whose was it?" he sneered.

"Jacobo. He knocked me to the ground."

"Why would he do such a thing? Jacobo is a man of the Church."

"He called me a whore and told me to eat dirt!" Isabetta sobbed louder at the memory of her humiliation.

"Do you blame him, after the way you've behaved?"

Shocked, Isabetta stared at him before our mother led her into the back courtyard where they spent the evening washing the dress. When my sister at last came to bed, I tried to reassure her. "Don't worry, Isabetta. From now on, I will walk you to work and collect you at the end of the day. If Jacobo tries to hurt you again, he'll have me to deal with."

My sister threw her arms around me. "Thank you, Alessandro. You're the only one I can trust to take care of me. I don't know what I would do without you."

"I'll always be here to protect you, I promise." My words have returned to haunt me again and again.

In the morning, I accompanied Isabetta to the seamstress's house, and at dusk I climbed into the olive tree opposite the gate to wait for her. I saw her following behind the others, carrying a heavy basket. As I leapt down to help her, Jacobo appeared from the side of the house. So engrossed was he with ill intent that he failed to see me approaching. As Isabetta passed by, he stuck out his leg, causing her to fall to her knees and drop the basket.

Within moments I was upon him. Despite him being at least twice my age, Jacobo was an easy opponent owing to his corpulence and my stronger build. I brought him crashing down and sat upon his chest, pulling up his cassock so that his privates were exposed to all the girls, who shrieked with laughter. Even Isabetta could not hide a smile of quiet satisfaction. "If you ever go near my sister again, you'll have nothing to show next time. Understand?"

When I at last let go of him, he ran up the lane stopping once to look back. "I'll get you for this, Alessandro! And your whore of a sister!"

I made to run after him but Isabetta held me back. "Let it be, Alessandro." I did as she asked, but I should have known we hadn't seen the last of Jacobo. In my arrogance, I was convinced that my heroic efforts had taught him a lesson. How wrong could I have been? All I succeeded in doing was jeopardising my sister's safety even more, but should not a brother defend his sister's honour? Even now I do not know what would have been the right course of action, but all my worrying amounts to nothing. I cannot change the past, especially not what happened the next evening.

I broke my promise to Isabetta. Instead of going straight to the seamstress's house, I stopped off at the *taverna* and became distracted watching the men play *tarocco*, the new card game of wands, cups, swords and pentacles. I arrived home to find that Isabetta hadn't returned. "I thought she was with you!" cried my mother, clasping her hands to her face. "Go! Look for her, Alessandro!"

I ran to her place of work but the seamstress confirmed that Isabetta had left at the usual time. I knocked on the door of every girl she worked with, but none of them knew of her whereabouts, until at last I arrived at Serena's house. "Did you see where Isabetta went after work?" I asked.

"No, sorry," Serena replied. I turned to leave, my shoulders stooping in defeat. "But I did see her talking to Jacobo. Perhaps he knows where she is."

"Jacobo!" I cried. Serena stepped back, startled by my angry cry, but there was no time for pleasantries. The pulse at the side of my head began to throb as I ran to the house on the hill. The bell of the private chapel was ringing to signal evening prayers. Led by Jacobo's father, the family were filing into the chapel as I came tearing into the courtyard. "Jacobo!" The family stopped

45

and glared at me. It was then that I noticed Jacobo's right cheek was swathed in a bandage, still seeping with fresh blood.

"Do you know that peasant, Jacobo?" asked his father.

"Your son has been bullying my sister and now she is missing," I shouted. "Where is she, Jacobo?"

Feigning ignorance, his bulging eyes stared at me with disdain. "I have no idea what this vulgar boy is talking about, Papa."

"If you don't tell me," I threatened, "I swear I'll beat it out of you!"

"Hold him!" ordered Jacobo's father, gesturing to the two gardeners standing by. Wiping the smirks from their faces, they dropped their spades and seized my arms.

"If I find out you've laid a finger on Isabetta, you'd better start praying to your God for salvation," I bellowed. Struggling out of the gardeners' hold, I ran out of the courtyard and ducked behind the wall to listen for any clues as to Isabetta's whereabouts.

"What a ghastly boy!" said Jacobo's mother.

"Vultures, the lot of them!" said his father.

"As if Jacobo would hurt anyone. How absurd that a man of God should be accused of such profanity," tittered his mother. "Come, let us pray for strength in our dealings with these tiresome peasants."

Swallowing my fury, I set off, darting along the craggy mountain paths, leaping over rocks and through streams, crying out her name. "Isabetta! Isabetta!" For what seemed like an eternity, all I heard was the echo of my own voice, until at last I stumbled upon a clearing in the woods. A river of water trickled down over a rocky outcrop, forming a clear pool at its base. Reflected on its surface were the branches of the overhanging trees, upon which a flock of ravens had alighted to sing their evening chorus. Below them lay my sister. Isabetta's head and chest were submerged face down in the water, her long hair fanning out like the intricate threads of a spider's web. Her dress was bunched up above her waist, the backs of her legs streaked with red mud from the riverbank.

As I crept closer, my breath trapped in my throat, I realised that the redness was not that of the earth. It was blood. Shocked into action, I pulled at Isabetta's shoulders, dragging her heavy head and chest out of the water. Cradling her in my arms, I brushed her wet hair aside and gazed down at the ethereal beauty of my sister. I remember how cold her body felt, her purple lips stark against her alabaster skin, her green eyes unmoving.

Isabetta was dead.

Throwing my head back, I howled, "No! Isabetta! No!" Then, rocking her corpse in my arms, I wept and wept until I had no more tears to shed. After a while, I became aware of the ravens. Never before had I seen so many gathered together. I watched as they took it in turns to swoop down and dive through the air in a myriad of dancing wings and shrill song. One by one they flew over us and away into the distance, until there was but one raven left sitting high upon the tallest tree. Time seemed to stand still as the bird gazed down at me from its lofty perch. I sensed that its beauty embodied the spirit of my dead sister and I felt myself grow calm, hearing her gentle voice whispering to me on the breeze, "I'm here. Look, I'm free at last." Then the raven flew away, carrying on its wings the purity of Isabetta's soul.

Dusk fell, save for the light of the maiden moon, whose milky tears rained down over my sister's body. Lowering my eyes, I surveyed the bite marks upon her neck and budding breasts, the bruising on her arms and the caked blood on her legs stemming from their apex. It was then that I realised her innocence had been brutally robbed before the water drowned her screams. I knew without doubt the identity of her rapist and murderer. Gathering her body in my arms, I began the long march back to the village.

As I approached the square, candlelight flickered through the shutters of the church and a chorus of voices filled the air, singing a dedication to the Virgin Mary. I strode through the doors, interrupting midnight Mass. All eyes turned and stared in horror as I walked up the aisle carrying Isabetta's bloody corpse. I heard my mother's screams, the cries of my grandfather, but I did not take my eyes from the murderer standing behind the altar. Jacobo flinched as I walked through the door, before covering his guilt in a mask of moral propriety.

"Punching Isabetta was not enough to quench your thirst, was it Jacobo? You had to rape her child's body and drown her in the river!" Silence filled the church, broken only by my footsteps on the flagstones. "Is the devil within you satisfied or has your lust for a virgin's blood grown now you have tasted its sweet nectar?" My voice echoed over the hushed congregation as I approached the altar and lowered my sister's body onto it. Jacobo's bloated face pulsated with a red stain that spread upwards from his neck to meet the bloody bandage still plastered to his right cheek, prompting me to turn towards the shocked villagers. "Ladies and gentlemen, witness for yourselves the redness of Jacobo's guilt, and the fresh wound upon his cheek where my sister tried in vain to defend herself." Turning back, I lunged over Isabetta's corpse and wrapped my hands around Jacobo's throat, intent on strangling every last breath out of him.

Padre Rambaldo began to strike me, demanding I release his apprentice, until my father and uncle pulled me back. "What the devil has possessed you, Alessandro?" he demanded, panting with the excitement of hitting me.

Rubbing his throat and struggling for breath, Jacobo launched his defence. "It is the spirit of his whore of a sister come back to haunt him from the depths of hell!" With a cry, I threw myself at him but the hands about my arms were unyielding. Jacobo puffed out his chest and continued to address the congregation. "Believe me, fellow Christians, when I swear with God as my witness that I have never laid a finger upon this deranged man's sister. As a true follower of Christ, I tried in vain to exorcise the devil from her, but fear I was too late. Clearly the girl was laden with his child and, fearing her fate, threw herself into the river, at which point her death caused her womb to empty itself of Satan's spawn. Hence, the blood we see upon her legs."

"Liar! My sister was a virgin!" I shouted.

"Silence!" Padre Rambaldo's booming voice echoed through the church. "I know Jacobo to be a man of undisputed faith in our Lord Jesus Christ and a true disciple of his teachings. You, Alessandro, are nothing more than a fornicator whom I once caught sucking at the loins of this girl laying before us. In fact, it would not surprise me if the child she was carrying was none other than your own bastard, and in her shame she took her own life. In so doing, she has committed the gravest of sins. Not only the sin of taking her own life before the time God chose, but also that of murdering her unborn child. As a punishment for her crimes, it is only fitting that her rotting flesh be removed from consecrated ground and cast into the pit of hell."

"No! My sister was innocent! Isabetta is innocent!"

"As for you, Alessandro, get out of my sight before I call upon the Inquisition to burn you in their pyres. Be warned that if you ever show your horned head in this village again, I swear on God's Holy Book that you will be tortured to death for your sins."

My father loosened his grip on my arm and I looked at him in disgust. "Are you to say nothing? Does the sight of your own daughter lying raped and murdered not compel you to defend her and fight for justice?"

My father continued to stare straight ahead. "That which the Lord ordains must be obeyed."

"You would believe the word of the devil in Christ's clothing rather than that of your own son and the bloody evidence of your murdered daughter? What man are you to accept the corrupt authority of these hypocrites who hide their own wickedness behind the sign of the cross? If these be the men to lead us to salvation, I would rather worship the devil. It is I who am ashamed to call myself your son."

"Seize the devil-worshipper! By his own admission he dances with Satan. Seize him, so we may watch him writhe at the stake!" Padre Rambaldo collapsed on the floor in a state of ecstatic frenzy. The congregation, terrified by the unfolding scene, reacted to the priest's words like dogs to their master, falling over each other in their attempt to catch me. Taking my chance, I ran along an empty pew and up a side aisle.

I turned back once to see my mother bent over Isabetta's corpse, clawing at her face, her eyes flitting wildly. Her mind had at last succumbed to the madness that stems from a life of injustice, bullying and loss. Instead, she discovered the peace that can come from wandering the path of the insane, devoid of understanding. I sometimes wish my own mind had followed a similar route and then my suffering and pain would have ceased. Instead, I carry with me wherever I go the image of Isabetta's bloody corpse on the altar, her murderer standing over her gloating in triumph. "One day, Jacobo, I will find you and I will have my revenge!" I vowed.

Then, with a last threatening look, I darted through the door to escape the mob that was almost upon me. From there I ran through the maze of alleys that wound their way between the houses and out into the woods. I headed towards the hollow tree and climbed up inside it. From my vantage point, I watched as the villagers scoured the streets for me, flaming torches held high above their heads. I waited until the crowd had at last dispersed, satisfied that I was nowhere to be found, and crept back to the house where I was born.

My grandfather was waiting for me. Beckoning, he handed me a sack filled with provisions. I embraced him, inhaling the smell of tobacco impregnated in his cheeks. I knew it would be the last time I would ever see this wise, old man who had loved me well and nurtured my dreams. "Here, take this, look after it." Tears streamed down his aged face as he pressed his guitar into my hand. "Play the songs I taught you as a child and remember us as it once was. Your old grandfather playing a tune while you and Isabetta knelt at my feet singing. She hasn't gone, Alessandro. She will always be here with us in our hearts. Time will help to heal the pain you now feel."

"Time doesn't heal, Nonno. It simply dulls our memories, so that only with difficulty can we picture our loved ones face or smell their scent, but it will never dampen the rage I feel nor quench my thirst for revenge."

"Listen to me, Alessandro. Now is not the time to seek revenge. You are angry and people make foolish decisions in anger. You must put your sister's murder out of your mind for the time being and get on with your life. When the time for vengeance comes, you will know, but you must be skilful, for there is an art to exacting revenge. Murder is too clumsy. It lowers you to the same depths as your enemy and achieves nothing but more bloodshed. If the avenger is to be victorious, then the abuser must be punished through the proper judicial processes. Go forth, my son. And remember, we will be watching over you always."

My throat ached from unspent tears as I hugged his frail body for the last time, while images of my sister's corpse continued to stab my mind. "What about Isabetta?"

My grandfather drew back in quiet contemplation. "I will see to it that she is buried beneath the hollow tree in the woods beyond, where you played together as children. That way you will always be able to find her. It may not be what the Church Fathers call consecrated ground, but I can think of nothing more sacred than returning Isabetta's body to the earthly womb of our Blessed Mother. As for you, Alessandro, head for the south. They say it is safer there from these priests who accuse us of devil-worship.

Retell the stories of old to those you meet and play my guitar. In this way, you will always find welcome wherever your journey leads you."

With a final embrace, I left to begin my long hike. I didn't look back until I had reached the highest ridge on the mountainside above our village. Stopping to catch my breath, I glanced back down towards the group of stone houses nestling in the valley beside the great lake, but I could only see darkness. The maiden moon lay hidden beneath a shroud of heavy cloud. In contrast, the snow-capped peaks of the mountains to the south shimmered in the distance. That night I began to journey along the paths I had always dreamt of exploring and indeed I have had many adventures along the way. The reality has been different in only one respect. My sister Isabetta accompanies me in spirit alone and I will not rest until I have avenged her death. Now, after twenty years of wandering and waiting, the time has at last come. In Santa Sofia, I will have my revenge.

* * * * * * *

A stunned silence followed the conclusion to Alessandro's story. At last, Federico spoke. "Alessandro, you have my deepest sympathies. The fate of your sister is a terrible tale." He paused before continuing. "Forgive me, though, for I still do not understand what your story has to do with Bishop Pazzini and the village of Santa Sofia."

Alessandro stared at him, his eyes burning with fury. "The name of the novice priest who killed Isabetta was Jacobo Pazzini. If I am not mistaken, the scar upon Bishop Pazzini's right cheek is the same mark left by my sister. Only by travelling to Santa Sofia and lying in wait to see him, will I be able to confirm what my instinct tells me is true."

A collective gasp rose up around the table. "Why waste time

waiting for him in Santa Sofia? Why not go straight to the city of Arunca and have our revenge!" declared Federico.

Alessandro shook his head. "I am grateful for your loyalty, Federico, but my grandfather was right. It would be foolish to act in haste and anger. Murdering Pazzini would not be punishment enough for his crimes. Instead, I must find a way to ensure that he is tried by the same Church in which he hides his evil. If not, I will have failed in defending Isabetta's innocence and her spirit will continue to haunt me."

"What will you do?" asked Stefano.

"First, I will travel to Santa Sofia alone and see how best to avenge my sister's murder. If I need you at any time in the future, I will let you know."

"If that is your wish, Alessandro, then we will remain here, but rest assured that you have an army of men waiting to fight with you," said Federico.

Alessandro stood up and clapped Federico and Stefano on the back. "My thanks to you both, not only for tonight, but for the past year of friendship. Matteo, I'll see you at dawn."

As he turned to leave, Alessandro caught sight of Sapia smiling at him. It had not taken long to discover which village he must travel to, nor which evil he must fight. Only time would unravel the remainder of her prophetic words.

Back in his room, Alessandro gathered his few possessions together in a sack before sitting on his bed to digest the evening's events, his eyes welling in sadness for Isabetta but also in gratitude for his friends' loyalty. Then he picked up his guitar, for music was his only respite when his thoughts were troubled. And he played the song he had written for every young girl who has been robbed of her innocence, left wondering if she was guilty of provoking the crimes against her pubescent body. Above all, he had written it for the spirit who walked his dreams. His sister, Isabetta.

See that young girl,
The unfastened dress,
With her lips bloodied red
And her hair a mess?

I run with her
To the mountain peak
To escape the evil,
The violent and weak.

Climb out of the valley of darkness,
The shadows can only bring pain.
In the skies you will find a healing light
Where the fear of his touch will wane.

Fly high on the wings of a raven
As it soars over your earthly fears.
Take me with you on the winds of change
To where the sun dries our tears.

See that woman,
A whore and a nun,
With her lips rouged brightly
Hair tight in a bun?

I walk with her
Through my dreams at night,
And pray that he'll leave us
Alone in the light.

* * * * * * *

Down the steep mountain path, in the foothills below San Martino, lay the village of Santa Sofia, where a very different scene was unfolding in the upstairs bedroom of a house.

"Lora, calm yourself and listen to me. Your babe is nearly here now. When the pain comes, I want you to push as hard as you can," ordered the midwife Rosa.

"I can't!" screamed the labouring woman, her arms flailing.

"Yes, Lora, you can! You must, else your babe will die."

"Get it out! Get it out!" Lora sobbed in desperation during the brief respite before the next onslaught of pain. Such was her suffering that if someone had handed her a knife, she would have carved open her own belly to deliver the child.

"Caterina, stand on the other side of Lora and place her foot against your hip," Rosa directed her assistant. "Now Lora, push against us. Push!" Another anguished scream rang out as Lora tried in vain to follow Rosa's instructions. "Don't waste your breath screaming, Lora, just pant. Pant!" cried Rosa. The pain subsided once more but the babe was no nearer to being born.

Caterina beckoned the midwife over to the fire. "Rosa, a whole evening has passed since Lora started pushing."

Rosa gave a deep sigh, smoothing her white hair from her damp forehead and wiping her hands on her cotton dress. From her many years experience, she knew that if a young woman as slender as Lora had laboured these two days past to no avail, the chances were she would not live until morning. As she watched, Lora began to thrash less, her screams turning instead to dull moans. Her mind and body could no longer tolerate the pain, and her spirit was already preparing to leave. "Quick, Caterina, go to my house and fetch my herbs. Let us at least give Lora some peace in her suffering."

Caterina ran downstairs, where Lora's mother Emilia and her

grandmother Agnesa were waiting. As usual, they were attired in their black widow dresses with lace handkerchiefs perched upon their tightly pinned hair. The father of the unborn babe was nowhere to be seen. A travelling musician by trade, he had disappeared as quickly as he had arrived, unaware of the legacy he had left behind. The women of Santa Sofia had exchanged many a wry smile over this sorry state of affairs, for Emilia and Agnesa were renowned for their snobbery and unkind remarks. Indeed, they had made Caterina's life very difficult for her since she had married Enrico. On her arrival at the Galletti family's farmhouse, he had demanded his aunt and cousin leave and return to the Gamba's terraced house on the square, only two years after he had allowed them to move into the farmhouse following his mother Francesca's death. Despite it being Enrico's sole decision, Agnesa and Emilia blamed Caterina for the decline in their standard of living, and went out of their way to make trouble for her. Nevertheless, Caterina's heart went out to them in the knowledge that they were soon to lose Lora.

"How is my daughter? Is the babe here? How much longer must she toil and are we to wait?" cried Emilia.

"Lora has laboured long and hard. The babe inside her is large and is unable to pass through her slender frame. It is with great sadness that I must urge you both to prepare yourselves, for there is little more we can do. I am hurrying now to gather some medicine which Rosa will use to lessen Lora's suffering. Perhaps then you would like to come and sit with her."

Emilia clasped her hands over her mouth, then grasped Caterina by the shoulders, shaking her. "What have you done? You and that wicked witch have killed Lora! And her babe still trapped in its warm nest."

Caterina pulled out of her reach. "I beseech you, Emilia, don't look at us as the cause of your daughter's passing. We have done everything possible to save her, and I share your grief for I have loved Lora like my own cousin. The perils of childbirth are known to all and none is more experienced in midwifery than Rosa. Now, let me go and fetch the medicine."

Caterina ran out of the house on the eastern side of the square, leaving Emilia to be comforted by her mother, who mumbled prayers to the Virgin. The deserted square was lit only by the dim light of the moon. Caterina headed south down the main street flagged on either side by stone houses, which seemed to merge together into one amorphous façade of wooden doors, wrought-iron balconies and flat roofs. Opposite a small shrine dedicated to the healing waters of a spring, Caterina turned right down a steep lane that wound past Rosa's house and through the woods to the Chapel of the Black Madonna. Running through Rosa's abundant olive grove, Caterina soon reached the farmhouse and leapt up the exterior flight of stone stairs. Bursting into the first floor room, she startled the man who was seated at the table, studying his books. "Niccolo, Rosa has sent me to collect her herbs."

The man stood up, the likeness between him and Rosa at once apparent. They shared the same brown eyes, although Rosa's flashed with defiance in a way that Niccolo's placid temperament seldom revealed itself. Of small stature like many men of the south, his hair was beginning to grey at the temples, giving him an air of authority. He frowned on seeing the anxiety etched in Caterina's beautiful features. "What's the matter? Which herbs does my mother require?"

"It's Lora. We're unable to deliver her child. She's dying, Niccolo. Rosa has sent me to fetch something to ease her suffering."

"It's not herbs you need, Caterina, but medicine," said Niccolo, reaching for his doctor's bag.

"Now is not the time to discuss the virtues of your medicine over Rosa's use of herbs. Pray, fetch her herbs and bring your own bag if you must, but hurry."

Niccolo acquiesced, driven by his affection for Caterina as well as by his filial desire to protect his mother. Rosa's belief in the ancient art of medicinal healing had caused her son many a sleepless night during the past years of the Inquisition, but until the recent arrival of Bishop Pazzini there had never been any real threat to his mother's life. Now, Niccolo had every reason to fear for her safety. Despite being old and frail, Rosa was still as stubborn as ever and intent on defying the new Bishop.

Running down the stone steps, Niccolo ventured into the main room of the farmhouse. On the far wall, he pulled aside a curtain and pushed open the wooden door that led into his mother's private room. Lighting a candle, he reached for the herbs he knew to be the ones his mother required, for she had spent many hours in his childhood fostering in him a fascination with all things medicinal. Little had she known that his interest would take him down the path of the now orthodox form of doctoring, with its belief that man was more capable of curing pain and disease than Mother Nature. It was the only subject upon which mother and son disagreed, for they had shared a close bond since the early death of Rosa's husband when Niccolo was just two years old.

"Come, Niccolo, we must go," urged Caterina.

Caterina and Niccolo soon arrived at Agnesa's house, which was situated at the end of the row of buildings on the right, providing her and Emilia with a far-reaching view over the square to the front. The windows to the back overlooked the main road running between San Martino and Arunca, where the church was sited. Despite bemoaning their lack of land, living in a house with such a commanding position was beneficial both to their need to feel superior and to their desire to gossip, for they could watch all the comings and goings of the villagers.

When Caterina and Niccolo entered the house, Agnesa and

Emilia were nowhere to be seen. Upstairs in the bedchamber, Rosa motioned to them to be quiet. She was seated on the bed, holding Lora's hand and wiping her brow. Lora lay prostrate with her eyes closed. Her breathing was ragged and her limbs still twitched in response to the pain in her abdomen, but she was no longer crying out.

"It's nearly time. Have you got my herbs?" asked Rosa.

"Mother, let me examine her."

Rosa glared at her son. "And what experience do you have in the birthing of children, Niccolo? Please do not seek to question my knowledge in this matter."

"It is not that I do not trust you, but with the arrival of Bishop Pazzini, it would be advisable if a doctor were to examine your patient," explained Niccolo.

Rosa looked away in anger, not at her son, but at the thought of all the midwives in the north who had been accused of witchcraft and burned at the stake. The Church Fathers looked for reasons to explain why evil and suffering happened in a world governed by their pure and perfect God. Their search arrived at the door of the devil, whom they believed to be a tangible being, guilty of seducing the weak to carry out his wicked deeds. Women, having been described throughout the Roman Church's teachings as being weaker than men, shouldered much of the blame. Old women who tended to those in labour were easy scapegoats if anything ill occurred. The death of the patient, or a deformity in the newborn child, could all be attributed to the devil-worshipping midwife who had attended the birth. Rosa shook her head in disgust at this theology, which polarised good and evil, pleasure and pain, light and darkness. Instead, she believed that both ends of the spectrum were part and parcel of the same divine light. For the fire that brings warmth and light is also that which burns, but from this very act of destruction stem the fertile ashes of rebirth. In Rosa's opinion, to separate these creative and destructive forces was to deny the essential truth of Mother Nature.

"Mother?" Rosa's musing was brought to a halt by her son's gentle prompting.

"Do what you must, Niccolo," Rosa agreed, knowing that he only sought to protect her from Bishop Pazzini's false accusations of witchcraft.

Niccolo nodded and approached Lora, who was now only moments from death. He examined her gently and felt the crown of the babe's head wedged in the cradle of her narrow body. Raising his eyes to his mother, he nodded. "It is as you say. The child is too large. There is nothing more we can do."

"And my herbs?" asked Rosa.

"I leave that to you, but if anyone asks, you must say that it was I who administered her medicine."

"Fetch a small bowl of water, Caterina, and warm it over the fire," instructed Rosa, before reaching for her *nanta* bag of ritual tools and pulling out a short wand of oak, which she had polished and carved with sacred symbols. Laying out the pouches of herbs upon the table, she closed her eyes and cast her wand over them, allowing the movement of its tip to guide her to which herbs she should use. Among others, she selected rue for its antispasmodic qualities, and began to extract various dried leaves from the pouches, rubbing them between her fingers to form a fine dust. A fragrant aroma filled the room as the powdered herbs dissolved in the warm water. Reaching for a spoon, the old wisewoman ladled the brew into Lora's mouth, urging her to swallow the soothing drink. Within moments Lora's pained expression softened, her muscles ceased to spasm and her breathing slowed. "Caterina, you can call Emilia and Agnesa now."

Caterina opened the door to discover the two women standing outside on the landing. As she motioned for them to enter, she wondered how much of their conversation the women had overheard. Emilia strode past Caterina towards her daughter's motionless body and threw herself upon the bed. "Oh, my poor Lora. What have these wicked women done to you?" But Rosa knew that Lora could no longer hear her mother's words for she could see her spirit, cradling that of her unborn child, walking into the loving arms of the Black Goddess Sofia.

Niccolo approached the bed. "Emilia, allow me to express my deep regret at your loss, and to assure you that I examined your daughter and found that Rosa was correct in her diagnosis. There was no possibility of Lora ever delivering her child."

"Well, of course you would say that. The witch is your mother," spat Emilia.

Niccolo gritted his teeth. "No, Emilia, I speak these words as a doctor, not as a son."

In the meantime, old Agnesa had approached the table at the side of Lora's bed where Rosa had left her herbs, and began to poke at the pouches with her stick. "What are these potions? Are they the ones you used to murder my granddaughter?"

Emilia turned towards the table and grabbed at the various pouches, holding them high in the air with a triumphant glare. "The evidence! I have the evidence! You will surely burn for this, Rosa. Just wait until Bishop Pazzini hears about this!" With Agnesa hobbling behind her, Emilia flew out of the bedroom without even a glance at her daughter's corpse.

"Leave her be," said Niccolo, reaching out to restrain Rosa, who was keen to retrieve her herbal remedies. "Let us wash and dress Lora's body, then leave Emilia and Agnesa in peace to mourn. They will calm down by the morrow, I am sure. The shock and their suffering have made them hysterical."

Caterina fetched some water and began to bathe Lora's lifeless body. "Perhaps, Niccolo, but I am not so hopeful. Emilia did nothing but bully Lora, especially when she grew big with child and brought shame upon the family. She didn't love Lora, not like a mother. There is more to her reaction tonight than meets the eye."

Rosa caught Caterina's gaze and nodded in agreement. Then she anointed Lora's forehead, chest and navel with olive oil, before helping Caterina to clothe her in a white, cotton dress. "What will be, will be, my children. Sofia weaves her cloth in mysterious ways and it is not for us to question her motives. Come, let us return home and rest awhile, for it has been a long and sorrowful night."

On their arrival back at the Lorini farmhouse, Niccolo poured some cups of wine and they settled themselves into the chairs beneath the *pergola*. They sat for a while, pondering the sad event of Lora's death and the futility of their efforts to save her.

Caterina gave a deep sigh. "It is at times such as this that I wonder if there truly is a divine Mother guiding us and, if so, to what end she delivers such loss and suffering."

Rosa stared at her niece, understanding the pain behind her question. "Something positive can usually be drawn from every negative experience, Caterina. Even those events that at first sight seem tragic and incomprehensible, in hindsight can be viewed as stepping-stones towards greater wisdom and strength. It is through periods of suffering that we can grow and move forward with greater compassion and love for ourselves and for others. People may lose their lives, but their deaths are rarely in vain. In some way their dying will have a positive influence on the community in which they lived, even if it is to bring about change. Death is always followed by rebirth. Something will come from Lora's death this night, you can be sure."

They pondered her words for a while until at last Caterina asked Rosa, "Was it so when my own mother died giving birth to me?"

Startled, Rosa watched Caterina as she picked at the petals of a fallen flower. She had waited twenty-nine years for her niece to ask her this question. At last she had the opportunity to help

Caterina to understand the events surrounding her birth and the subsequent repercussions on her life. Rosa signalled to Niccolo, who kissed his mother's cheek and bade Caterina goodnight. Silence followed Niccolo's departure as Caterina continued to pick at the deep red petals of the flower. Rosa waited until she looked up. "Are you sure you are ready to hear this, Caterina?"

"Yes." Caterina swallowed the tears gathering in her throat. "The loss of my mother has been on my mind much of late. Perhaps it would help if I understood what happened."

Rosa nodded and prayed for guidance from Sofia and from Caterina's own mother, whose spirit she could see standing in the olive grove behind her daughter. Then she told Caterina the story of her birth.

* * * * * * *

It was a warm summer's evening like tonight when you entered this lifetime, Caterina. Your mother had laboured long and hard like Lora, but after many hours she was able to give birth to you. She cradled you in her arms, holding your pursed lips against her breast to suckle.

Then the bleeding started. Your grandmother Maria and I tried to stem the flow with every means known to us, but it was relentless. Your mother knew it was her time. She remained calm throughout the ordeal, treasuring the few moments she had with her newborn child, until she drifted into the waiting arms of Sofia.

I was devastated by her loss for she was very dear to me, being both my niece by blood and fellow priestess, as well as my sister-in-law by marriage. No one was more distraught, though, than your father. He adored your mother and never came to terms with her loss. Perhaps you are right to suspect that a part of him held you responsible for her death. But try to understand that when someone suffers the loss of a loved one, they will often seek to blame someone as a means of assuaging their grief and anger.

Nevertheless, your father loved you, Caterina. I know that it is hard for you to believe when he showed you little affection, but I know it to be true. He was simply too frightened to nurture your relationship in case he lost you as well. His final act before he died, of arranging your marriage to Enrico, stemmed from good intent. On his deathbed, he told me that his only wish was to see you taken care of, and he thought that his old hunting friend Enrico, heir to the Galletti farmstead, would be the one to look after you. He couldn't have predicted that Enrico would subject you to such violence. In fact, he would be horrified to know that the man he left in charge of protecting you is the same man who inflicts such appalling wounds on your body.

I am telling you this because I am fearful for your safety. You appear to accept Enrico's violence as if it were your deserved punishment. Caterina, listen to me. Tonight you witnessed for yourself the dangers implicit in childbirth. Your cousin Veronica's mother also died the same way. You are not to blame for your mother's death. The Black Goddess we serve is both the crone of death and the midwife of birth, precisely because the two stand side by side at the same crossroads. When a woman is labouring to deliver a child, she and her babe dwell in the centre of these crossroads, where only the thinnest veil separates the world of the living from that of the dead, and only Sofia can decide which path they both will take. It is beyond any of our control.

Stop punishing yourself for something that was not your fault and start believing that you are worthy of being loved. If not, you will continue to remain trapped within a marriage where your husband is your abuser, not your lover. Harness the anger you turn on yourself and use it to fight for your freedom. Don't forget that the Black Goddess of Wisdom is also a warrior who upholds justice when the right order is out of balance. Think of

Paolo and what it would mean for him to see his mother shake off her veil of passive acceptance and rise up as the warrior woman I know you to be. Find her, Caterina, before it's too late.

* * * * * * *

Rosa searched Caterina's face for a sign of the courageous spirit she knew lay locked inside her niece's pain, but Caterina's eyes remained devoid of emotion. Only the way in which she dug her nails into the palms of her clenched hands belied the distress she was struggling to control. Standing up, she made to leave. "I must go, Rosa. It's late."

Rosa reached out and grasped her arm. "Wait. Don't leave in anger."

Caterina continued to stare into the distance. "I'm not angry, Rosa, just tired."

"Yes, you are angry. With yourself. With me for not saving your mother. With your mother for leaving you. With Sofia for depriving you of your mother."

Caterina's mouth began to tremble and her eyes filled with tears. Rosa let go of her arm and instead took hold of her clenched fist, uncurling the fingers and lacing them through her own as she pulled Caterina forwards. "Come, there is someone I want to show you." Caterina allowed her aunt to lead her through the olive grove towards an old, stone well. Peering into the water, Rosa gestured to Caterina to do the same. "Now, tell me what you see."

For a while, Caterina saw nothing but the fragmented reflection of the waxing moon upon the water's surface. Then, between the rippling shadows of the overhanging trees, a figure emerged. A woman dressed in white and barefoot, with flowing hair entwined with flowers, appeared in the reflection. Caterina gasped. "What do you see?" asked Rosa.

"A woman," answered Caterina.

"Who is she?"

"I don't know."

"Listen and she will tell you," said Rosa.

Caterina's mind wandered through the veil separating the physical world from the spiritual realm. There she listened to the voice telling her what she needed to hear, until the images on the water's surface faded to moonlight. "It was my mother," she said, giving Rosa a tremulous smile.

"Yes."

"She said she still walks beside me."

"Yes. As does Sofia. As do I. You are never alone, Caterina. Take strength in that. Remember that the Black Goddess forces us to change by challenging us. She strips us bare so that her seed of wisdom can grow in the tilled soil of our souls. But you always have a choice whether you remain trapped in the underworld or whether you fly to freedom above."

Caterina wrapped her arms around Rosa's small, stout body and breathed in her scent, which evoked memories from her childhood spent at the farmhouse with Rosa, Niccolo and her father. Pressing a kiss to her temple, she whispered close to Rosa's ear, "Forgive me for my anger."

Rosa tightened her hold. "There is nothing to forgive."

With a final embrace, Caterina turned and began walking back through the olive grove. Rosa watched her progress until a movement in the sky above distracted her gaze. An owl flew past and Rosa whispered a prayer for Lora's soul on the breeze of its silent wings. Like the raven, the owl was a messenger of death, guiding the soul to the Black Goddess of Wisdom in the underworld, in the same way that the dove carried the soul back to the realm of the living. The owl was also a portent for battle and as Rosa readied herself for bed, she could not help but wonder whether the bird's appearance alluded to Caterina's struggle for self-worth, or whether there was some larger battle looming.

On reaching the square, Caterina turned left past Niccolo's consulting room and continued along the westerly road that ran straight to the coast. Once she had passed the orchard and reached the woods that circuited the hill above the chapel, Caterina turned right down a dirt track that led across her husband's barren land to the farmhouse in the distance. Its bare, whitewashed walls were covered in dirt, creating the semblance of a large, inert tomb rising up from the earth, in stark contrast to Rosa's myriad of rambling roses, which covered the walls of her house with vibrant bursts of colour. There were only three houses sited outside the centre of the village where the majority of people all lived huddled together. The third belonged to the Orsini family, now headed by Caterina's grandparents Bartolomeo and Maria Colombe, which was situated behind their son Dionisio's *taverna* on the north side of the square. The Lorini and Galletti families had once been landowners with farmhouses set amid flourishing olive groves. Where Rosa had worked hard to cultivate the land following her husband Agnolo's premature death, Enrico had squandered much of his family's wealth on wine and the acquisition of guns, for his greatest enthusiasm besides drinking was hunting.

Arriving at the farmhouse, Caterina opened the door quietly so as not to wake him. Creeping up the darkened staircase, she stopped at her son's bedroom and peered around the door. Paolo lay sleeping, his locks of fair hair falling forward over his eyes, his round cheeks flushed. Caterina felt her heart swell with maternal love, and knew that she would fight to the death to protect this angel who brought such joy and laughter to her otherwise troubled life.

Caterina felt behind the door for the pouch of sand that hung there on a hook. A village superstition warned of an evil spirit who stole into the bedrooms of children at night and sucked out their breath, causing them to die in their sleep. To prevent this from happening, mothers hung pouches of sand behind the doors of their children's bedrooms, so that the spirit would have to count every grain of sand before it could enter the room and steal the child's breath. As this task was impossible to complete before the first rays of dawn banished the evil spirit to its lair, the children were deemed to be safe. Caterina smiled at her relief on finding the pouch, but the smile was wiped from her face in an instant.

"Where have you been this late, sneaking around so that I might not know of your treachery?" demanded Enrico, seizing her shoulder and slamming her against the stone wall of the landing. "Whose bed have you been warming tonight, Whore?"

Caterina's eyes glazed over as she disassociated her mind from her body, allowing her spirit to wander to a place where it could not feel the pain that she knew her body was about to suffer. She had learnt over the past seven years of marriage that there was no use protesting her innocence. Any words uttered by her would only serve to inflame her husband's rage. Better, instead, to remain mute and compliant until Enrico had exorcised the voices that taunted him with his wife's imaginary infidelities, demanding she be punished.

And so, it began. Grabbing his wife by her hair, Enrico dragged her into their bedroom and threw her on the floor. Caterina curled up into a ball, placing her hands over her head to protect herself. She heard him undoing his belt and flinched at the first whip of the hard leather on her back. Again and again he struck her, calling her a whore and a slut with every blow of the belt, until at last he fell on the bed, panting from exertion. Caterina waited until his breathing became slower and deeper, when she could be sure that he had passed out. Wincing from the pain, she crawled out of the room. Then, wrapping her shawl about her, she lowered herself onto the deep stone seat of the landing casement and pulled the drape behind her. As she leant her head back against the wall, the maiden moon reached out to touch her cheek through the open shutter. In response, Caterina's eyes searched the stars, but not even their sublime beauty could arouse a response within her. Instead, closing her eyes, she escaped into the numbing abyss of sleep.

Thursday

12 August 1583

Santa Sofia

Caterina was soon woken by the dawn discord of church bells. Gazing out over her uncle Giorgio's butchery into the village square, she watched her father's only surviving brother, Padre Francesco, opening the church doors. On the lintel, she could just make out the carving of San Michele slaying the serpent-dragon, a symbol of the Roman Church's attempt to control and ultimately destroy the old religion of the mother Goddess and her son-lover God, which had existed for millennia before the birth of Christianity and was indeed its foundation myth. The frail priest hailed a greeting at Caterina's grandmother Maria, who was making an offering to the statue of Ceres, the Roman Goddess of the Harvest. The statue had been erected many years before the Roman Church came to power, but the priests had not removed it, unwilling to offend their new flock. Instead, they had built a large, cumbersome church beside it, quite out of proportion to any other building in Santa Sofia.

On the north side of the square, Caterina's uncle Dionisio was already setting up for the day, wiping the tables that lay beneath the *taverna's* large *pergola*. Tommaso had arrived in his horse-drawn cart and was ringing the cowbell above his head. The wooden doors of the houses along *Via Principale* opened as the womenfolk hurried to buy his fresh milk and cheese. Through the open doorways, children could be heard in the inner courtyards of the old stone buildings, their shrill laughter bringing a smile to Caterina's face.

"Mamma?"

Caterina drew back the curtain to see Paolo's sleepy face framed in the doorway of his bedroom.

"Is it time to get up?" he asked.

"Yes, my love," answered Caterina, reaching out to enfold him in her arms and breathing in the sweet smell of his hair. "Run along and get dressed while I make your breakfast."

Caterina watched as Paolo wandered back into his room and then crept into her own bedroom. Enrico was nowhere to be seen. His absence at least gave Caterina some privacy in which to bathe her wounds without having to endure his mockery. Hiding the welts beneath a dress, she offered up a prayer to Sofia before going downstairs.

Caterina tried not to look at Enrico, who was slumped in a chair by the hearth. She could not, however, ignore the stale smell of sweat and alcohol. Presuming him asleep, Caterina went into the kitchen to prepare Paolo's breakfast. Rubbing a piece of hard baked bread with garlic, she sprinkled it with crushed plum tomatoes, olive oil and basil. Paolo soon joined her and nibbled at the *bruschetta*. It was the last slice of bread and Caterina knew she would have to ask Enrico for money to buy another loaf, for it was too hot to bake her own. Keen to avoid a confrontation, she tiptoed over to his chair and reached into the pocket of his coat for some coins.

"Trying to steal from me now, Whore?" he growled, seizing her arm.

Caterina lowered her eyes. "I didn't want to wake you. I need some money to buy bread."

"More bread? You only bought some the other day. Why do you need to go to the bakery again so soon?" Enrico paused, searching for an answer. "So it is the golden-haired baker Aurelio you have set your lustful sights on. No doubt it was him you were fornicating with last night."

Perhaps it was the way in which Caterina's head hung low and her shoulders stooped, or perhaps it was because he felt too tired and ill to pursue his line of attack, but nevertheless, Enrico muttered something under his breath and closed his eyes. Caterina remained still, uncertain of his motive. She had learnt from past experience not to trust him when he appeared to acquiesce. With the slightest provocation he could rise up again. Step by step, Caterina backed away from him, reaching for Paolo's hand, and headed towards the door.

"Mind you come straight back, Caterina. None of this trifling with men."

Caterina jumped, startled by his booming voice, and glanced back at him. Enrico was staring into the fire, but not with the eyes of a man who sought to understand the language of the flames. Rather, with eyes that festered with the bitterness and misery of a man who had never known love.

Hand in hand, mother and son strolled down the track towards the village square, which was bustling with the cries of vendors selling their fresh produce and women bartering for goods. As they passed the orchard behind Niccolo's consulting room, they waved to the farm labourers boarding the carts which drove them to the flat plain of fertile fields between the foothills and the coast. The pastoral scene soothed Caterina's anxiety and she responded with increasing gaiety to the greetings hailed at them.

"Mamma, why is Papa always so angry with you?"

Paolo's question caught Caterina off guard. "Is that the way it seems to you, Paolo?"

"I hate him! I hate what he does to you!"

Caterina stopped and bent down so that her face was level with his. "Whatever do you mean?"

"I saw him, Mamma," Paolo sobbed. "I saw what he did to you with his belt."

Caterina gazed into his troubled eyes, shocked by his admission. She had tolerated Enrico's violence, safe in the knowledge that Paolo was unaware of it, but how could she allow it to continue now? And yet, what choice did she have? As Caterina stroked the tears from Paolo's cheeks and kissed his forehead, she cursed Enrico for causing his suffering. "Paolo, I need you to try to understand. Sometimes Papa feels unhappy and he drinks wine to make himself feel better, but instead it makes him angry and sometimes he gets angry with me."

"Then why does he drink wine if it doesn't make him feel better?"

"Well, sometimes your father doesn't have the strength to stop himself, but he doesn't mean to hurt me. The best thing we can do is to make Papa happy and then he won't get angry."

Paolo looked at his mother with suspicion, then lowered his eyes beneath her gaze. "I will try, Mamma, but only because you want me to."

"Good boy. Now, dry your tears for it is too beautiful a day for sadness," said Caterina, standing up. "I know, why don't we go to the woods and gather some flowers for Rosa? She is preparing the chapel for Sunday's festival. Would you like to help her?" With a small smile tugging at his mouth, Paolo nodded and reached up to take his mother's hand. Leading him out of the square, Caterina became aware of the curious stares of the villagers standing nearby. Ignoring them, she walked Paolo along *Via Principale* and down the lane past Rosa's house to the woods. Then they continued to climb down the steep path through the trees to the chapel, stopping now and then to pick some wild flowers.

At the end of the path, they passed through the moon portal. It was constructed from wood, with a large beam lying horizontally across two upright posts. When the moon was full, it appeared to rest upon the beam, as if creating a gateway into a magical lunar realm. The portal opened into a circular garden surrounded by steep wooded ridges. It was as though a divine hand had carved out a basin of rock and planted a garden of paradise in its stead. A grove of olive and fig trees, interspersed with rose bushes, formed a wall of foliage and flowers on the outer circle of the garden. In the central open space, the villagers gathered to worship around a sacred well and apple tree. Clinging to the hillside on the farthest side of the garden was a small, stone chapel. To the right, the ground fell sharply away down a ravine, which swirled with water from the river that cascaded down the mountainside.

"Mamma, why is the chapel so far away from the village?" asked Paolo, who was tired from their walk.

"Why don't we sit on that bench and rest a while, and I will tell you," replied Caterina.

Once they had quenched their thirst with some cool water from the well, Caterina told Paolo the story of the chapel.

* * * * * * *

Once upon a time, the people who lived here prayed together in a sacred cave, behind where the chapel is now built. They worshipped a Black Goddess of Wisdom, whom they called Sofia. One day, a Church Father arrived in the village and forbade the people to worship the Goddess in the cave. Instead, he ordered them to build a large church dedicated to the Roman Church's Father God.

Forced to obey the priest, the villagers began to build a church. They started to lay the foundation stones, but when they returned to work the following morning, they discovered the stones had been crushed into grains of sand. This happened for three days in a row, until on the fourth day Sofia appeared to the mute shepherd girl Angela.

"Tell the villagers not to build a large church in my garden. If the new priests must be obeyed, ask them instead to build a small chapel dedicated to the Black Madonna, in whose image I shall continue to shine within the Roman Church. Tomorrow, a line of ants will show them where the foundations must be."

Angela asked Sofia by what means she could tell the villagers these words, and then realised to her astonishment that she could speak. The young shepherdess ran as fast as she could back to the village square, where she told the villagers what Sofia had said. Everyone was amazed by the miraculous healing of Angela's voice and knew that this must indeed be a sign from the Goddess.

In the morning, all the villagers crowded into the garden, where they discovered a long, black chain of ants marching in straight lines around a small area in front of the cave. The wisewoman of the village understood. "Sofia wants us to build the chapel in front of the cave, so that we can continue to worship her in secret as we have always done, deep within the cave-womb of her earthly body."

And that is how the chapel came to be here in Sofia's garden of paradise, close to the sacred cave and far away from the main church where the Roman Church's priests worship their Father God.

* * * * * * *

Paolo frowned. "I don't understand, Mamma. Why did the priests not want them to pray to Sofia in the cave?"

"No one really knows, Paolo, but what I do know is that the further we stray from worshipping the divine Mother, the more violent and angry our world becomes." The two of them sat in silence for a while, Caterina brooding on the future of her people, while Paolo struggled to understand the meaning of her words. Sensing his discomfort, Caterina stood up. "Shall we go and look for Rosa inside the chapel?" Taking his hand, she led him towards the chapel, guiding him to safety past the steep drop into the ravine.

"Why is there a mermaid above the door?" asked Paolo.

Caterina glanced up at the stone carving of a mermaid, her tail spread wide in the act of birth. "The mermaid is the symbol of fertility and new life. She is often found where sacred water flows. There used to be many sanctuaries dedicated to the ancient Fish Goddess, but the priests built churches on them and dedicated them instead to Christ the Fisherman." Pushing open the door, Caterina stepped inside the coolness of the chapel. Subdued rays of light filtered through the stained-glass windows on either side, illuminating their images. Caterina gestured to them. "The Tree of Life represents the Goddess as Patroness of the Harvest and the wisdom of her harvest myth."

"Why is that big snake wrapped around the tree?" whispered Paolo.

Caterina smiled at his apprehension. "See how the serpent looks like a babe's umbilical cord when it is lying in its mother's watery womb? That's why the serpent became a symbol for the waters that flow deep within the earth, nurturing the vegetation and ensuring a bountiful harvest. The serpent's role is therefore to protect the Goddess's role as Patroness of the Harvest and her wisdom."

Paolo turned to the other window. "And the stag?"

"The stag is the Horned God of Spring, who is joined each year with the Goddess in the sacred marriage," replied Caterina, pleased that Paolo had at last reached an age when he was eager to learn more about the ancient myths and symbols of his ancestors. "Their union ensures the rebirth of all life for the following year. Then he is hunted down by the Wolf of Winter and sacrificed, before being reborn again in the endless cycle of life, death and rebirth."

Paolo continued walking down the narrow aisle as he listened to his mother, rubbing his hands over the carved pew ends, towards the round, stone altar at the end. He was transfixed by the glittering black altar cloth and the stag horn candelabra upon it. "Mamma, what are those silver crosses on the altar cloth?"

"They're swastikas," replied Caterina. "A very ancient symbol. The four equal sides represent the four stages of the moon and of the vegetal growth from seed to shoot to flower to fruit, as well as the four seasons."

"And who's she?" asked Paolo. Caterina gazed up at the painting of the Black Madonna. She was not surprised Paolo did not recognise her. This painting was far removed from the pious images of the Virgin found in Roman churches. Seated upon a lion throne, she was depicted offering a naked breast to her son, drops of milk flowing from her nipple. Above her head shone the sun, while her crown was interspersed with the twelve astrological stars. She wore a silver headband of seven moons to represent the seven days of the waxing moon and the seven moving planets. And she was dressed in a turquoise mantle, denoting her affinity to the sea and water. Against her side rested the bow and arrow of the Virgin Huntress, virgin in that she was beholden to no one but her own wild nature. Beneath her feet lay the crescent moon and a coiled serpent, while wild animals such as the bear and wolf surrounded her in a protective circle.

"That, Paolo, is the Black Madonna. And in that alcove, is the real thing."

Paolo glanced over at the ancient, wooden statue. "Is that the one the men will carry in the procession on Sunday?"

"Yes, my love."

On either side of the statue were two large vases overflowing with fragrant blooms. From behind one of them, Rosa's head appeared. "Ah, Caterina and my dear Paolo," she said, enveloping her young nephew in her arms.

"Mamma told me about the sacred cave behind the chapel. Is it still there, Rosa? Can I see it?" asked Paolo.

Rosa glanced at Caterina and nodded. Paolo was old enough now to be trusted. Rosa set him on the floor and stared into his eyes. "The sacred cave is still there, Paolo, but only a few people know about it. If we let you come inside with us, you must promise that you will not tell anyone."

"I promise, Rosa. I promise, Mamma, I won't tell." Paolo's heart began to pound with a mixture of fear and excitement as Rosa swung the painting of the Black Madonna sideways to reveal an iron key hanging from a hook. Taking the key, Rosa fetched a candle and stepped into the shadows of the far corner. Pulling aside a thick curtain, she motioned to Paolo and Caterina. Behind the curtain was a small wooden door, set into the rock of the mountainside. The door led into a long, narrow tunnel carved out of the rock, its sides engraved with spiral images of serpents, which leapt out at Paolo in the flickering candlelight. At the end of the tunnel was another solid door, above which was painted the head of a growling lioness.

"Why's that there?" asked Paolo, his voice trembling.

Caterina squeezed his hand. "The lioness is the ancient protector of the Goddess's cave. There's nothing to fear."

Rosa unlocked the door and swung it open to reveal a large, cavernous chamber, lit by the flames of a fire fed with oak wood. The uneven roof of the cave rose in places to the height of the tallest tree, before plummeting so low that an adult was forced to crawl through the gap to reach the chambers that lay deep within the labyrinth. To the right, stone steps led down to a pool of water glistening clear and green in the candlelight. The overhanging walls of rock were stained white, red and black, and painted with symbols of regeneration such as the bird, serpent, butterfly and frog. To the left was the moon stone, a tall, black obelisk. It was surrounded by a spiral of smaller black stones embodying the souls of the dead waiting to be reborn. Between these stones, footsteps had been worn into the floor by generations of spiral dancing intended to carry the dancers' souls into the invisible world to commune with the spirits of their ancestors. In the centre of the cave stood a large statue of the Black Goddess, carved from the mountain's rock.

"Look, Paolo, at the lion throne upon which Sofia is seated." Caterina gestured to the statue that Paolo was staring at, eyes wide open in awe. "In her right hand, she is holding the root of a flower which blossoms into the lily upon which a dove is seated. Do you know what these symbols mean?" Paolo shook his head, stunned into silence by the grandeur of the statue and the mystical resonance of the cave. "The root is the symbol of the Goddess as the source of all things. It is through her wisdom that our souls can blossom like the lily and fly to freedom on the wings of the dove."

"What about the goat at her feet? Is that the devil?" Fear stifled Paolo's voice so that he was barely audible. Rosa pulled him into the cradle of her lap as she knelt among the abalone shells filled with libations of seawater, salt and wine. "Let me tell you a story, Paolo, which I hope will allay your fears."

* * * * * * *

There is no devil, only the Goddess and the Horned God. Since the beginning of time, the Goddess has been symbolised by the serpent, and the Horned God by the goat, stag and bull. It was only when the Roman Church came to power that it claimed the serpent and the goat were creatures of the devil, because it was afraid of the power of the Goddess and Horned God.

The Church Fathers even wrote a story in their bible about the serpent and the first man and woman in the garden of paradise. In the story, the woman Eve is tempted by the serpent to eat the apple from the Tree of Wisdom, and by doing so, Eve is believed to have brought about all evil and suffering in the world. Of course, none of this is true. The story is just one of the ways in which the priests tried to frighten people into believing in their Father God. Above all it was a warning to any women who continued to worship the Wisdom Goddess that they would be found guilty of evil-doing and punished.

This means that if the Bishop of Arunca ever discovered your mother and I still worshipped the Goddess in this cave, he would accuse us of carrying out the devil's work and would punish us. That is why we must keep this cave a secret and you must not tell anyone what you have seen today.

* * * * * * *

"I promise, Rosa," said Paolo.

"Good boy," said Caterina. "Now why don't you stay and help Rosa with the flowers, while I return to the square to buy some bread? I'm sure Rosa won't mind walking you back to the house in time for lunch."

Rosa led the way out of the cave and into the chapel, returning the key to its hiding place behind the painting of the Black Madonna. Kissing Paolo goodbye, Caterina began the slow climb back through the woods.

On reaching the corner of the square by Niccolo's consulting room, Caterina was greeted by her young aunt Elena. Her ample bosom was heaving from her rush across the square, her ruddy cheeks even more flushed than usual.

"Have you seen him?" she asked.

"Seen who?" replied Caterina.

"The stranger, talking to Dionisio by the *taverna*. Donata said she saw him arrive on the fish-seller's cart."

"Oh." Caterina tried to appear interested but all the while she was aware that she had been gone from the house a long time and her husband would be growing suspicious.

"I wonder who he is?" mused Elena.

"Maybe he's one of the musicians come to play at the dance," replied Caterina.

"Oh, I do hope so. How pleasant it would be to spend an evening admiring his handsome face."

The arrival of a new man in the village was certain to encourage Elena's daydreams of marriage and children. Caterina sympathised with her aunt's loneliness, but she was anxious to get home. Making her excuses, she headed across the square towards the bakery, lowering her head to avoid any further interruptions, and promptly cried out as she collided with another pedestrian.

"Forgive me."

Caterina looked up to find herself staring into the eyes of the stranger, and quickly lowered her gaze. When she didn't reply, the stranger continued. "Are you hurt?"

"No. Thank you." Glancing about to see if her husband had witnessed their meeting, Caterina turned and ran towards the bakery.

Although Enrico had not seen them, they had not gone unnoticed by the two women waiting on the balcony outside Niccolo's consulting room. "Will you look at that whore? Lora's body lies barely cold and that witch's assistant sees fit to flirt with a man who, I might add, is not my cousin Enrico." Emilia raised her arched eyebrows, while her mother Agnesa scrunched up her eyes in an attempt to sharpen her vision.

"Who is he, Daughter?" asked Agnesa. "I cannot tell from this distance."

"I have not seen him before, Mamma, but by the look in his eyes I would say he is enamoured with the whore. The guitar he carries suggests he is another travelling musician and, as we know to our cost, such gypsies are partial to seducing village girls."

Agnesa closed her eyes in concentration. "This may be to the benefit of our plans, Daughter. Persuading Bishop Pazzini to charge the old witch Rosa with Lora's murder should be easy enough, but having revenge on her young and beautiful assistant Caterina will prove more difficult. Perhaps this stranger's arrival will bring about her downfall without us needing to bring her to trial. Report any further meetings between Caterina and the stranger to Enrico, for it is rumoured he chastises her errant ways with violent means. If we were to incite his rage enough, he might deliver a fatal blow."

Emilia clapped her hands together. "Oh, Mamma, how clever you are. Justice will be ours!"

At that moment, the door opened to reveal Niccolo standing on the threshold. "What can I do for you in your hour of mourning, Emilia and Agnesa?"

Emilia pushed past her mother. "You and that witch of a mother have already done enough," she hissed, showering his face in spittle. "My mother and I are here to tell you that we travelled to the city of Arunca early this morning and spoke with Bishop Pazzini. He is outraged by your mother's use of witchcraft to kill Lora and has sworn to bring the devil-worshipping serpent before the Inquisitor."

Niccolo's eyes filled with anxiety. "Emilia, I beseech you. My mother did no wrong last night. Everyone knows her to be an honest woman, skilled in the art of midwifery and healing. Please, I beg of you, be mindful of spouting false accusations, for these are dangerous times in which we live and too many innocent women in the north have already died at the hands of the Inquisition."

"Hah! Your mother is not innocent, Niccolo," cried Emilia. "I have heard rumours that she worships the goddess Diana in a secret cave near the chapel, and I swear that I have seen her flying through the night sky on a broomstick."

Niccolo slammed his hand down on the wooden balustrade of the balcony. "Enough of these lies! You bitter fools can plot and slander as much as you like, but you are the only two people in this village who would not defend my mother. Now, please stop wasting my time."

The two women gasped, for they had always thought the doctor a gentleman. Evidently he was as wicked as his mother, they agreed as they gathered up their baskets and left. Niccolo glanced down at the small crowd of villagers who had gathered to listen to their confrontation. Ignoring them, he strode to the far end of the balcony overlooking the apple orchard, and called out to the man he had earlier spotted over Emilia's shoulder. "Luca?" He waited for a while as the man made his way through the trees, looking about him as if to ward off some hidden danger. At last, he climbed up the stairs to the balcony and scurried into the consulting room. Niccolo closed the door, motioning to Luca to sit down, but he was restless and paced the room, running his fingers through his long, shaggy hair. "What is it, Luca?"

The young man's eyes darted around the room as he pulled at the heavy beard covering his face. "It's the full moon on Sunday."

"How are you feeling?" asked Niccolo.

"They frighten me, these feelings I have when our mother moon is laden. Will you help me?"

"Of course." Niccolo opened one of the wooden cabinets and drew out a jar of pills, handing it to Luca. "Here, take these. They will help to calm you." Luca pocketed the jar and left as silently as he had arrived. Distracted, Niccolo closed the door behind him and sat down at his desk. He felt for Luca and would usually have spent more time talking with him, but Emilia's words had unsettled him and he was anxious to warn his mother. Locking the door, he headed home in search of Rosa.

In the meantime, Caterina had chosen a flat, circular loaf of hard bread and was handing her coins to Aurelio when the stranger walked into the bakery. "I believe you dropped these when we collided earlier," he said, holding out a small posy of woodland flowers, which Paolo had picked for her.

"Oh, thank you. They were a present from my son."

"So this is what you get up to when my back is turned?" bellowed a familiar voice from behind her. Dread filled her eyes and she lowered them from the stranger's gaze as Enrico reached out to seize Caterina's arm, squeezing the tender flesh and causing her to gasp out in pain.

The stranger stepped forward. "Release the lady at once."

Enrico stared in disbelief at his audacity. "This is no lady. She is a whore and my wife. And as my wife, I have every right to treat her as I choose, especially when she has accepted flowers from the lecherous likes of you."

"The flowers were a present from her son. I merely returned them to your wife after I caused her to drop them earlier." But the stranger's attempt to assuage Enrico's wrath only succeeded in incensing him further.

"So this is not your first meeting of the day? My, you have been busy, you slut!" Enrico's hand tightened on Caterina's arm, causing her to gasp again.

"Enough! I will not stand by and watch a lady be so abused." The stranger reached out and tried to prise Enrico's hand from Caterina's arm.

"Stop, please!" cried Caterina. The stranger stilled and looked at her, but she avoided his questioning gaze, tears falling from her eyes. "Forgive me, Enrico. Please, let us leave now."

Enrico ignored Caterina, still enraged by the stranger's interference. "What is your name, boy?"

"Alessandro."

"Well, Alessandro, I will warn you only once. Stay away from my wife or else you will live to regret the day you ever laid eyes on her." Keeping his grasp on Caterina's arm, Enrico pulled her out of the bakery, glaring at the stranger who had dared to question his ownership of his wife. To Enrico, such behaviour by a man was unforgiveable. There was an unwritten law governing the fraternity of men that no man ever questioned another's treatment of his wife. In Enrico's opinion, and that of the Church, his wife belonged to him and as her master he could deal with her in whatever way he saw fit.

Alessandro followed the old brute as he dragged his young wife past the butchery on the corner, only coming to a halt when Enrico disappeared with her down the road Matteo had taken to the coast. Memories of his sister flooded his mind. The woman even possessed a physical resemblance to Isabetta, with her pale skin and long, sun-lightened hair. Only the eyes were different, the woman's clear blue colouring a reminder of the marauding Turks who had left their mark on previous generations in the south. Alessandro may not have succeeded in protecting Isabetta, but he had sworn he would never make the same mistake again. Even if the woman was unknown to him and the abuser was her husband, he could not walk away and allow such violence to continue. Perhaps this was the woman in need of his help whom the prophetess Sapia had spoken of.

As if able to read his thoughts, a man stepped out from the shadows of the butchery doorway and crept up behind Alessandro. "It is not for you to save that one. Only she can save herself."

Alessandro looked around in surprise at the young man who stood to his side and behind him, as if hiding in his shadow. For a moment, Alessandro's eyes widened in shock and then softened at the sight of the young man's skin, which was covered in a thick mat of hair. He had met a wolf-man similarly afflicted a few years earlier. Undeterred by his appearance, Alessandro was interested to discover what he knew about the woman and her husband. "You know the young woman?"

"I know everyone in the village. Her name is Caterina and she is married to my late mother's cousin Enrico. They live in the Galletti farmhouse off the coastal road."

Alessandro suspected that the wolf-man's knowledge of Santa Sofia could be of assistance and sought to make his acquaintance. "What is your name?"

"Luca, but some people call me Lupo, the Wolf, owing to my disease." Luca lowered his head in shame.

"You are not alone, Luca. I have met another like you," replied Alessandro, holding out his hand. "My name is Alessandro and I am a travelling storyteller. Why don't you accompany me to the *taverna* for some lunch?" Alessandro gave an encouraging smile and motioned to Luca to follow him. Luca wavered, suspicious of Alessandro's kindness, for few people would be generous to a stranger unless they desired something in return. He studied Alessandro for a while, deciding whether or not to trust him, but in the end, his curiosity got the better of him and he shuffled alongside the storyteller, making sure to stay within his shadow.

As they made their way back towards the *taverna*, a large man wearing the red vestments of a bishop marched past them in the direction of the church. Alessandro stopped short, his pulse quickening and his breath coming in bursts. The years had robbed him of his hair and he was more obese than ever, but there was no mistaking the bulging eyes and the scar upon his right cheek. Through clenched teeth, Alessandro spat out the name of his sister's murderer. "Jacobo Pazzini."

Luca sneered. "The devil himself." Rage blinded Alessandro and he took a step forward, but a furry hand reached out to grasp his shoulder. "Now is not the time."

Alessandro remembered his grandfather's words and stopped. With a last look at Bishop Pazzini's retreating back, he turned to Luca. "It's as if you can read my mind. How are you able to do this?"

Luca looked down at his feet. "As an outcast few people speak to me, but I see and hear everything. I study people and in understanding them, I sense their needs. I cannot read your mind, but I know that it is not a good idea to confront someone in anger."

"You speak with wisdom, Luca," said Alessandro, seating himself at one of the tables set outside the *taverna*. "Come. Pull up a chair."

Luca hesitated. "I would prefer to stay in the shadows."

"Then I shall move the table into the shade," replied Alessandro. Encouraged by his kindness, Luca stepped beneath the row of wooden poles entwined with lush green vines. Other than Padre Francesco, Rosa and Caterina, and of course Niccolo, few people acknowledged Luca. His own grandmother Agnesa and aunt Emilia would have nothing to do with him, revolted by his discoloured skin and excessive body hair. The men sat down and Alessandro ordered two bowls of vegetable soup and a jug of wine from Dionisio. The landlord looked suspiciously at the wolf-man, but brought them their refreshments nonetheless. "Tell me, Luca, why did you call Bishop Pazzini the devil?" asked Alessandro.

Luca leant across the table and whispered in a low voice. "Two months ago, on his first visit to Santa Sofia, he committed a terrible crime against a friend of mine."

"This friend would not happen to be a young woman?" Alessandro asked.

Luca glanced at him in astonishment. "Why, yes."

"Did he attempt to rape and kill her?"

Luca nodded, wary of revealing the identity of the victim, for she was still in hiding and only a trusted few knew about the attack. "How do you know?"

Alessandro studied Luca's face and recognised the same desire for revenge in the wolf-man's eyes. It was then that he knew he could entrust Luca with the secret of his sister's fate and his reason for coming to Santa Sofia. "Jacobo Pazzini raped and killed my sister twenty years ago. I am here to have my revenge."

An array of emotions washed over Luca. Sorrow for Alessandro's sister, relief that his own half-sister had survived, and then anger once more. "Why come to Santa Sofia?" he asked Alessandro.

"The fish-seller Matteo told me that the Bishop is attempting to stop your pilgrimage to the chapel on Sunday. I therefore knew that he would be coming here, away from the safe protection of his Bishop's palace in Arunca, where it would be easier to execute my plan to bring him to justice."

Luca nodded in agreement. "What is your plan?"

Alessandro shrugged his shoulders. "I do not have one yet. All I know is that I must somehow produce enough evidence to bring Bishop Pazzini before the court of the Inquisition to be tried and punished for his crimes."

Luca let out a long sigh. "That is going to be very difficult."

"I know," agreed Alessandro. The two men sat pondering the matter for a while, until Alessandro made a hesitant suggestion. "Perhaps your friend would testify against the Bishop? I have no evidence of the crimes he committed against my sister, but your friend survived a similar fate." Luca shook his head in denial, but Alessandro was impatient. "Isn't it worth a try?"

"You don't understand. I know she would help us, for she is a very strong and brave woman, but I have already discussed the possibility with the wisewoman Rosa. She explained that the courts would not accept her testimony."

"Why not?" asked Alessandro.

To answer his question, Luca would have to reveal his sister's identity. He paused, debating whether or not to trust him, but then it occurred to him how much Alessandro had risked in talking to him. "Veronica is my half-sister," he explained. "We live with my father Piero, a shepherd, in a hut on that hill you can see rising up between the apple orchard and the woods leading down to the chapel. As a woman and a peasant, the courts would disregard her testimony against the Bishop. We are powerless to seek justice."

Alessandro gazed at Luca in sympathy, now understanding the bond that existed between them for they were both brothers of Jacobo Pazzini's victims. Then he ran his fingers through his hair in exasperation. "There must be another way." They both fell silent in contemplation until at last Alessandro spoke. "Tell me about the Bishop and the festival. Why is it so important for the villagers to worship at the chapel and not the church?"

Luca was touched by Alessandro's request, for it was rare that anyone cared to listen to him. "Many years ago, our ancestors revered a Black Goddess of Wisdom called Sofia. They worshipped her in a cave behind where the chapel now lies. When the Roman Church arrived, the moon priestesses continued to pass on her wisdom in secret to the next bloodline of priestesses. The wisewoman Rosa, her great niece Caterina, and Caterina's aunt Elena currently hold that responsibility."

"Do the other villagers know of this?" asked Alessandro.

"Over time the memory of Sofia and the cave was lost," continued Luca. "Only two other people besides Veronica and me know of its existence – Rosa's brother-in-law Padre Francesco and her son Niccolo. I would suggest that these are the only people you trust at this moment with your secret. It is not that the other villagers are malicious, but they are wont to talk."

"Matteo said the Bishop knows about the cave," remarked Alessandro.

"He has heard rumours. No doubt from gossips like Emilia Cesi."

"He thinks they're worshipping the goddess Diana."

Luca nodded. "That's because the Romans celebrated the Black Goddess Diana on the fifteenth of August and the Festival of Santa Sofia was held on the same date. When the Roman Church came to power, the priests built the chapel and encouraged the villagers to worship Santa Sofia and the Black Madonna instead of the Black Goddess Sofia. They even held a Mass on the same day combining the image of Sofia as God's Holy Wisdom with the celebration of the Assumption of Mary. Although ancestral memories have been lost, the tradition of holding the festival at the Chapel of the Black Madonna remains strong. Several times on the eve or night of the festival, a miracle has occurred, and the villagers are anxious that if they stop worshipping at the chapel, the divine Mother will no longer bless them with her healing. This is why the villagers are so angry with Bishop Pazzini for insisting Padre Francesco holds Mass in the main church."

"What about Padre Francesco? What's his view?" asked Alessandro.

"He supports our desire to worship at the chapel and even allows Rosa to accompany him in her role as priestess," explained Luca. "He is a secret Gnostic follower of the Early Church and reveres Sofia as the Christian Wisdom Goddess. He is up in arms at the Bishop's demands. It remains to be seen whether or not the procession to the chapel will take place."

Alessandro smiled at Luca in gratitude. "Thank you, my friend. Your explanation will serve me well. Have you not thought of using your talent for storytelling? As a travelling storyteller and musician, I would recommend the life."

Luca glanced about at the neighbouring diners. "Do you not see how everyone stares at me? How could I venture to strange parts when people react with such fear?"

Alessandro smiled and waved his guitar at Luca. "As long as you can tell stories and entertain your hosts with a song or two, I am sure you would find welcome wherever you wandered."

Luca shook his head. "Alas, I don't know how to play an instrument. My nails are too long and pointed."

"Then they are perfect for playing the guitar as you use your nails to pluck the strings. Why don't I teach you some tunes as payment in kind for your help?" Luca's face broke into a broad smile, revealing the reddened teeth he tried to keep hidden from view, but his excitement was too great to contain. Alessandro was touched by his reaction, but his thoughts soon returned to the task at hand. "You say I can trust Padre Francesco?"

"Most certainly," said Luca. "He is a good priest."

"I did not know such a thing existed."

Luca understood Alessandro's bitterness, but he also knew that not all priests shared such a cruel, dogmatic attitude. "Padre Francesco explained to me that, like the Cathars, he believes in discovering the Christ within through the wisdom of Sofia. To him, religion is a pathway to individual, spiritual transformation, not a political power like the Roman Church of today. He is deserving of your trust."

Alessandro stood up, leaving some coins for Dionisio.

"Where are you going?" asked Luca.

"To speak with Padre Francesco and see what Bishop Pazzini wanted with him," replied Alessandro.

"Shall I come with you?" asked Luca.

Alessandro shook his head, holding out his guitar to Luca. "Why don't you go and practice a while. You'll find me here this evening entertaining the villagers at the monthly *veglia*. Perhaps you'll join me in a song or two?" Luca gawped, filled with trepidation at the prospect, but took hold of the instrument, cradling it in his arms like a newborn babe. As Alessandro headed off to the church, Luca crept around the corner of the *taverna*, keeping in the shadows until he reached the edge of the woods that backed onto the Galletti and Orsini plots of land. There he paused to look for any sign of Enrico, who often trained his gun upon his cousin, before running into the forest to pluck at the strings and sing to his heart's content.

The heavy door of the church was ajar and as Alessandro drew near he could distinguish two voices, one clearly identifiable as that of Jacobo Pazzini. Alessandro felt his heart begin to pound, but taking a deep breath he crept through the open door and ducked behind a stone tomb to listen to their conversation.

"There is another matter on which I wish to speak with you, Padre Francesco," said Bishop Pazzini. "Word has come to me this morning from two ladies of the village. They claim that the midwife Rosa Lorini has sold herself to the devil and by her sorcery has brought about the death of the girl Lora Cesi."

Alessandro thought he could detect a slight tremor in Padre Francesco's voice as the priest responded. "Your Excellency, I can assure you that I am well acquainted with the midwife Rosa for she is my sister-in-law, and I know her to be a woman of high moral standing and unquestionable expertise. These women are sorrowfully mistaken if they believe Rosa to be capable of murder."

Bishop Pazzini continued as if he had not heard Padre Francesco. "These women also believe that it is Rosa who worships the goddess Diana in a secret cave near the chapel. They say that she wields much power over the village during the Festival of the Assumption."

Padre Francesco swallowed hard and asked God's forgiveness for the lie he was about to tell. "Your Excellency, I know of no cave and it is I alone who leads the religious service during the festival. It appears to me that these poor ladies are somewhat deluded. Perhaps in their grief they have become confused. Rather than pay any attention to their words, I suggest we pray for their troubled minds to find peace."

Bishop Pazzini glowered at Padre Francesco. The priest's refusal to implicate Rosa was frustrating his own plans to arrest the woman. Before coming to the church to speak with Padre Francesco, he had gone to inspect the woman's property on the pretext of questioning her. To his satisfaction, the Bishop had found the house unoccupied, which allowed him time to assess the value of the farmstead. Rosa owned a large, fertile olive grove, which would provide him with a modest income if he were to successfully prosecute her and seize ownership of her land. All he needed was enough evidence to persuade the reticent Inquisitor to put her on trial, but the witness statements from two old women were not going to be sufficient on their own. With a last glare at the uncooperative priest, Bishop Pazzini marched towards the door, hurling a final order over his shoulder. "Keep an eye on the midwife, Padre Francesco. I shall make sure to attend Mass on Sunday, and if I see anything suspicious in her behaviour, I won't hesitate to report her to the Inquisitor." With that, Bishop Pazzini sailed past Alessandro in his hiding place and slammed the door behind him, the sound reverberating through the empty church.

Alessandro heard Padre Francesco give a deep sigh and appeared from behind the tomb, startling the priest. "What needs you hiding there? Who are you?"

Alessandro gave a respectful bow. "I am Alessandro, a travelling storyteller by trade. I beg a few moments of your time, Padre."

Padre Francesco's eyes flitted towards the door as he wiped his brow. "Could you come back later? There is someone I must see."

"The midwife Rosa?" asked Alessandro.

The priest eyed him with suspicion. "What do you know of Rosa?"

"Only what the Bishop said," replied Alessandro.

"Well the Bishop is misinformed and I would beg of you not to repeat any part of our conversation that you may have overheard," said Padre Francesco, moving towards the door.

"May I accompany you to the house of the midwife?"

"I think not. It is a private matter on which I must speak with the lady," replied the priest.

Alessandro remembered Luca's words, urging him to trust Rosa and Padre Francesco. "Padre!"

The old priest turned back, his expression impatient.

"I know things about Bishop Pazzini that might be of help to you in protecting Rosa," explained Alessandro. "He committed crimes against my sister."

Padre Francesco looked at him in surprise.

"Please," asked Alessandro, "allow me to accompany you to Rosa's house and I will tell you both my story. Luca has already heard it and has agreed to help me bring Bishop Pazzini to justice."

Alessandro's reference to Luca convinced Padre Francesco of the stranger's sincerity, for Luca was an excellent judge of character who trusted few people. "Come with me then, Alessandro, and we will hear your story."

Padre Francesco led the way out of the church to Rosa's farmhouse. On their arrival, an elderly lady with her white hair swept up in a bun, came out to meet them and took both of the priest's hands in her own. Padre Francesco smiled down at her, the warmth in his eyes leading Alessandro to wonder about the nature of their relationship.

"Rosa, I need to talk with you where we cannot be overheard."

The anxiety in Padre Francesco's voice caused Rosa's smile to falter. "What is it? What's happened?"

"Not here. Let us go inside."

Rosa motioned to Padre Francesco to enter the house and looked up at the stranger standing behind him.

"Forgive my rudeness," said Padre Francesco. "Rosa, this is Alessandro. He has a story to share with us."

Rosa smiled in welcome. "Come in, Alessandro, and go through to the back room."

Alessandro followed Padre Francesco as he made his way through the main room of the house into a small room lit only by candles. It was warm and welcoming without being oppressive. A collection of paintings depicting a host of animals and pagan goddesses hung on the walls, and the wooden shelves were laden with various tincture bottles, pouches and artefacts. Alessandro felt a sense of calm enfolding him.

Rosa entered the room carrying a tray of rose tea and *focaccia* cake, followed by Niccolo. "Alessandro, this is my son Niccolo. He is the village doctor." Alessandro stood up and shook Niccolo's hand. He appeared to be slightly older than Alessandro and of smaller stature, his eyes shining with the same kindness as those of his mother.

"Now, Francesco, tell me what is troubling you," insisted Rosa.

"The Bishop has just been to visit me..." began Padre Francesco.

"Not him again," said Rosa. "I am bored of hearing stories about that dreadful man. Let us speak of something uplifting."

"Rosa, please listen to me. This is important," begged Padre Francesco. "It would appear that Emilia and Agnesa have charged you with being a devil-worshipper. They have accused you of the murder of Lora."

"I know. Niccolo told me earlier. Now, can we talk of something else? Why doesn't Alessandro tell us his story?"

Padre Francesco slapped his hands on his knees. "Rosa, enough of your obstinacy! This is serious. The Bishop has warned me to keep an eye on you and if he sees anything suspicious on Sunday, he is going to report you to the Inquisitor."

Rosa shrugged her ample shoulders. "Then let him. For some forty years, you and I have led the villagers' worship at the Festival of Santa Sofia. No Bishop is going to make me stop now with idle threats of torture and death by burning."

Padre Francesco shook his head with regret. "These are not idle threats, Rosa. I did not want to tell you until I was sure, but the Bishop confirmed today that an *auto-da-fé* is to be held in Arunca on Tuesday. This public ceremony, the first of its kind in the south, will witness the burning of four women and a man. The Inquisitor has been forced to find them guilty of heresy on account of Bishop Pazzini's evidence." His news was met with stunned silence from the others. Even Rosa was sapped of her usual defiance.

Alessandro cast his mind back to Sapia's prophetic words and realised that these must be the burnings he was destined to prevent. "If the burnings are to be held on Tuesday, then we must move fast," he said. "The story I am about to tell you will reveal the extent of Bishop Pazzini's evil. If you desire to protect Rosa and the people fated to die on Tuesday, then all I ask is that you join me in devising a plan to bring the Bishop to justice."

Rosa looked at Padre Francesco and Niccolo, who both nodded their heads in agreement. "Pray, tell us your story Alessandro."

Dusk had fallen by the time they began the walk back to the village *taverna* where the monthly *veglia* was due to take place. Its purpose, like the seasonal festivals, was to give the villagers respite from their hard-working lives. Usually, the evening of storytelling was held on the night of the full moon, but the festivities planned over the weekend meant it had been brought forward. While Padre Francesco and Niccolo walked on ahead, Alessandro fell into step beside Rosa, musing on the successful outcome of his day. On hearing his story, the others had all agreed to consider how best to produce enough evidence against Bishop Pazzini to hand him over to the courts, thereby invalidating the evidence he had presented against his latest victims and liberating them from their death sentences.

"Tell me, Alessandro, what do you hope to gain from bringing your sister's murderer to justice?"

Rosa's sudden question took Alessandro by surprise, prompting him to answer without reservation. "An end to this feeling of emptiness, of searching with no fulfilment, of my guilt, of the nightmares that plague my sleep."

Rosa fell silent in contemplation before responding. "Your guilt will not disappear until you accept that you could not have protected Isabetta. It is my belief that each soul chooses the experiences it will endure according to the lessons it needs to learn or to teach others in each consecutive lifetime. It is not for us to seek to control another's destiny or to alter their soul's path."

Alessandro's eyes lit up with anger. "Are you implying that my sister chose to be raped and murdered?"

"Sometimes Sofia works in mysterious ways that are unfathomable to us. Why do mothers die in childbirth? Why are children born with painful afflictions? Why do some people suffer more loss than others? Each soul has something different to give and to receive. Perhaps the soul of the child who dies comes to teach its mother how to endure loss and therefore how to comfort others who also suffer loss."

Alessandro glanced at Rosa and saw the wistful look in her eye. "You speak as if from experience."

Rosa gave a sad smile. "Yes. My daughter Madelena died when she was two, only four years before my husband was killed in an accident on the farm. At the time, I could not believe that anything good could come from their loss. I cursed Sofia and swore that I would no longer serve her as a priestess. But it was in this dark cave of pain that I discovered her light of wisdom. If I had not entered that cave, then I might never have found my true strength. The deaths of my daughter and husband were the catalysts for my own journey of spiritual transformation. I am grateful for their teaching, even though it entailed suffering their loss. In the same way, I am sure that Isabetta's violent death will bring about something positive in your life." Alessandro raised his eyebrows in disbelief as Rosa continued. "The emptiness you feel stems not only from your loss of Isabetta but also from the loss of your connection to your soul. Your sense of searching is your soul's desire for reunion, not just for revenge. Fulfilment will only come through healing your pain and releasing your fear, so that they no longer prevent your soul from experiencing love, both for yourself and with others."

Alessandro could see the lights of the lanterns hanging from the *pergola*, reminding him of the night of storytelling that lay ahead. "I'm looking forward to the *veglia* tonight."

Rosa smiled at his attempt to steer their conversation. "Yes. The path to healing is to be found in the creative realm. Playing your guitar and telling your stories must give your soul chance to express itself."

"It brings me peace."

"Then you have experienced union with your soul."

Alessandro smiled at the wisewoman's persistence. "Luca told me about the cave. May I see it?"

"Of course. As long as you keep it secret," replied Rosa. "Why not come and visit us there tomorrow morning?"

"Us?"

"My niece Caterina will be helping me to prepare the chapel for Sunday's service."

Images of the young woman with blue eyes played through Alessandro's mind. In his haste to gather support against Jacobo Pazzini, he had forgotten about Caterina's predicament. Gladdened by the knowledge that he would see her the following day, Alessandro accepted Rosa's invitation.

At last they reached the *taverna* and found every table beneath the *pergola* full of villagers discussing their concerns about the festival and the Bishop. While Rosa took her place in the chair beside the hearth, Alessandro joined Luca in the shadows, retrieving his guitar to repeated thanks from the wolf-man.

"Come, children, gather round and I shall tell you a story about Befana, our Harvest Mother," said Rosa. The children crept forward, urged on by their parents, and sat down on the straw mats in front of Rosa, which the innkeeper's wife Cristina had provided for them. When they were all settled, Rosa began.

* * * * * * *

On Sunday we will celebrate the Festival of Santa Sofia, where we give thanks to our Blessed Mother for her love and wisdom, and for the bountiful fruits of the harvest. Tonight, I am going to tell you a story about Befana, a fairy and ancient Mother of the Harvest, and her sister Hecate, an old, wizened crone, rather like me.

One day a young girl, just like you Fiora, was gathering corn in the fields when, as if from nowhere, an old woman appeared, dressed in long, black robes. Fiora leapt back in fright for she assumed the stranger to be a witch, but then the old woman said, "Have no fear, child. My name is Hecate and I am the sister of the good fairy Befana. Take this apple to quench your thirst."

On hearing that Hecate was Befana's sister, the girl's fear vanished, for Befana was indeed a good fairy, who filled her stocking with presents every sixth day of January. So the young girl, who was very thirsty from her hard work in the fields, accepted the juicy apple from Hecate and took a bite.

At once, the ground beneath her opened up and she fell headlong into a deep pit. The poor girl was very frightened and began to sob. Her head hurt from the fall, and as dusk fell she felt so alone. Indeed, she feared she would never be able to escape until, glancing up, she noticed a light flickering from above and cried out, "Help me! Help me!"

Just then, a radiant light filled the gloomy hole and a beautiful woman appeared, dressed in turquoise robes sparkling with silver stars. "I am the good fairy, Befana, Mother of the Harvest. Come with me, child, and I will see you home to safety."

Moments later, the young girl found herself standing outside her house. Her mother opened the door and embraced her daughter, "You were lost but now you are found. Come, sit by the fire and warm yourself." The young girl approached the hearth to find a stocking hanging from the chimneybreast, overflowing with harvest fruits.

And so, children, the message I bring to you tonight is this. Do not be afraid of eating from the black crone Hecate's fruit of wisdom and falling into the dark pit of fear, for the good fairy Befana will always find you and bring you back to the light, where you will discover great gifts. In the same way that the seed must germinate in the darkness of the earth before growing into grain, so must we all experience difficult times if we are to grow wise and strong. But remember children, you are never alone. Our Blessed Mother is always with you.

* * * * * * *

Rosa finished her story and smiled down at the children, their eyes open wide. The villagers applauded their wisewoman before gathering their offspring back onto their laps. "And now," said Rosa, "I give you our travelling storyteller, Alessandro."

A further round of applause followed as Alessandro took his seat in the chair by the hearth. "Good evening, ladies and gentlemen. Tonight, allow me if you will to continue the harvest theme of this evening's *veglia*, and to bring alive for you the ancient Greek myth of Demeter and Persephone."

"Storyteller, what of your travels?" asked the innkeeper Dionisio, who was keen to discover the secrets of his new lodger's past. "Could you not tell us of the many places you have visited?"

"The most important thing my travels have taught me, Dionisio, is that every place is the same. They may look or smell different, but the people living in them experience the same emotions of joy and pain, love and hatred, peace and anger in the infinite cycle of birth, life and death. If I were to tell you a story of a place I have visited, it would be the story of your own village, only painted in a different light. Instead, I would prefer to tell you one of the myths of old that my grandfather taught me as a child, for it is through these stories that we can learn the truth about ourselves."

* * * * * * *

Demeter, Goddess of the Harvest and of the fertility of the ploughed field, sailed to Greece from the ancient land of Crete, where people lived freely and at peace. She came with her daughter Persephone, Maiden of the Corn, and this is their story.

One day, Persephone was walking in a meadow, picking flowers with her friends, when the goddess Gaia produced a narcissus from the earth. As Persephone bent to pick the narcissus, the earth opened up beneath her and her uncle Hades, Lord of the Underworld, dragged her down on his immortal horses.

Persephone sobbed in fear, but her cries were not heard by her father Zeus, only by Hecate dwelling in her cave, and by Helius, son of Hyperion. Her mother, Demeter, was distraught and flew in the form of a bird over land and sea for nine days, searching for her daughter. On the tenth day, Hecate told her that she had heard Persephone's cries, and Helius confirmed that Zeus had given her to his brother Hades as his wife.

Now Demeter was angry with Zeus and left Olympus to wander the earth disguised as an old woman in black robes. She came to Eleusis and told the daughters of Celeus that she had come from Crete and was looking for work in a house. The women took pity on her and invited her to care for their baby brother. Demeter nursed the baby Demephoon as a god and tried to make him immortal by placing him in the fire each night. One night, his mother Metaneira saw what Demeter was doing and cried out in fear. The goddess grew angry because Metaneira's fear would now keep the child mortal, and ordered Celeus to build a temple where she could teach them her rites. Celeus obeyed her and the child Demephoon flourished.

However, Demeter was still in mourning for her daughter Persephone, and caused a great famine to cover the earth. Zeus sent Iris and all the other gods and goddesses with gifts to placate her, but Demeter still refused to return to Olympus or to allow any fruits to grow until she had seen her daughter. So Zeus sent Hermes to ask Hades if he would let Persephone go. Hades agreed but gave Persephone a honey-sweet pomegranate to eat, to ensure that she would not spend all her days with her mother.

Persephone was reunited with her mother Demeter, and after they had shared a loving embrace, Demeter asked her if she had eaten anything, for then she would be forced to stay in the underworld for a third of the year, returning only in the spring. Persephone confirmed that Hades had made her eat a pomegranate, and so from that day forth she was destined to spend the winter in the underworld with Hades, emerging only in the spring to be reunited with her mother Demeter.

Hecate joined them in their joyous celebration and became Persephone's lady-in-waiting, while Zeus sent Rhea to bring Demeter back to Olympus and instructed her to allow the harvest to be fruitful once more. Demeter agreed and at once fruit, flowers and corn sprung up from the earth, while she taught the Kings of Eleusis the secrets of her mysteries to ensure that they would never be forgotten.

And so, my friends, may you draw comfort in the coming

winter from the knowledge that the corn maiden Persephone will be growing beneath the earth, appearing in springtime as the new shoots and maturing into the ripened grain of Demeter, Black Mother of the Harvest. May you remember them in your prayers this Sunday, and give thanks for the wisdom of their mysteries and for the bountiful fruits of their harvest.

* * * * * * *

Alessandro came to the end of his harvest story and bowed in acknowledgement of the applause, before picking up his guitar and playing a medley of traditional Neapolitan songs to the delight of the villagers. For once they were able to shake off the gloom that had descended on their lives since the arrival of Bishop Pazzini. After a while, Alessandro encouraged Luca to come out from the shadows and to sing a song of his choice, while Alessandro accompanied him impromptu on his guitar. Daunted by the suspicious stares of the villagers, Luca faltered at first but then grew in confidence, giving a moving rendition of the ballad his mother used to sing to him when she was nursing him as an ailing child. The words always reminded Luca of how much she had loved and nurtured him, despite his many afflictions, before she died and left him in the care of his father Piero.

> I watch you lying there
> Wondering why I am hurting you.
> How can I explain to you that
> Mamma's trying to make you better?
>
> Ravens fly,
> Sofia cries,
> There's only betrayal in your eyes.

Ravens fly,
Sofia cries,
I wish I could just say goodbye.

But that's a Mamma's role.
We hurt and heal.
We wipe your tears,
And we swallow our own.

Luca glanced up to find his listeners staring at him in astonishment. Bowing, he scuttled into the shadows to sit and treasure the significance of what he had just done. He, Luca the wolf-man, had sung in public. Veronica would never believe him.

Alessandro continued to play for a while longer to ensure his free lodgings, his songs carried on the breeze over the rooftop of the bakery and through the open casement to the woman seated on the stone seat, a smile upon her lips as she listened to the rich tones of the storyteller's voice.

Friday

13 August 1583

Santa Sofia

Alessandro rose early the next morning. As he stepped outside the *taverna*, he caught sight of a group of six men standing in front of the butchery. Enrico was there, a long, intricate rifle slung over his shoulder. Beside him was a large man, whom Alessandro recognised as the butcher Giorgio, Dionisio's elder brother. Once the men had set off on their hunting trip into the forest behind the *taverna*, Alessandro made his way to the chapel.

As he approached the moon portal, Alessandro could hear Rosa's raised voice coming from the chapel garden. "Paolo told me that he witnessed your beating, Caterina." Silence followed as Alessandro hung back in the shadows of the trees. "Do you not realise what effect this will have on him? By tolerating Enrico's violence, you are teaching Paolo that it is acceptable to be abused. Do you want him to grow up believing that he, like his mother, deserves to be punished and not loved?"

"Of course not!" Alessandro could detect the anger and frustration in Caterina's voice.

"Then stand up to Enrico and protect Paolo, before it is too late." Just then, Rosa spied Alessandro standing by the gate. The wisewoman hailed him a greeting as Caterina turned in surprise to see the stranger behind her. Rosa approached Alessandro, extending her arms out in a warm welcome. "Come, I would like you to meet my niece. Alessandro, this is Caterina."

Alessandro smiled at Caterina. "We meet again. I must offer you my apologies for any upset I may have caused you yesterday."

"It was nothing," dismissed Caterina.

Rosa looked on intrigued, while Caterina chose to avert her eyes from Alessandro, following the flight of a butterfly.

"I hope that your husband's wrath soon cooled?"

Caterina ignored his probing question, offering him a wan smile instead. An uncomfortable silence ensued until Rosa stepped in. "Caterina, why don't you show Alessandro around? We were speaking only yesterday of the chapel and cave. I am sure he would be interested to see them." Caterina glared at Rosa, who in turn ignored her. Then, obliged by her innate sense of courtesy, Caterina motioned to Alessandro to follow her.

As they neared the chapel, she warned him to take care on the narrow path that ran along the edge of the ravine. Alessandro stopped and leant over the low wall, which was all that protected them from falling down the steep drop.

"Isn't this a dangerous place to have a chapel?"

Caterina nodded. "I worry about the children when they come to worship, but there is always someone here to watch them. Besides, the villagers couldn't have defied Sofia's wish and this is where she wanted the chapel to be."

"Has anyone ever fallen down the ravine?"

Caterina glanced at the stranger, but seeing only a keen interest, she told him the story of the soldier.

* * * * * * *

Legend has it that during one of the many wars, a soldier fell down the ravine and lay on the rocks below with every bone in his body broken. The goddess Sofia appeared to him bathed in light, and gave the soldier two thorns to climb back up the ravine. The soldier shook his head in defeat, for he knew the two thorns would never support his weight. Sofia urged him to trust in her, and so the soldier stood up and began to climb up the steep wall. To his astonishment, he discovered his broken bones were healed and the thorns were as strong as pick axes, enabling him to scale back up the ravine. When he reached the top, he sank to his knees in front of the chapel and removed his uniform, laying it on the altar as a way of giving thanks to the divine Mother. Since that day, many people have experienced Sofia's miraculous healing power, and every one of them has left their favourite garment in gratitude.

* * * * * * *

Alessandro gazed down at the beauty of the woman beside him, whose blue eyes shone as she spoke. When she had finished, Caterina looked up and smiled, glad of Alessandro's interest. "Would you like to see the soldier's uniform and the other garments?"

"Very much," replied Alessandro, as Caterina led him into the chapel and down the narrow aisle. To the right of the altar was a large alcove carved into the mountain's rock, with an iron gate across the front. Through the bars of the gate, Alessandro could make out rows of garments, including wedding dresses, military uniforms and baptism gowns. There was a mystical air about the costumes, which hung together as proof of the divine Mother's healing power. "Have all the owners of these garments experienced a miracle?" he asked.

"Yes, all of them. The miracles usually happen around the Festival of Santa Sofia. Perhaps you will be fortunate enough to witness one this year," Caterina said, shivering from the cool air in the chapel, which was in sharp contrast to the warmth of the sun.

"You're cold," remarked Alessandro, reaching out and touching her bare arm. Caterina recoiled. Her father had denied her physical affection as a child, and the rare times her husband had forced his unwanted attentions on her, she had been left feeling bruised and dirty. Never before had she experienced the gentle touch of a man, and Alessandro's gesture confused her. "Forgive me. I have offended you," said Alessandro, dropping his hand and looking away.

Caterina saw his discomfort and sought to reassure him. "There is no offence. It is merely your kindness that is my undoing." Before Alessandro could respond, Caterina turned to fetch the key and headed towards the secret door, but her words had not gone unheeded by Alessandro. "I will show you the cave now. As Rosa has no doubt mentioned, you must not speak to anyone of what you are about to see. There are many who would not understand and would accuse us of witchcraft." Alessandro nodded, finding it difficult to concentrate on Caterina's words when his senses were spinning from the perfumed smell of her skin. "Alessandro?" prompted Caterina. Offering her a strained smile, he gestured for her to lead the way down the tunnel, but the sway of her hips did little to lessen his desire.

On entering the cave, Caterina picked up the broom of protection from the doorway and used it to waft the incense, filling the cave with the smoke of purification. Meanwhile, Alessandro wandered to the back of the cave and peered through the narrow gap into the next chamber. "Do you use this as well?"

"Yes. It is where the bones and ashes of the moon priestesses are buried to await their rebirth."

Alessandro gazed over at the luminous green pool. At the water's edge lay several clay pots with their spouts formed like birds. "What are those?" he asked.

Caterina joined him on the steps leading down to the pool. "They contain sea water, the essence of the moon. As priestesses of the Black Goddess of the night, we draw our power from the moon."

"Why are they shaped like birds?" asked Alessandro.

"Birds, like the rain, fall through the sky, alight on the earth and sink into the waters of the underworld, uniting the three different realms," explained Caterina.

Alessandro's gaze then turned to the majestic statue in the centre. "The bird upon the lily is a dove."

"Yes. The soaring spirit…" she began.

"…of freedom," Alessandro finished.

Caterina looked at him in surprise. "How do you know?"

"My grandfather taught me well," explained Alessandro. "The dove accompanies the ancient goddesses Aphrodite and Persephone in the myths of old." Caterina smiled. It was not easy in those treacherous times to find others with whom she could share her beliefs. Alessandro noticed that Caterina had begun to let her guard down and seized his opportunity. "It would seem that you have need of the dove's power to free yourself." Caterina's face fell and she turned away. She would not be drawn, even by Rosa, to discuss Enrico's violence nor the unrealistic notion of leaving him. "I see I have offended you once more. Forgive me."

Caterina's expression was blank. "There is nothing to forgive. Shall we go?"

Alessandro followed Caterina out of the cave and into the chapel garden, attempting to break the uncomfortable silence with idle conversation. "What are your plans this afternoon?"

"Along with the rest of the village, I will be making sauce for the year ahead, using the tomatoes we harvested last week," replied Caterina.

"Perhaps I could lend a helping hand?"

"I am sure the villagers would be grateful for your help."

Alessandro was sensitive enough not to insist further, but felt frustrated by Caterina's refusal to allow him to voice his fears for her safety. Vowing to find Caterina later that afternoon and attempt to speak with her once more, Alessandro bade her farewell and headed towards the portal.

Just then, Rosa stuck her head out from behind a rose bush and called out to him. As he turned towards her, he caught sight of Caterina walking back inside the chapel. Rosa recognised the look in Alessandro's eyes and smiled to herself. "I appreciate your concern for Caterina's welfare, Alessandro, but you can no more save her than you could save your sister. Protecting Caterina will not resolve your feelings of guilt concerning Isabetta's murder."

Alessandro's eyes lit up with anger. "How can you stand by and watch her be so abused?"

Rosa shrugged her shoulders. "I cannot create the strength and courage that she needs to stand up to Enrico. I can only encourage her to believe that she has it and show her why it is important to use it."

"How can she fight Enrico when he is stronger than her?"

"Enrico is weak like all bullies, in the same way that your father was. In understanding this, you may be less inclined to replace one form of control with another."

Alessandro frowned in confusion. "Whatever do you mean?"

Rosa gave a sigh, knowing that her words were difficult for Alessandro to hear. "Your desire to control Caterina's destiny stems from your fear of not being able to control life, but you will never succeed in doing that. Learn to trust in life and relinquish control. By believing in the divinity of your own soul, you will no longer fear those mortals who seek to control you. They have no real power over your soul's destiny. Draw strength from Mother Earth, whose nurturing waters can multiply into the destructive flood of the Great Dragon, belittling the insignificant power of men and institutions such as the Church. Put your fears of this moment in the greater perspective of all your past and future lifetimes, and allow them to become meaningless in proportion. Trust that you will cope with whatever life throws at you and let go of your fears."

At that moment, Caterina stepped out of the chapel and Alessandro made a quick retreat into the woods, more to escape from Rosa's unsettling words than to avoid her niece. In the stillness of the forest, he contemplated her advice, shaking his head in bemusement. He had never considered the possibility that he was frightened of anything, let alone that he may be trying to exert the same control that he had so despised in his father and the priests. Perhaps Rosa spoke the truth. Perhaps it was not his place to save Caterina. Indeed, when he had tried to protect Isabetta, he had only succeeded in endangering her further. That experience had made him wary of the dangerous consequences of such impulsive behaviour. He would not jeopardise Caterina in the same way. However, he could follow Rosa's example and help her to see that Enrico's violence was unacceptable.

On his return to the square, Alessandro set about finding Luca to help him with his plan to spend the afternoon with Caterina. He did not have to venture far, for soon he could hear the chords of his guitar and Luca's lilting voice coming from the apple orchard. "Luca?" The hairy face of the young man appeared from behind a tree. "I need your help." Luca listened to Alessandro's request. He loved Veronica's cousin Caterina and did not want to be party to anything that might endanger her. On the other hand, he too was desperate for her to escape from her husband's violence. With Enrico away on a hunting trip, it would be a perfect opportunity for Alessandro to speak with Caterina. Noting the sincerity in his eyes, Luca felt reassured by Alessandro's concern and decided to help him. Nodding his head in agreement, he made his retreat, running through the shadows of the orchard towards a row of peasants' huts that clung to the bottom of the hill.

At that moment, Niccolo stepped out onto the balcony. "Alessandro!" He looked up to find Niccolo beckoning to him. "Come. I need to speak with you." Alessandro climbed up the stairs and followed him into the consulting room. "Please take a seat." Alessandro settled himself into a chair opposite Niccolo, wondering if he had come up with an idea about how to bring Bishop Pazzini to justice. Niccolo, however, was keen to discuss other matters. "I wanted to thank you, Alessandro. Your offer of friendship has warmed the heart of a lonely young man. Never before have I seen Luca with such joy in his eyes."

"It is nothing," replied Alessandro. "I am merely repaying him for his kindness in helping me."

"Nevertheless, your attitude towards Luca may help to change the way in which the villagers perceive him." Alessandro smiled, casting his mind back to old Sapia's prophetic words and realising that he had found the outcast who would benefit from his friendship. A strained silence followed as Niccolo busied himself rearranging some jars on his table, and Alessandro waited. "There is another matter I wish to speak to you about," Niccolo at last said.

"Yes?" Alessandro was growing impatient.

"It concerns Caterina."

Niccolo seemed once more to be at a loss for words, and Alessandro fell upon a reason for his hesitancy. "You are in love with her?"

"Heavens, no!" cried Niccolo. "She is my cousin. After her mother died giving birth to her, she and her father lived with my mother and me at the farmhouse. We were brought up like sister and brother." Alessandro felt a sense of relief, while Niccolo struggled with how to tell Alessandro of his fears without offending him. "It is just that I am concerned for Caterina's safety. Her husband has a violent temper, and I am worried what he might do to Caterina if he were to find her talking with another man."

Alessandro now understood what was troubling Niccolo. "You heard what happened yesterday in the bakery?"

"Yes, Aurelio told me. My mother also mentioned that you were going to visit them at the chapel this morning. It is not that I wish to intrude, Alessandro, but Caterina is a woman with whom a man could fall in love at a glance. Such infatuation might render him blind to the dangers he puts her in by courting her attention."

"I understand your concern, Niccolo, but let me reassure you that I am not some lovesick youth. Like you, I seek only to help Caterina."

"Then I would urge you not to endanger her further by seeking out her company."

Alessandro sighed and shook his head. "On this matter, I cannot give you my word. I must meet with her again and persuade her to find the strength to stand up to Enrico."

"How do you intend to do that?" asked Niccolo.

"By telling her the story of Isabetta's fate. Perhaps the horror of such events will help Caterina to realise that she must leave Enrico, before it is too late."

Niccolo recalled Alessandro's story from the previous afternoon and understood his motive for wanting to tell Caterina about the fate of his sister. Perhaps it was what Caterina needed to hear in order to find the strength to break the chains that bound her. "Something needs to be done. My mother and I have tried but to no avail. Nothing we say seems to make a difference, so I will give you my support."

Alessandro stood up and offered Niccolo his hand. "Thank you."

As they shook hands, Niccolo leant forward, lowering his voice. "About the Bishop. My mother seems to think she may have the answer, but she needs to speak with someone first. I will keep you informed of any progress."

"Your mother's plan may be my only hope, for I have begun to despair of ever bringing Jacobo Pazzini to justice."

"Have no fear. My mother walks the path of wisdom."

The door of the consulting room had just closed when Luca reappeared at the bottom of the stairs, carrying a heavy iron object in his hands. Alessandro leapt down the stairs and grasped it from him. "Ah, you have it! You are a friend indeed Luca. I'll meet you here later." Alessandro glanced about, but seeing no one watching him, he headed past the apple orchard, carrying his bounty with care. His actions, however, did not go unnoticed by the woman in the house on the corner.

As Alessandro walked along the track to Enrico's farmhouse, he could see Caterina sitting under the *pergola*. Already the vines that crept around the wooden posts were beginning to wilt in the heat of the August sun, their fruit swollen with juice like the tomatoes that Caterina was feeding through the crusher. She looked up on hearing his footsteps and frowned. Alessandro placed the cage on the table, gesturing to the three white birds it contained. "The doves are to make amends for upsetting you this morning." Caterina gave a slight smile but her eyes remained guarded. "You don't like the birds?" asked Alessandro.

"I do. I am most grateful, Alessandro. It is just that I cannot accept your gift."

"Why not?"

Caterina moved away from Alessandro on the pretence of stoking the fire that was warming a large cauldron of water. "You should not be here. What if my husband returns and finds you?"

Alessandro followed her. "Luca has assured me that Enrico will not return from his hunting trip before nightfall, so he need never know that I was here. If you will only listen to the story I have to tell you, then I swear that I will leave you alone." Caterina glanced up at the urgency in Alessandro's voice. What story could he possibly need to tell her? Suspecting a trap, she shook her head. Alessandro stepped closer towards her. "Niccolo suggested that I come to see you. He thinks it is important that you hear what I have to say."

On hearing her cousin's name, Caterina stilled. She looked over Alessandro's shoulder into the distance to reassure herself that Enrico was nowhere to be seen, then sat back down on the bench and gestured to Alessandro to follow suit. "I suppose it is unlikely that Enrico will return before dusk, and if Niccolo thinks I should hear your story, then I will listen to it." Alessandro sat down on the bench opposite Caterina and watched as she continued to feed the bright red tomatoes from a basket into the funnel, turning the wheel of the grinder so that the juice from the fruit spurted forth into a large, wooden bucket at the foot of the table.

"Where is your son?" he asked.

"He is with all the other children of the village, picking basil leaves in the fields so that we can add them to the sauce."

"You love him very much."

"Yes," Caterina replied with a smile. "Paolo is my life. I carried him, gave birth to him, suckled him. He is part of my life-blood and I feel his pain and joy as if it were my own. I would risk my life to protect him but I fear that something will happen to him beyond my control."

"I am sure that every mother experiences the same fear. It's what often drives women to have large families, so that if something befalls one child there will still be others to love." Caterina's eyes filled with tears and she lowered her head, but not before Alessandro had seen. "Forgive me. I have an unerring ability to upset you."

Caterina paused to compose herself. "It is not your fault. It is just that I dream of having another child but I know I never will."

"Why not?" asked Alessandro.

Caterina hid behind her hair. "It is a story not worthy of your attention."

"I am a storyteller, Caterina. My livelihood depends on

listening to and telling stories. They are what bind us together. Stories are how we express our fears and joys, creating a sense of unity through shared experience. Pray, tell me your story."

Caterina took a deep breath and began to speak in much the same way that Alessandro spoke of his sister's murder. He recognised it as the voice of mourning, for it was often only possible to speak of a traumatic event as if it had happened to someone else. Such was the way in which Caterina told her story to Alessandro that afternoon beneath the *pergola*.

* * * * * * *

It was two years after the birth of Paolo and a child had been growing in my belly for five months. One evening I was delayed, helping Rosa to deliver a child, as often happens at night. Enrico had been drinking as usual and his anger had grown into a rage as the hours passed, imagining I was with another man. As I crept into the house, he grabbed me by my hair and threw me onto the floor. He kept slapping my face, accusing me of being a whore and a slut. I was crying, begging him to stop. "Please, Enrico, not when I am with child."

"With child?" he bellowed. "There's no child in your belly. Only the devil's spawn of another man, which I swear by God I will rid you of tonight."

I screamed and begged him again and again, but to no avail. He struck my head each time I tried to crawl away and kicked my belly until an excruciating pain wracked my body and I began to bleed. On seeing the blood, he howled in triumph like a beast feasting on the pleasure of a kill. He left me there on the floor and passed out in bed upstairs. I managed to crawl out of the door and up the lane. My uncle Dionisio heard my cries from the *taverna* and carried me to Niccolo's consulting room, where he and Rosa nursed me.

I lost the baby and since that day I have not conceived. The injuries to my body were too great. That is why I know I will never have another child. Now perhaps you can understand why Paolo is even more important to me than ever. Without him, I would never again feel the joy of loving a child.

* * * * * * *

Alessandro could not find the words needed to offer Caterina solace, for there were none. Instead, he seized the opportunity to persuade her. "Now do you see why you must leave him?"

Caterina gave a bitter laugh. "Rosa. Niccolo. Now you. You all tell me I must leave my husband. None of you say how I should do this or where I should go. Why? Because there are no answers. If I were to leave Santa Sofia, Enrico and Bishop Pazzini would hunt me down and bring me back. As long as the robbers and murderers hadn't found me first. If I refused to return to my husband's house, the Bishop would have me thrown into a nunnery. A woman cannot live alone unless she is a widow. Do you not understand? I am not a man. I do not have the freedom like you to wander the earth with no fears or responsibilities. I am a woman, a wife and a mother. I have no rights. I am the property of my husband. I have nowhere to run to and I have a child to protect." Caterina was now shaking with rage. "And what of you, Alessandro? Have you asked yourself why you never stay in one place for long? Running away is not the answer. You may think you are free because you travel, but I could not imagine a lonelier way of life. I may have a cruel husband but I have Paolo, my family, my community. What do you have Alessandro? Are you truly free?"

Alessandro remained silent. Caterina's words had struck a chord, but he ignored his own feelings. Instead, moving to sit beside her, he took her hand in his and stroked her fingers. She did not recoil this time, as if in need of his touch. "The story I want to tell you, Caterina, might prove to you why you must find the strength to defy Enrico and Bishop Pazzini."

* * * * * * *

When I saw you yesterday, with your fair colouring and white dress, you reminded me of my sister Isabetta. Like you, she was passive and accepting of her fate. Instead of rising up against our father and the village priest, she allowed their bullish treatment to sap her spirit, until she had no strength left to fight or to follow her dreams. Such was her frailty that she fell into a trap set by Bishop Pazzini who raped and murdered her.

I understand how difficult it was for Isabetta and is for you to stand up to violent men and to the Church's authority. I blame myself for not protecting Isabetta when I still had the chance. My instinct now is to reach out and save you, but Rosa insists that only you can find the courage to defy Enrico. That is why I am here, in the hope that Isabetta's story will help you to see how important it is to find your strength. If not for yourself, then for Paolo.

I have never been able to forgive my mother for not protecting us. Her betrayal has left me wary of trusting anyone. You are right. I am lonely. But it was my mother's acceptance of male violence that led me to be so. Do you want Paolo to suffer the same fate as me? Perhaps I should not judge my mother so harshly. Perhaps being a woman made it impossible for her to stand up to my father and the priests, but you are different from her. She was alone, whereas like you said, you have your family, friends and community. Draw strength from their love, ask for their help, and find the courage to stand up to Enrico and protect your son. Or one day your husband may strike a fatal blow, leaving Paolo without a mother.

* * * * * * *

Caterina brushed the tears from her cheeks and stroked Alessandro's hand. Beneath his strong façade, she could see the pain of the boy betrayed by his father and mother. "You would do well to forgive your mother, Alessandro. I am sure that if she had thought she could have protected you, she would have done. You must also forgive yourself for you are not to blame for Isabetta's death." As she spoke the words, Caterina understood that she too was not to blame for her mother's death. Glancing up at the doves fluttering in their cage, she felt an urge to free them.

"I thought perhaps you could set them free on the night of the festival, to symbolise the liberation of your own soul."

Caterina smiled through her tears. "Paolo will love them."

As if on cue, the little boy came running down the track. "Mamma, Mamma!" Caterina went to meet him, stooping to cradle him in her arms. "Who's that?" Paolo asked, catching sight of Alessandro over his mother's shoulder and fearful of the stranger's presence.

Caterina led him over to the table. "This is Alessandro. He is a travelling storyteller who has come to entertain us with his stories and songs."

Paolo eyed Alessandro with suspicion, but on seeing the birdcage on the table, he climbed up onto a bench and reached up to stroke the doves through the iron bars. "What beautiful birds. Are they ours?"

Caterina paused, fearful of what Enrico would do if he discovered they were a gift from Alessandro, but on seeing the excitement in Paolo's eyes, she could not bear to disappoint him. "Yes, Paolino. Alessandro brought them for us to set loose on the night of the festival, so that they may fly to freedom like the dove on Sofia's statue."

"Like Rosa said."

"Yes. Paolo, would you do something for me?"

"What, Mamma?"

"If Papa asks you who gave us the birds, would you tell him that Rosa did?"

Paolo looked at her in confusion. "Why?"

"Well, I think Papa might be angry if he knew Alessandro had given them to us," explained Caterina.

"Oh." Paolo was too young to understand, but he was old enough to know that he would do anything to protect his mother. "I promise, Mamma."

"Good boy. Now, what do you say to the kind gentleman?"

Paolo looked up at the stranger with smiling eyes. "Thank you, sir. The birds are beautiful."

"You are very welcome, Paolo. Their beauty reminded me of your mother," replied Alessandro.

Paolo smiled, gladdened by Alessandro's kindness towards his mother. Caterina, on the other hand, blushed at the compliment and sought to change the subject. "Come, Paolo, why don't you show us all the basil leaves you have picked today." Caterina reached for the basket that Paolo had discarded on the ground in his excitement at seeing the doves.

Paolo struck a bashful pose. "I won the prize for picking the most leaves." Caterina's eyes opened wide with the delight of a mother who takes pride in her child's every feat. "Tomorrow evening after dinner, I am to lead the first dance with Fiora."

Caterina hugged her son. "I'm so proud of you, Paolo. I know how hard you've been practising with the dance group. What an honour to lead the first dance and to partner your beautiful cousin Fiora." Then Caterina lifted the birdcage off the table, hanging it from the branch of the single olive tree in front of the farmhouse. "Come now, if we don't get these bottles filled, corked and boiling in the pot, we will not be going to the dance."

Paolo sat down on the bench with his basket of basil leaves on the table in front of him, while Caterina removed the crusher to make room for the large bucket of tomato juice that Alessandro was lifting off the ground. Then Caterina arranged some old, washed wine bottles in front of her, as Alessandro assumed his position at the end of the table. First, Caterina ladled the tomato juice from the bucket into a bottle. Then, Paolo stuffed a bunch of basil leaves into it. Lastly, Alessandro pressed a stopper down hard into the bottle, before placing it into the large cauldron of boiling water hanging over the fire. An evening's duration of being boiled would ensure the preservation of the tomato sauce for the year ahead.

Dusk was falling by the time the three had filled and corked every bottle, their enjoyment of the shared pastime evident in their easy chatter and laughter. Caterina watched her son as he grew in confidence with Alessandro. Perhaps Alessandro and Rosa were right, she thought. Perhaps there was a way to protect Paolo from the violence that had become a part of their everyday life.

"I should be going," said Alessandro at last. "I'll look forward to watching you perform tomorrow evening, Paolo." Caterina smiled up at Alessandro, whose presence that afternoon had opened a window of opportunity in her mind. "Until tomorrow, Caterina." Alessandro turned and began walking back down the track towards the village square. Caterina watched him as he left, turning once to call out over his shoulder, "Mind you keep your wings unclipped." Caterina smiled to herself with the joy of a captive who has tasted her first sip of freedom, oblivious to the fact that she was about to be recaptured by the hunter.

Meanwhile, Alessandro crept back past the orchard towards Niccolo's consulting room, observed once more by the woman behind the shutter.

"Alessandro!" He turned to see Padre Francesco approaching him from the church. "Could you spare a moment of your time?"

"Certainly, Padre," replied Alessandro.

The old priest was now level with Alessandro and glanced up at the house on the corner where Emilia and Agnesa lived. "Not here. It isn't safe. Come with me to the vestry."

Alessandro's concern grew as he followed Padre Francesco into the church and the privacy of the vestry walls, noticing the agitated way in which the priest began to pace to and fro.

"What's worrying you, Padre?" asked Alessandro.

"It's Rosa. She's adamant that we hold the Festival at the chapel."

"What do the villagers want to do?"

"They are confused and frightened," explained Padre Francesco. "Word has spread about the burnings on Tuesday in Arunca. Even if they do ask me to hold the service at the chapel, it would be madness for Rosa to join me in leading the prayers. Bishop Pazzini could not send the whole village to the stake, but if he were to witness Rosa in her role as priestess, he would have all the evidence he needs to try her for heresy."

"Why does Rosa still insist on such a dangerous course of action?" asked Alessandro.

Padre Francesco stopped pacing to sit down on one of the benches, where Alessandro joined him. "Rosa believes that it is her duty as one of a long line of priestesses to lead the villagers in their prayers to our Blessed Mother. It is not that I am critical of her for wanting to fulfil her spiritual role, for they say that in the Early Church some women rose to the level of bishop, but times have changed. The Church is not what it once was. The true teachings of Christ, who loved and honoured women, have been distorted so as to propagate fear and hatred of them. I am powerless in this wave of Inquisition madness to protect Rosa. If only she would swallow her pride and lie low for a while, until these troubled times are over and Bishop Pazzini is no more."

Alessandro nodded his head, the mention of the Bishop

prompting him to wonder whether Rosa had made any progress with formulating her plan. "Did Rosa mention the idea she has had to bring Bishop Pazzini to justice?"

"Yes, forgive me, I have a message for you. We are all to meet at Rosa's house for dinner to hear what she has to say."

"Well, perhaps we could try to persuade her to see sense then."

Alessandro stood up to leave, but Padre Francesco reached out to grasp his arm. "Alessandro, I think it would be better if one of us spoke to Rosa alone before dinner. If we all try at the same time, she will only grow more stubborn. Perhaps as an outsider you might have more success."

Grateful for their willingness to help him overthrow Bishop Pazzini, Alessandro agreed. "If you think I could help, then I would be glad to speak with Rosa."

Padre Francesco smiled with relief. "Thank you. You will no doubt find her in the chapel recess at this hour."

Alessandro looked at him in confusion, trying to picture the recess. Then it dawned on him that Padre Francesco was referring to the cave. Alessandro smiled at his discretion and gentle nature, which was a healing balm to the anger he felt towards the priesthood. "Then I shall look for her there."

As Alessandro entered the square, he caught sight of Enrico and the other men returning from their hunting trip, carrying a large boar to the butchery. Several men playing *tarocco* outside the *taverna* leapt up to marvel at the size of the boar, which would be roasted the following afternoon in time for the village feast that evening. Leaving the boar in the butchery cellar, the men wandered over to the *taverna* and ordered some jugs of wine to celebrate the success of their hunt. Keeping to the shadows, Alessandro quickly made his way down *Via Principale*.

As he stepped into the chapel garden, Alessandro felt a slight shiver coarse through his body. A heavy silence hung amid the deserted grove of trees, save for the distant sound of water cascading into the ravine. Flickering flames of candlelight filtered through the chapel windows, sending shadows dancing across the rose bushes. Alessandro made his way into the chapel to find it deserted. Pulling aside the heavy curtain to the left of the altar, Alessandro noticed that the small, wooden door was ajar. Shutting it behind him, he used his hands to guide him along the tunnel wall towards the second door which he knocked upon. Within moments, Rosa came to stand on the other side of the door. "Who's there?"

"It's me. Alessandro."

Rosa turned the key. "Come in. I am just tending to the fire." Rosa led Alessandro into the cave where she bent over to stoke the embers that lay between the feet of the statue, cradled in the curve of the serpent's body.

"Do you come here each night?" asked Alessandro.

Rosa looked up at Alessandro from her crouched position. "The fire of the Black Goddess must always be kept alight. Now that she has been banished into the womb of the earth, it is even more important that we stoke up her flames."

Alessandro was reminded of the final riddle of Sapia's prophecy and realised that this must be the fire she alluded to. "Is that why you are still determined to lead the prayers on Sunday?"

Rosa studied Alessandro with a faint look of disappointment. "Francesco sent you." Then she knelt back on her heels, patting the ground beside her. "Come, sit, and I will tell you why I must fulfil my duty."

* * * * * * *

We live in an age when wars are being fought and people are being tortured and killed, all in the name of God. This is not what religion was intended for. Our ancestors who worshipped the Black Goddess in this cave did not seek to kill those who perceived the divine in a different image. They did not hold women responsible for all the suffering in the world and punish them for it. They strived to be loving, compassionate and tolerant, upholding those values that Christ later endorsed.

Alessandro, you must understand that I am not opposed to those who follow the true teachings of Christ. If I were, I could not have as much love and respect as I do for Padre Francesco. No one need abandon the Christian faith to be inspired by Sofia, for her divine wisdom is the bridge between all religious traditions. It is the Roman Church and priests like Bishop Pazzini that enrage me. Their unjust doctrines and violent methods are not fuelled by a love of the divine, but by a desire to grow evermore powerful and rich. This greed is exactly that which Christ despised in the Pharisees.

Even though deep inside all of us we know this to be wrong, more often than not we stand aside and do nothing, until we ourselves are threatened. Whether it is from fear or from a feeling that it does not concern us, still we do not question the Church's doctrines. In so doing, we lend credence to the beliefs that the divine is male, that man is superior to woman, that there is only one truth, thereby encouraging devotees to make war with those who hold a different truth. As a priestess of the Black Goddess, I believe it is my duty to stand up to the Church and to challenge its authority, so that those who continue to be oppressed and threatened with violence or death may find their liberation.

The extortionate ground rents and tithes the priests demand from our farming communities leave us crippled by debt, exhausted from our labours and without sufficient food to nourish our children. It is a priestess's responsibility to remind her fellow peasants of their right to freedom from such tyranny.

The Church desires to burn women like me in its fires because we embody the very wolf energy that it finds so threatening, but it is this denial of the dark side of life that leads to acts of evil. If there is to be peace in our world, then wholeness must be restored through the unity of darkness and light, women and men, Goddess and God. If our view of the world order does not change, then society never will. Sofia must return to redress the balance.

Like Isis, Cybele, Demeter, Artemis and Athena before her, Sofia is the light of hope that shines within the darkness. As one of her few surviving priestesses, I believe it is my responsibility to ensure that her light is never extinguished. One day, the Black Goddess will return in her full glory, bringing with her the wisdom of how to live freely in peace with ourselves, each other and the earth. The embers of her fire are still glowing and each day that we fan the flames is another step closer to her rebirth, when the boiling lava deep within the rocks of her body will explode up in a volcanic rush so violent that the hot ashes will fall upon every land, fertilising the earth so that the seed of the Black Goddess and her divine wisdom can grow once more.

* * * * * * *

Her passion riled, Rosa paused to catch her breath. Alessandro gazed at her in awe, inspired by her revolutionary fervour, which was so similar to his own. Then he remembered his promise to Padre Francesco. "Rosa, I understand your desire to stand up to the Church and Bishop Pazzini, for I myself have sworn to do the same, but why do you insist on a course of action that will ensure your death at the hands of the Inquisition? What good would you be to Sofia then? Surely there is some other way you could keep her fire alight without risking your life?"

Rosa looked at him in surprise. "There is no other way, Alessandro. Although the villagers only perceive me as their wisewoman assisting Padre Francesco at the festival, they still honour my role as a traditional part of their ritual. I would be betraying them if I neglected my duty. Moreover, I would be delivering the Black Goddess into the hands of the Roman Church. If I must die then so be it, but at least I will have died being true to Sofia and to myself."

"I understand your reasons, Rosa, but who would carry on your role of protecting Sofia if you were to die?"

"Caterina will. I have been training her now for many years and she is wise in all the ways of the Black Goddess. The only thing left for Caterina to do is to discover her true strength. Then she can pull herself out of her prison, in much the same way that you need to." Alessandro's body recoiled in defence as Rosa now steered the conversation towards him. "I recognise the same energy of the wolf burning in your eyes, Alessandro. We share the same desire for freedom. Yet the wolf inside you remains trapped by your fears." Silence fell as Rosa waited for a response that was not forthcoming. After a while, Alessandro looked up and Rosa caught his gaze. "Tell me, Alessandro. If you do not believe or trust in the wisdom of the Black Goddess, why do you tell stories about her?" Alessandro shook his head, unsure of how to answer Rosa, who continued to share her understanding with him.

* * * * * * *

Your stories reflect your dream world and wisdom comes in dreams. As you said at the *veglia*, the myths of old teach us the truth about ourselves. The myths you tell are those that provide resolution for your own soul's dilemma. The answer you have been searching for all these years is hidden in the myth of Demeter and Persephone.

It is not just a vegetation myth for harvest time, Alessandro, but one concerning the rebirth of the soul. In the same way that our souls are reborn after death in consecutive lifetimes, so are they spiritually reborn throughout each lifetime from the darkness of pain into the light of wisdom. Like the maiden Persephone, you are lost in the underworld, cut off from your soul, longing for reunion. You remain trapped by your pain and fear because you have ignored the teachings of the Black Goddess Demeter, or Sofia as I call her. You have forgotten that it is her wisdom that can teach you how to set yourself free.

A word of warning, though, Alessandro. Once you have left the underworld, do not expect to never enter it again. Like Persephone, your soul will return one way or another every year of your life, for it is through enduring and learning from challenging experiences that we grow again like the grain. However, with each descent, you take with you greater wisdom and strength, and therefore fall less far and for a shorter time. Have no fear, for you will always be accompanied by the wise crone Hecate. Trust that dawn always follows night and you will never become trapped again.

* * * * * * *

While Alessandro had been listening to Rosa's words, the dancing flames of the fire had drawn him into a meditative state. Like when Sapia had spoken to him, he had heard Rosa's voice as if it came not from her, but through her. Casting his glazed eyes upwards towards the statue of Sofia, he saw her smile and stretch her arms out to him. "Trust in me, Alessandro. I am always here, loving you, guiding you." His eyes filled with tears and he lowered his head onto his knees. Rosa stroked his back, allowing him to release all his grief, fear and loneliness from the last twenty years. They sat there for a long time until at last Alessandro raised his head.

"She spoke to me," he said. Rosa nodded. "I heard her voice," he continued. Rosa smiled. Then Alessandro fell silent, for there were no words to describe what he had just experienced. Only a sensation of relief, a lightening of the load, and light. Blinking, he glanced about the cave and pressed his hands upon the cold hardness of the rock to ground himself. Then he looked at Rosa. "Thank you."

Rosa returned his smile. "True healing works on a soul level. And now it is time for you to be reborn out of Sofia's womb-cave of transformation. Come. As the midwife of your soul, I will guide you back down the birth-canal tunnel." Pushing herself up from the floor, Rosa placed another oak log on the fire, before taking Alessandro's hand and leading him out of the cave. Once Rosa had locked the door behind them, Alessandro sensed the stifling weight of the confined space pressing down on him. Rosa pulled him through the second door and he burst forth into the bright, open space of the chapel. Alessandro glanced up at the painting of the Black Madonna and whispered a prayer of thanksgiving to Sofia, whose wisdom had guided him out of the cave. Then he turned to find Rosa standing behind him, her face wrinkled in a smile of satisfaction. "It is time we returned to my house. There is someone waiting there to meet you. I will tell Padre Francesco that you tried your best to persuade me but that I am a stubborn, old hag."

Alessandro laughed, offering her his arm for the climb back to the farmhouse.

As Alessandro and Rosa strolled through the olive grove, they could see the *pergola* ahead of them, illuminated by lanterns hanging from the posts. Padre Francesco and Niccolo were seated on chairs beneath the vines.

"I see my guests have not arrived yet. Good, that gives me time to finish preparing the meal. Make yourself comfortable, Alessandro, and I will join you anon." Rosa disappeared inside the house to indulge in her favourite pastime of cooking, which she considered to be a process of alchemical transformation. Washing the clams and baby squid she had bought from Matteo earlier, she added them to a large pot of tomato sauce warming over the fire. Outside she checked on the progress of the two chickens she had earlier immersed in clay pots filled with water, now bubbling from the heat of the fires beneath them. All that could be seen of the chickens were their bony, yellow feet poking out of the pots, and the pathetic sight saddened Rosa. That afternoon she had performed the sacrifice, kneeling down to give thanks to Sofia before cutting the chickens' throats and sprinkling their blood onto the earth. The ritual was intended to atone for the death of the birds by fertilising the earth they fed from. In the nearby vegetable patch, she pulled several ripe *melanzane* and *zucchini* from the earth to slice and add to another pot of tomato sauce simmering over the fire. With all the preparations now administered to, Rosa headed into her bedroom to change into a fresh dress, before rejoining the men beneath the *pergola*.

Just as Niccolo was pouring his mother a cup of wine, he looked up to see Luca approaching with a young woman, whose sensual features so captivated his attention that he spilt some wine on the table, causing Rosa to smile to herself. Although Niccolo had known of her existence through Luca, he had never met Veronica before, isolated as she was with her shepherd father Piero. Welcoming her with a warm embrace, Rosa took both Luca and Veronica by the hand and led them over to the table. "Alessandro, Niccolo, I would like you to meet Luca's sister, Veronica. She is the brave, young woman who has agreed to help us bring Bishop Pazzini to justice."

Alessandro looked at Luca in confusion, remembering their discussion from the previous day. He already knew that Veronica's testimony would not stand up in court, but how else could she be of help? Then he noticed the bruises still evident on Veronica's bare arms. "I'm Alessandro," he said with a warm smile. "You have my deepest sympathies for enduring such an ordeal."

"Luca told me the tragic tale of your sister," replied Veronica.

"I am only sorry that she was unable to escape. It is you who have my deepest sympathies."

Niccolo, who had been standing by the table listening to the dialogue with an expression of growing confusion and concern, now approached. "Veronica, are you hurt? Do you require medical attention?"

"I'm fine now, thanks to your mother's healing hands."

Niccolo stared at Rosa. "Mother?"

Rosa's eyes flashed with defiance. "Veronica was frightened. She didn't want anyone to know that she had survived the attack in case the Bishop returned to finish the job. Her wounds were such that I was able to treat her without your help."

"The Bishop attacked you?" cried Niccolo.

"Come, everyone take their seats and I will serve the first course," said Rosa. "Then Veronica can tell us her story."

Veronica approached the table, kissing the hand of Padre Francesco who was seated at the end. The priest smiled and stroked her hair. "I am very proud of you, Veronica. You have recovered well."

"You knew of this too?" asked Niccolo.

"It's my fault, Niccolo," said Veronica. "I asked them not to tell anyone."

Niccolo shrugged his shoulders beneath Veronica's gaze, and pulled out the chair next to Padre Francesco for her. Then he sat on her other side, while Alessandro and Luca took the chairs opposite them, leaving space for Rosa at the other end. She soon appeared with steaming bowls of thick seafood sauce and a basket of bread, the smell of basil and tomatoes filling the air. Padre Francesco gave thanks to Sofia as Patroness of the Harvest for the food before gesturing to them to begin eating, at which point Veronica began to tell them her story.

* * * * * * *

It was two months ago, on the day of Bishop Pazzini's first visit to Santa Sofia. Dusk had fallen and I was just leaving the chapel after having added more wood to Sofia's fire. The Bishop appeared at the door and asked me what I was doing. I explained that I had been blowing out the candles in the chapel, but I could tell that he wasn't listening to my words. Instead, his eyes were roaming over my body and he began to rant like a madman, accusing me of being a whore sent by the devil to tempt him. I backed away in fear, but there was nowhere I could run to. He lunged at me and tore at my clothes. I tried to fight him off but he was so heavy. Then he took the cross from the altar and began to beat me with it, bellowing that he would strike the devil out of me. The blows weakened me until I could no longer prevent him from wreaking his evil lust on my body.

When he had finished, he lifted me up and carried me out of the chapel to the wall above the ravine. Dazed and weak, I begged him to set me free, but he just laughed and pushed me off the wall, causing me to tumble headlong into the river below. The water caved in around me, swallowing my screams. I closed my eyes, believing I would drown. Then, something happened that I still cannot explain. I felt several hands upon my body, pushing me upwards until my head broke the surface of the water. Clinging to a rock, I looked up at the edge of the ravine, expecting to see the Bishop leering down at me but he had gone. Within moments Luca's head appeared over the wall. He climbed down and carried me back to the safety of our father's hut, where Rosa treated my wounds.

Since that day I have been in hiding, frightened of what the Bishop might do if he discovered I was still alive, but powerless to bring him to justice. Until now. Rosa came to see me today and we discussed her idea. I believe it has a good chance of working, and I am willing to try anything if it means preventing Bishop Pazzini from harming another woman.

* * * * * * *

Everyone present except for Niccolo had known of Bishop Pazzini's attack on Veronica, but still they sat in silence, moved by the retelling of her ordeal. Niccolo glanced at the bruises still marring Veronica's arms, desirous to reach out and soothe her pain. Instead he placed his hand over hers in sympathy. Veronica saw the compassion in his kind eyes, and her wide mouth curved up in a smile that lit up her face. Niccolo breathed in her scent, noticing how the tendrils of her hair clung to the faint dampness of her skin from the heat of the summer evening.

"Rosa, what exactly is this idea of yours?" asked Padre Francesco, interrupting Niccolo's reverie as Rosa began to gather up the empty bowls.

"Patience, Francesco. Allow me first to serve the chicken and then I will tell you all about my plan." Veronica stood up to help Rosa and they soon returned with six plates laden with succulent pieces of *melanzane*, *zucchine* and chicken, a smell of garlic now filling the air. When all her guests were enjoying the fruits of her labour, Rosa cleared her voice. "As you are all aware, the courts will disregard Veronica's testimony, so the only way we are going to ensure the Bishop's conviction is if he is forced to reveal his guilt."

Padre Francesco choked on his wine, while Alessandro and Niccolo gazed at Rosa in disbelief. "How on earth do you expect to force a confession from the Bishop?" asked Padre Francesco.

Rosa glared at him. "If you would just listen, then I will explain."

* * * * * * *

If we defy the Bishop on Sunday and still hold the festival at the chapel, then he will be bound to come down there to rant and rave at our heathenness. While he is occupied in chastising us, Veronica will appear before him in the trees beside the ravine. She will be wearing the same white dress she wore on the night of the attack, covered in pig's blood to simulate her own shed blood. Believing Veronica to be dead, the Bishop will think it is her spirit returned to haunt him.

Having heard Alessandro's story, we are all aware that Bishop Pazzini is incapable of feeling remorse, and so I am not hopeful that on seeing Veronica he will confess to his crimes. But what we can be sure of is that the Bishop fears the devil. He will most likely believe that the apparition has been sent by the devil to wreak vengeance upon him, and will be driven by shock and fear to reveal his guilt. The Church may be able to ignore the testimony of one woman, but they could not discard the testimonies of every person in the village who will have witnessed the Bishop's guilt.

* * * * * * *

Rosa came to the end of her explanation and looked up with triumph at her guests. The men stared back with varying degrees of reticence and a heated debate ensued. Typical of Italians in the south, the group of friends discussed the matter in such heated tones that a foreigner would have assumed they were sworn enemies.

"Mother, it's far too risky for Veronica," said Niccolo.

"It's my choice, Niccolo," said Veronica. "I was the one whom the Bishop attacked and I want to see him punished."

"How can we be sure that Bishop Pazzini will reveal his guilt?" asked Alessandro.

"It is a risk we will have to take," replied Rosa. "Do you know of any other options open to us?"

"You do realise, Rosa, that we would have no choice but to hold the prayers at the chapel?" asked Padre Francesco.

"That was always my intention."

"What of the villagers? What if they are too frightened to stand up to the Bishop and ask me to hold Mass in the main church?"

"Then we will have to work at persuading them to defend their ancient customs and defy Bishop Pazzini," said Alessandro.

"But such a course of action could endanger Veronica's life," said Niccolo.

"As your mother pointed out, what other option do we have?" replied Alessandro.

"Niccolo, this is my decision," repeated Veronica. "I will be quite safe. As soon as I have appeared before the Bishop, Luca will help me to escape back to our father's hut. Bishop Pazzini has no idea where I live."

"Luca, have you agreed to take part in this scheme?" asked Niccolo.

"It's what Veronica wants me to do."

"Padre Francesco?" asked Niccolo.

"If the villagers agree to us holding the prayers at the chapel, then this may be our only chance of preventing the burnings on Tuesday," replied Padre Francesco.

"Well, if you are all decided, then at least allow me to insist that you do not lead the prayers, Mother. If Bishop Pazzini sees you in your role as priestess, he will try you for heresy."

"Niccolo, if our plan is successful, Bishop Pazzini will be on trial himself for rape and attempted murder. The courts would ignore any accusation he might make against me," replied Rosa.

"So you are still determined to lead the prayers with me?"

"Yes, Francesco. You of all people should understand why."

"I tried to persuade her," said Alessandro, "but..."

"I'm a stubborn, old hag," Rosa finished with a smile. "Now we are all agreed, please raise your cups and let us ask for Sofia's blessing on a successful outcome."

They all stood up, Niccolo with a reluctant shrug, and held

their cups aloft, the light of the burgeoning moon reflected in the surface of the wine. "Blessed Mother, fill our cups with your wisdom and strength so that we may find the insight and courage necessary to bring Bishop Pazzini to justice. Blessed be." The six of them drained their glasses and set them back on the table. When the moment had passed, Rosa cleared the empty plates and cups from the table. "It's late and we must conserve our energies for tomorrow's dance. Veronica, would you like someone to accompany you home?"

"I'll see to that, Mother." Niccolo stepped forward before Luca could offer and held out his arm to Veronica. Bidding the others goodnight, they soon disappeared into the shadows of the olive grove as they made their way towards the steep hill overlooking the chapel garden.

Alessandro and Luca watched their progress and exchanged knowing smiles. "Come, Luca. Let's return to the *taverna* and see if we can persuade the villagers to defy Bishop Pazzini. Thank you, Rosa, not only for your kind hospitality, but for providing me with a way to bring my sister's murderer to justice. I may not be able to have him prosecuted for Isabetta's rape and murder, but if your plan is successful, Bishop Pazzini will be tried for attempting to commit the same crimes against Veronica. At long last, I may be able to lay Isabetta's spirit to rest. Goodnight to you both." Luca gave a small bow of appreciation and followed Alessandro out into the lane, leaving Padre Francesco and Rosa alone to wash the dishes together, the priest laughing in exasperation at the glint of triumph in the wisewoman's eyes.

As Alessandro and Luca approached the end of *Via Principale*, they could hear Enrico's booming voice coming from around the corner by Niccolo's consulting room. Hanging back in the shadows, they stopped to wait for him to go home, then heard a woman's voice.

"It is as I say, Enrico. I saw the storyteller going to your house in the early afternoon. He was carrying a birdcage containing three doves. He didn't reappear until dusk when he no longer had the birdcage. It pains me to say this cousin, but I fear your wife is cuckolding you again." Enrico roared with anger before charging off as Emilia scuttled back across the square into her house.

"The interfering cow! Why are my whereabouts of any concern to her?" demanded Alessandro.

"I suspect she is searching for a way to avenge the death of her daughter Lora, who died in childbirth on Wednesday. Caterina and Rosa were assisting her. I imagine Emilia has stirred Enrico's wrath on purpose. No doubt she's hoping that he will beat Caterina," replied Luca. Alessandro cursed out loud and strode towards the dirt track leading to Enrico's farmhouse. Luca ran after him, grabbing at his arm to hold him back. "No, Alessandro! You will only incite Enrico's rage and endanger Caterina and Paolo further. We would have to take them away with us tonight and how then could we carry out our plan to trap Bishop Pazzini?"

Alessandro stilled, torn between his conflicting desires to protect Caterina and to bring Isabetta's murderer to justice. At last his body slumped and he shook his head with regret. "You're right, Luca, for I have waited more than twenty years to see Jacobo Pazzini punished for his crimes. Two more days and I will be free to help Caterina to leave her husband, if she at last finds the strength."

With one last look up the dirt track, Alessandro turned back to Luca. "Let us put our trust in Sofia that all will be as it needs to be." Then they walked over to the *taverna*, where they came upon the Colombe men sitting with some of the huntsmen, who were still enjoying a jug of wine. Like most of the men in the village, if they were not out hunting or working the fields, they were to be found at the *taverna*, playing *tarocco* and having heated debates about the problems of the world as they knew it.

"Come, sit yourself down, Storyteller," said Dionisio.

Alessandro fetched a stool to join the men, while Luca sat down at a nearby table on his own, content to listen to the men's conversation from afar. "What subject are we discussing tonight, my friends?" asked Alessandro.

"None more important that the sowing of our fields," replied Dionisio's aged father Bartolomeo, whose kind but defiant eyes were so similar to those of his sister Rosa.

"How interesting," said Alessandro with a smile. "Pray, enlighten me."

"You will take note, no doubt, when I mention that Bishop Pazzini is involved," said Dionisio, who knew of Alessandro's interest in the Bishop, for he had overheard him mentioning his name to the wolf-man the previous day.

Alessandro shrugged his shoulders, feigning disinterest, for he did not want the villagers to know about their plan to overthrow the Bishop. The story of his sister's murder and of Veronica's rape would only serve to stir up the villagers, and he didn't want anything to jeopardise their plan. He therefore remained silent, allowing the eldest Colombe brother Giorgio to explain their grievance. "Bishop Pazzini has taken it upon himself not only to tell us where we should hold our prayers, but also how we should cultivate our land."

"He has insisted that we must not allow any of the fields we lease from him to lay fallow this year," interrupted Bartolomeo, who took pride in being the most experienced farmer in the village, "and that after the harvest we must plough and sew each one. He has also forbidden us to plant our seeds at the new moon and harvest at the full, for he claims that farming by the moon's cycle is devil's work."

Bartolomeo broke off to relight his pipe, leaving Giorgio to finish explaining to Alessandro. "If we do as he says, the earth in the fields that should be left to rest this year will be sapped of any goodness, and will be of no use to us or to him in the future. We tried to explain this to the Bishop, but he just accused us of being lazy for not wanting to cultivate all the fields."

Bartolomeo once again chipped in, inhaling on his pipe, "Lazy! He should try working with us in the fields. He'd soon realise what a life of luxury he leads in the city."

"As if a man of the city and the Church knows anything about farming," agreed Dionisio.

"What do you suppose Bishop Pazzini is up to?" Giorgio asked Alessandro, who grasped the opportunity to rile the men against the Bishop.

"The Bishop has no respect for Mother Earth. His only ambition is to become more powerful through the wealth obtained from your harvest. The larger the harvest, the more money in ground rent he will earn. Combine this with the tithes on the grain collected by the parish church, and the Bishop will have a very prosperous year."

Bartolomeo looked at Alessandro in disbelief. "Does he not realise that by exhausting the earth, it will not matter how much power and money he has, if he has no food to eat?"

"Men like Bishop Pazzini think only of themselves and of the present," replied Alessandro. "They are consumed by their need for power and wealth to the detriment of all else."

"What do you suggest we do then?" Georgio asked.

Alessandro stood up to make his leave and leant forward with his palms flat on the table, as if to emphasise the importance of his words. "It seems to me that your only option is to defend your traditional ways of life and stand up to Bishop Pazzini." As Alessandro retired to bed, his response was met by a loud cheer from the men. The sound erupted through the silence of the night air, bustling through the metal bars of the birdcage, which hung from the olive tree outside Enrico's farmhouse, its door open and the doves gone.

Saturday

14 August 1583

Santa Sofia

Caterina awoke to the sound of Paolo's screams and ran downstairs to find him sobbing on the kitchen floor. Cradling him in her arms, she asked, "Paolo, what is it?"

Between sobs, Paolo repeated the same words over and over, "The doves, the doves."

There, hanging from the door's lintel by their tethered feet were the three doves, their necks broken and eyes staring lifelessly. Caterina held Paolo close, covering his eyes.

A movement behind them heralded the arrival of Enrico. "See what happens when you accept gifts from your lover?" he cried, laughing at her distress.

For once, Caterina could not hold back her disgust. To beat her was one thing, but to upset Paolo by killing the doves was too much to bear. "How could you be so cruel?"

"It wasn't me who committed the gravest of sins, fornicating with another man while your husband was out hunting to provide for the village." Enrico was now beside himself with rage and pulled Caterina towards him by her hair.

"No!" Paolo leapt up, reigning pitiful blows against his father's arm. "I hate you! I hate you!"

Enrico stilled in surprise. It was the first time Paolo had revealed the hatred he felt towards his father. Enrico let go of Caterina's hair and stared at Paolo.

149

Caterina pushed herself up and put her arm around Paolo. "Now do you see what you have done, Enrico? You have turned your own son against you with your bullying."

"Enough! If anyone has set the boy against his father it is you with your viper's tongue." Enrico made to strike Caterina again, but seeing the tears on Paolo's face, he stopped and instead stormed out of the door. Caterina and Paolo watched as he marched down the track towards the square. Once Paolo had quietened, Caterina urged him to go and get dressed. In the meantime, she untied the birds and laid them on the table. Wiping tears from her eyes, she sat for a while, gazing at the birds whose freedom had been so cruelly taken from them. Caterina wondered if this was a sign that she too would never be able to spread her wings and escape from Enrico. She had been foolish to listen to Alessandro and Rosa, and to believe for a single moment that she could set herself free. Then she thought of Paolo and how she had roared at Enrico with the ferocity of a she-wolf protecting her cub. Perhaps all was not lost, for she could feel the strength of the Virgin Warrior stirring within her.

A knock at the door broke her reverie and Rosa peered into the kitchen. Caterina moved into her reassuring embrace. After a few moments, Rosa set Caterina at arm's length and searched her limbs for bruises. "How are you? Alessandro was worried. He sent me to make sure you had come to no harm."

"For once, Enrico took his revenge out on something other than me." Caterina pointed to the birds.

"The doves Alessandro gave you," said Rosa.

"Yes, but how did Enrico find out? Alessandro was gone long before he came home. Enrico could not have known that he had been here. Or that the doves were a gift from him."

"Alessandro overheard Emilia talking to Enrico last night," Rosa explained. "She warned him about Alessandro's visit and his gift for you."

"Why would she do such a thing?" asked Caterina, then groaned, clasping her hand to her head.

"What is it?" asked Rosa, taking her by the arm and guiding her into a chair.

"A sharp pain in my temple."

"*Malocchio*. The evil eye. Let me help." Rosa collected a bowl and filled it with water from the well outside, while muttering the secret prayers she had been taught by her mother. Each priestess could only pass on the rites of divining the evil eye to two female blood relatives, and Rosa was in the process of teaching both Caterina and Elena. First, she rubbed her thumbs over Caterina's eyelids. Then, she picked up a flask of olive oil and poured three drops into the bowl of water, before studying the way in which the droplets of oil dispersed to form patterns on the surface of the water. "It is as I thought, Caterina. These drops here, one bigger than the other, show that there are two women, one stronger than the other, who are plotting against you."

"Emilia and Agnesa?" asked Caterina.

"It is not for me to say. Only you know the truth. Over here, there is another, much larger source of evil. It is a man. He will cause you great suffering but you must be strong, Caterina. Follow the path of Sofia's wisdom and you will come to no harm."

"Who is the man?"

"I cannot tell you, but his identity will become known to you on the night of the festival. Now, close your eyes, while I try to rid you of the effects of their ill feeling." Rosa stirred the oil in with the water then moved her fingers over Caterina's eyes and temples, drawing sacred symbols and muttering the secret prayers that were known to only a few. When she had finished, she threw the contents of the bowl into the hearth. "It is done."

Caterina thanked Rosa, already feeling the pain in her head subsiding. "I wish I knew what I had done to cause Emilia and Agnesa to hate me so much."

"You were right the other night," said Rosa, sitting down on the stool next to Caterina. "There was more to Emilia and Agnesa's reaction than mourning Lora's death. We both know they did not love Lora. They despised her for the shame they felt she had brought on them. Their desire to hurt us is rooted in past grievances from long ago."

"What grievances?" asked Caterina.

Rosa poured herself a cup of water before telling Caterina the story of Agnesa and Emilia.

* * * * * * *

Before I married Agnolo, Agnesa had her sights set on him. Not because she loved him, but because her eldest brother Paolo was set to inherit the Galletti farmhouse. His wife Francesca, your late mother-in-law, was a cold, uncharitable woman who would not have allowed Agnesa to remain at the farmhouse once she had married. Even at the tender age of eighteen, Agnesa knew she could not tolerate the humiliation of living in a small house in the village. Instead, she looked to the only other large farmhouse belonging to a family with eligible sons and that was the Lorini's.

At the time, I was unaware of her intentions. In fact, if I am honest, it was Agnolo's eldest brother, Francesco, whom I had always cared for. But when Francesco took his orders as a priest, it was Agnolo who courted me. He was kind and gentle, like Francesco, but more suited to working outdoors on the olive farm than pursuing a spiritual path. I grew to love him very much and it seemed only natural to accept his proposal of marriage. Little did I know that my actions would provoke a feud between Agnesa and myself, which has lasted for some fifty years. A year after our wedding, Francesca forced Agnesa to marry Michele Gamba, who worked in the mill and lived in a house on the square. As if this was not bad enough for the proud, ambitious Agnesa, Michele died only a few years later, leaving her with little income. This is the real reason why Agnesa desires to have me tried as a witch. Not because she believes I killed Lora, but because she blames me for stealing what she believes to be her rightful position — mistress of the Lorini farmstead.

As for you, Caterina. You are a victim of their anger simply because you are your mother's daughter. History has a strange way of repeating itself. Twenty years after I married Agnolo, your mother Cicilia married his youngest brother Guido. Agnesa's plans to marry her daughter Emilia into the Lorini family and rule the farmstead were thwarted. I shudder to think what my life might have been like. Thankfully, Guido was captivated by my niece, leaving Agnesa and Emilia in the Gamba house on the square. Like her mother before her, Emilia was forced to marry a farmer by the name of Luigi Cesi, who also died young. But as luck would have it, they only had to wait a year before Enrico's mother Francesca also died, when he allowed them to move into the Galletti house. At last they were able to enjoy a position of superiority, until Enrico married you and forced them to leave two years later. By attempting to bring about your disappearance, they are seeking not only to return to the Galletti farmhouse, but to have their revenge on your mother.

So you see, Caterina, their hostility towards us goes back many years and is rooted in greed and jealousy. There is nothing we can do to change their minds. We can only feel pity for them that they have wasted their lives chasing empty dreams of status and wealth. Try not to feel threatened by their ill-feeling towards you. Remember what I taught you and place salt in your pockets before you leave the house tonight. It will help to dampen the force of their evil eye on you.

* * * * * * *

Rosa reached for her *nanta* bag and pulled out a miniature pair of silver scissors and a small red horn made from rue. "Here, take these charms for protection."

As Caterina pocketed the charms, Paolo walked back into the kitchen and Rosa reached out to embrace him. "Now, Paolo, I have a suggestion to make which I hope will help you to feel better about the sad fate of your doves." Paolo's eyes filled with tears once more at the sight of the birds' carcasses, which Rosa was placing inside her basket. "Dry your tears and come with me. We will take the doves to Sofia's cave, where we will offer them into her fire. The smoke will carry their spirits to join her dove, with whom they will be forever free, flying on the wings of the Mother Bird Goddess." Paolo wiped his eyes and took hold of Rosa's hand.

Caterina smiled in appreciation of Rosa's ability to bring healing to those in pain. "Thank you."

Rosa held Caterina's gaze. "Remember, Caterina, what the dove symbolises. It is the awakener of erotic love, the harbinger of peace and war, and the companion of the Virgin Warrior. A priestess of the Black Goddess embodies all these qualities. In killing the doves, Enrico not only sought to exert his control over you, he challenged everything that Sofia stands for. The question you need to ask yourself is whether you have the courage to embrace the warrior within and defend the Black Goddess as well as yourself? Call to her, Caterina, and she will help you to stand in your power." Then she glanced down at Paolo. "I'll bring him back in time to get ready for the dance." Caterina nodded and watched as Rosa led Paolo down the track. Then she disappeared inside the house to make the final alterations to Paolo's costume and to ponder on Rosa's words.

Rosa and Paolo strolled up the coastal road towards the square. As they passed the orchard, Alessandro called out and Rosa led

Paolo into the privacy of the trees.

"How is she?" asked Alessandro.

"Rest assured for once the brute left her alone," replied Rosa. "Instead, he took his anger out on the doves you gave her." Rosa pulled the cloth away from her basket to reveal the bodies of the dead birds. "We're going to give them a proper burial in Sofia's sacred fire, aren't we Paolo?"

Paolo looked up at Alessandro with sorrowful eyes. "I'm sorry my father killed your doves."

Alessandro crouched down so that he was level with Paolo. "Don't worry, Paolo. I will find you some more doves for tomorrow evening."

"Really?" said Paolo, but then his eyes filled with fear like those of his mother. "But if my father finds them, he will be very angry."

"Well, what if I left them by the side of the chapel, so that you could find them at the festival? That way, you wouldn't have to keep them at home where your father might see them."

"Thank you, sir, thank you," said Paolo, taking Alessandro's hand as they wandered into the square, before Rosa led him off to the chapel.

The square was heaving with villagers making preparations for the evening's dinner and dancing. In front of Niccolo's consulting room, a temporary wooden stage was being constructed. Here the musicians would play and the children would descend from the balcony to perform their traditional dances. In the middle of the square, Aurelio and others were helping Dionisio to set up long wooden tables, where all the villagers would later dine. Giorgio and Enrico were standing outside the butchery, building the fire over which the boar would be roasted that afternoon.

Keen to avoid a confrontation with Enrico, Alessandro skirted round to the easterly side of the square. Bartolomeo was directing several men standing on ladders, who were tethering ropes to Agnesa's wrought-iron balconies. Another group were carrying the other ends of the ropes across the square to tie them to the awnings of the bakery and butchery. Alessandro stopped to help Bartolomeo hold the ladders steady for the men. Behind him was a group of women seated around a table, preparing *gnocchi* for the first course, and he listened intrigued to their ensuing conversation.

Emilia was seated at the head of the table, wearing an apron over her black widow's dress and a white handkerchief on her head. They did little to protect her from the flour, which flew up in the air every time she pounded a large lump of dough. On either side of her, the aged Agnesa and Maria were bent over, straining to see the round pieces of dough that Emilia had produced, so that they could flatten them into long strips. Next to them sat Elena and her aunt Donata, who seldom left her house due to caring for her paralysed son Rafaello. Her husband Zanobi had deserted them shortly after his birth, as some men do in such circumstances, but at least she had help from her family, especially Elena. They were in charge of slicing the strips of dough into small squares, which they brushed down in a flurry of flour to the end of the table. There, Cristina and three other women sat, creating the *gnocchi* by dragging their fingertips through the pieces of dough, until they curled up into the shape of shells. These were then laid with great care onto long wooden boards, to be cooked later in large vats of tomato *passata* sauce.

"Bartolomeo came home last night insisting that we should defy the Bishop and hold our prayers at the chapel," said Caterina's grandmother Maria, a small, timid woman who was not one to speak her mind like her husband Bartolomeo. However, she was devoted to the divine Mother as Patroness of the Harvest, and laid offerings at the statue of Ceres every morning during the month of August. "I have to agree with him. If we break with tradition, our Blessed Mother might not see fit to protect our harvest from storms or floods. In these times of plagues and famine, should we not offer our prayers at the Madonna's chapel?"

"What nonsense!" Emilia's booming voice startled Maria. "Bishop Pazzini has decreed that Padre Francesco will hold midnight Mass in the main church, and we must respect His Excellency's wishes."

Agnesa nodded her head in agreement, but Elena was not about to stand by and watch her mother being bullied by a pompous snob such as Emilia. "I agree with Mamma. Our loyalties should lie with the Black Madonna, not with the new Bishop of Arunca, who is nothing more than her servant."

"I also believe we have a duty to worship our Lady at her chapel," said Donata, "but what of the burnings on Tuesday? What if the Bishop was to punish us and send us all to the pyres?"

"If we all decided to worship at the chapel together, Bishop Pazzini could not punish the whole village," Elena reassured Donata, who dwelt in a permanent state of exhaustion and anxiety from caring for Rafaello.

Just then, cries of excitement erupted in the square as the cart carrying the troupe of musicians arrived from Arunca. All the villagers stopped what they were doing and gathered around the cart to welcome the men, asking them which songs they would be singing and what news they brought from Arunca. Even Agnesa and Emilia joined the crowd, but not to welcome the musicians. Instead, they set about giving the men a stern lecture on how to conduct themselves with regard to the village girls. Their absence from the table gave the Colombe women chance to speak in private.

"I see Caterina has more bruises," remarked Elena.

"Yes, I noticed them too," said Cristina.

Elena glanced across the square at Enrico and Giorgio. "Why does my brother tolerate his company? Giorgio is Caterina's uncle and yet he spends so much time with Enrico."

Maria looked over at her eldest son. "That is the way of men, Elena. They depend upon each other to provide for the village. When Giorgio goes shooting with Enrico, he does not see him as a man who beats his niece, but a fellow huntsman. It doesn't mean that he agrees with Enrico's violence so don't judge your brother too harshly." Elena raised an eyebrow.

"What I don't understand is why she stays with him," said Cristina.

Maria glanced at her daughter-in-law as she rolled a ball of dough beneath her palm. "For the same reason he beats her."

"Whatever do you mean, Mamma?" asked Elena.

"Enrico's mother Francesca was a cruel woman who gave her affections freely to other men but not to her son. In Caterina, Enrico has found a woman to punish for his mother's betrayal," explained Maria.

"But what does that have to do with why Caterina tolerates him?" asked Cristina.

"Caterina was also deprived of her mother's love. Like Enrico, she is angry. Unlike him, she turns her anger inwards, blaming herself as women are sometimes wont to do. What greater punishment could she have than his beatings?"

"You mean Caterina thinks she deserves to be treated in this way?" asked Elena.

Maria nodded. "Until she forgives herself, she will stay with him to receive her punishment."

"I think perhaps you are right, Mamma," said Elena.

"Is there nothing we can do?" asked Cristina.

"Help her to feel stronger by giving her love and support," replied Maria.

At that moment, Agnesa and Emilia returned to the table and the Colombe women stopped discussing their family matters, wary of giving them any fodder for gossip. Having listened with interest to the women's conversation, Alessandro wandered over to the *taverna*. Then, collecting his guitar, he joined the musicians on stage to practise the traditional folk songs.

All around them, the children were playing, growing more and more excited as the day progressed towards late afternoon. Dionisio's three young sons climbed up onto the flat roof of the *taverna* and began throwing stones down onto their friends below as they practised their dance steps. Alessandro chuckled as Dionisio shouted at the boys to climb down, which they did, only to be sent reeling to their mother. The women were gathering up their children to take them home, where they would wash and dress them in the elaborate traditional costumes. As all the villagers drifted home to prepare for the evening, the square grew quiet, save for the notes of a poignant ballad being played by the musicians. Alessandro looked up to see Luca signalling to him from the orchard and broke off from playing, promising to rejoin the musicians on stage during the dinner.

Alessandro followed Luca into the shadows of the orchard, where Niccolo and Veronica were seated beneath an old, gnarled apple tree.

"Have the villagers reached a decision yet, Alessandro?" asked Niccolo.

"Not that I know of," replied Alessandro. "I overheard a group of women discussing what they should do. All of them, except for Emilia and Agnesa, are inclined to worship at the chapel, but some are still fearful of Bishop Pazzini. It remains to be seen whether their fears will triumph over their loyalty to the divine Mother."

The friends exchanged anxious looks. Luca hopped from one foot to another, causing Niccolo to wonder whether he had taken his medicine.

"When will we know for sure?" asked Veronica.

"Padre Francesco has asked the villagers to advise him of their final decision tomorrow morning," answered Alessandro.

"What if they refuse to worship at the chapel?" Niccolo asked.

Alessandro shrugged his shoulders. "All we can do is hope that this evening's festivities will fill them with a sense of pride in their community, encouraging them to hold fast to their traditions." At that moment, the musicians launched into their first rendition of the night, heralding the start of the evening's entertainment. Alessandro turned to leave, followed by Luca, and glanced over his shoulder at Niccolo. "Are you coming?"

"No, you go on ahead. I'm going to keep Veronica company here, so that she can listen to the music and watch the dancing."

In appreciation of Niccolo's kindness, Veronica took his hand, causing his cheeks to redden and Alessandro to smile.

"I'll meet you anon, then. Enjoy the music."

Alessandro strode back to the square with Luca, who disappeared into the shadows below the balcony from where he could watch the musicians. Seated in a semi-circle at the back of the stage, the musicians were dressed in the traditional costumes of the Festival of Santa Sofia, which were provided for them each year by the villagers. Silk white shirts with full sleeves peered out from beneath black waistcoats braided with gold thread. Around the waistbands of their black trousers, red sashes were tied to match the red kerchiefs about their necks. Alessandro knew that his only chance of avoiding a confrontation with Enrico was to blend in with the musicians, so he found and donned a costume in Niccolo's consulting room.

A few minutes later, Alessandro emerged to take his place on stage with the musicians, from where he had a panoramic view of the square. The ropes that had been pulled taut above the tables were now adorned with oil lanterns. Their flames illuminated the assortment of gold, red and black silk flags and garlands of flowers, their sweet perfume filling the air. The whole square seemed to undulate in the breeze with a sea of colour. The benches on either side of the long, wooden tables were now full of villagers talking loudly to each other between mouthfuls of *gnocchi* dripping with rich tomato and basil sauce. In the foreground, Alessandro caught sight of Enrico marching into the square, with Caterina and Paolo following behind. Enrico headed straight for the butchery to give Giorgio a hand with carving the roasted boar, while Caterina led Paolo up the stairs beside the stage and into Niccolo's consulting room, where the other children were gathering before their performance. When she reappeared on the balcony, Caterina glanced down and gave Alessandro a fleeting look, before joining Rosa at the foremost table.

Within moments, Caterina became aware of the hostile eyes staring at her, and felt for the grains of salt and protective charms in her pockets. Emilia and Agnesa sat across the table, glaring at Caterina and Rosa, who whispered, "Ignore them, Caterina. Don't allow anything to spoil this evening's merriment." Drawing a secret hand gesture of the five-pointed star for protection, the old wisewoman of the village stood up and banged her bowl upon the table. A hush fell over the expectant crowd and everyone turned to listen to her.

"Gentlefolk of Santa Sofia. Welcome to the festival of our Blessed Mother. May your celebration of her fertile bounty this night fill your prayers of gratitude tomorrow evening, when once more we shall make our pilgrimage to her place of worship in the chapel garden. Let the dancing begin."

Rosa's words of encouragement brought forth their desired effect, causing a loud chorus of cheering and applause to erupt. The villagers raised their cups of wine in a toast to the Blessed Mother, which was followed by a dramatic drum roll from the musicians. Caterina watched with pride as Paolo emerged from Niccolo's consulting room and climbed down the stairs onto the stage, holding Fiora's hand to lead the first of the children's dances. Paolo was wearing a smaller version of the musicians' costumes, but Fiora was dressed in the girls' more lavish attire. Over their white shirts, the girls wore red silk bodices beneath black jackets edged in gold. About the waists of their varying coloured, full skirts were tied red and gold silk aprons, and upon their heads each girl wore an elaborate headdress of lace draped over gold tasselled hair pins.

Enrico looked up from the plate of boar meat he was eating outside the butchery and caught sight of his son dancing on the stage. Paolo was one of the youngest of the children dancing. Enrico felt his heart swell with pride on watching his earnest attempts to remember the complicated steps of the dance. Casting his mind back to the morning, Enrico was filled with remorse and an urgent desire to ask God's forgiveness for upsetting his son. Approaching Padre Francesco, who was seated at the far end of the long table, Enrico bent down beside him.

From the stage, Alessandro watched as Padre Francesco looked at Enrico in astonishment, then stood up and led Enrico to the church. Alessandro wondered what Enrico could need with the priest, but his absence from the evening's entertainment offered Alessandro an opportunity to have some food. He jumped off the stage to get a bowl of *gnocchi*, only to be grabbed by Elena and forced to join the large group of villagers now dancing.

The muffled laughter and music reached Enrico as he sat in the confessional box beside Padre Francesco. He had been silent for a while, struggling with how to express his confused emotions to the priest.

"What is troubling you, Enrico? Is it Caterina?"

"No, Padre, I feel no remorse for my wife. She is the devil in disguise of the foreign woman who offers help to sailors in the stormy night, then leads their ship onto the rocks."

Padre Francesco raised his eyebrows heaven-bound, recognising the influence of teachings from priests like Bishop Pazzini.

"Make no mistake, Enrico, God does not favour men who beat their wives. You must stop abusing Caterina or suffer his judgement."

"Your opinion about my wife is of no concern to me. I am here about Paolo. If I have any love inside me, then it is for my son. Today he told me he hated me and I am here to beg God's forgiveness for upsetting him. Tell me how I can make amends."

Despite his concerns about Enrico's treatment of Caterina, Padre Francesco believed he was sincere in his feelings for Paolo. "This love you feel for your son is to be applauded, Enrico. Why do you not tell him how you feel? Or demonstrate your love for him by spending time with him?"

Enrico nodded, realising that he never saw Paolo without his mother. Perhaps away from her influence, his son would grow to love him once more. "You're right, Padre. Am I forgiven?"

Padre Francesco replied with care. "God always forgives those who truly repent, but he is unable to forgive those who refuse to acknowledge that they have committed a sin."

"I am truly sorry for causing Paolo pain."

Padre Francesco's message was lost on Enrico, who remained oblivious to any crime he had committed against Caterina. The priest sighed at Enrico's lack of comprehension, but was compelled to absolve his sin. "Then God will forgive you for it." After reciting the confessional prayers, Enrico left to rejoin the festivities.

Just at that moment, Alessandro found himself thrown together with Caterina, who froze, but the nature of the formation dance forced them to remain partnering each other.

Through the sea of moving bodies, Emilia caught sight of the couple. Glancing back towards the church, she spied Enrico and ran to meet him. "Come quickly, cousin. It's that whore of your wife. She's dancing in the storyteller's arms."

Enrico let out a bellow of rage and marched over to the

group of dancing villagers, brushing couples aside until he found Alessandro and Caterina, whom he threw to the ground. Paolo screamed but Alessandro was upon Enrico in moments, wrapping his arm around his neck and reigning blows into his face. From the orchard, Niccolo heard the cries of the women and children, and ran into the square.

Amid the commotion, everyone failed to notice the arrival of Bishop Pazzini in his horse-drawn litter, save for Luca, who ran out of the shadows and grabbed Alessandro's arm. "Hurry, Alessandro, the Bishop is approaching. Run and hide before he recognises you." Alessandro looked up to see Jacobo Pazzini making his way towards the group of people surrounding him. He hesitated, torn by his guilt of having endangered Caterina and his desire to protect her.

Niccolo understood his dilemma. "Go, Alessandro. We will do what we can to protect Caterina. Hide in the orchard with Veronica and we will find you there later." Alessandro gazed into Caterina's sorrowful eyes before letting go of Enrico. Then, turning on his heel, he ran through the crowd into the shadows, just as Bishop Pazzini broke through the throng of agitated villagers, brandishing his staff.

"What the devilment is going on here?"

"It is nothing, Your Excellency, just a small misunderstanding." Padre Francesco, who had followed Enrico out of the church and witnessed the fight, was eager to pacify the Bishop.

Emilia, who was driven by a very different motive, forced her way through the crowd until she stood in front of the Bishop. "A misunderstanding! I'll tell you what foul sin has been committed here tonight!" she cried, pointing at Caterina, who had been helped up by Niccolo. "That whore has been fornicating for the whole village to see with a man other than her husband. It is as I told you, Your Eminence. She has the devil sucking at her loins and deserves to be burnt at the stake."

Padre Francesco again tried to calm the situation, but only after giving Rosa a warning look to keep quiet. "Your Excellency, Caterina has committed no crime tonight. With my own eyes, I have seen her do no wrong other than watch as her son led the children's dancing."

"How would you know what your niece was doing, Padre Francesco, when you were listening to my confession in the church?" challenged Enrico, despite Padre Francesco's recent kindness to him.

Bishop Pazzini turned to glower at Padre Francesco, his bulbous eyes protruding from beneath bushy eyebrows. "Is this true, Padre? Are you defending your niece with lies?"

The villagers held their breath, frightened by the aggressive way in which the Bishop was questioning Padre Francesco, for a priest to be found guilty of lying to his Bishop was tantamount to heresy. Padre Francesco was well aware of this and struggled with his response. "No, Your Excellency. It is just that I know Caterina to be a good woman, but Enrico is a man prone to unjustified violence against his wife."

"Padre Francesco, you know full well that whatever punishment a husband decides to mete out to his wife, the Church supports him. This man is the whore's husband and I shall leave it to him to decide upon her fate." Turning to Enrico, the Bishop pointed his staff at Caterina. "Take her home and do what is necessary to strike the devil out of her." Enrico nodded in satisfaction, pulling Caterina by her arm, and headed down the road past the orchard where Alessandro was hiding in the trees.

Paolo cried out and tried to follow his mother but was held back by Rosa, who whispered, "It is better you come and stay with Niccolo and me tonight."

"But Papa will hurt Mamma. I must stop him." Paolo tried to struggle free from Rosa's grasp but was too weak. Instead, he began to cry tears of fear and frustration. Niccolo motioned to

Luca with his eyes to follow Caterina. Luca slunk back into the shadows, vanishing into the night to ensure her protection. "See, Paolo. Our friend Luca has gone to take care of your mother. He will make sure no harm comes to her." Paolo grew calmer and sagged into Rosa's arms.

"Padre Francesco," continued Bishop Pazzini, "your loyalty to the Roman Church has been put into question tonight. It is my duty to suspend you *a divinis* from all your duties as a parish priest, until such a time as I have ascertained that you understand the teachings of the Church you serve."

The villagers gasped out loud in dismay, for the priest was loved by all. He believed that God's power was given equally to everyone, and did not seek to oppress them with convoluted dogma and extortionate tithes. Instead, he encouraged them to love and support each other, for he understood how important this was in a community where people depended on each other for survival. He also respected their traditional rituals, even though they were based upon the yearly vegetation cycle, for he believed that all spiritual paths, if founded on the concepts of love and wisdom, flow from the same divine source. And he treated every woman he met with the same amount of respect as any of his male parishioners. Another priest as tolerant and kind as Padre Francesco would be hard to come by.

Padre Francesco hung his head in acquiescence. To disagree with the Bishop would only serve to jeopardise his priesthood further. His love of Christ was such that he would suffer any hardship to ensure his ability to continue spreading the divine Son's words of Sofianic wisdom.

The Bishop lifted his hands to Padre Francesco's neck and removed his white collar, holding it aloft for all to see. "Tomorrow, I will fulfil the role of priest left vacant by the departure of Padre Francesco and I will hold midnight Mass in the main church."

The square rang with shocked cries from the villagers. Some, like Bartolomeo, tensed as if desperate to shout out and defy the Bishop, but were held back by more fearful relatives such as Maria. None wanted to jeopardise the safety of Padre Francesco further by causing the Bishop to question his control over his flock, although Padre Francesco had not once sought to wield power over them. The cries of disbelief faded to shrugs of silent defeat as the villagers made their way back to their homes, their evening of merriment lying in tatters of fluttering flags and wilting blooms. The musicians packed away their instruments and headed over to the *taverna* where they were staying. They joined the group of men hiding in the shadows beneath the *pergola*, waiting for the Bishop to depart so that they could draw up some chairs and discuss the evening's events. With a warning glare at Padre Francesco, Bishop Pazzini climbed back inside his litter and instructed the horseman to take him back to his palace in Arunca.

Rosa looked up into Padre Francesco's defeated eyes. Linking her arm through his, she took Paolo by the hand. "Come, you can both stay with Niccolo and me tonight."

Padre Francesco held back. "Thank you for your kind offer, Rosa, but perhaps it would not be wise."

"Where will you stay then, old man? At this present time, you are no longer a priest of the Roman Church and therefore you cannot stay in church lodgings. The Lorini farmhouse is still your home and, anyhow, we have much to discuss."

Padre Francesco smiled in exasperation. "How is it that you always have your way?"

Rosa chuckled but then her thoughts returned to Caterina and she called out to Niccolo, "What about Caterina?"

"You go on home. I'll wait here for word from Luca."

Rosa nodded and led Padre Francesco and Paolo along *Via Principale*, watched by a woman from the shadows of her doorway.

On arriving at the farmhouse, Rosa settled Paolo on a straw mattress in Niccolo's room, stroking his furrowed brow until he fell asleep. Padre Francesco had poured a couple of tumblers of wine and Rosa joined him at the table beneath the *pergola*. A comfortable silence fell between them as they both contemplated the events of the evening.

"Even as a young boy, all I ever wanted was to serve Christ," Padre Francesco at last said. "He seemed to me the essence of godliness on earth. He walked among us, felt our pain and suffering, and taught us the values of humility, love and forgiveness. He remained loyal to his beliefs in the face of extreme adversity. He stood up to cruel tyrants like Bishop Pazzini, but showed only love and kindness to the outcasts of society, the prostitutes, lepers and unloved. How can I, as a follower of Christ, allow this bishop to wield his power over my flock? Yet how can I oppose him when he holds such a powerful position within Christ's own Church?"

"The Roman Church, which claims to be the Church of Christ, is not in fact a Church that Christ would be proud of," replied Rosa. "Its priests have manipulated his teachings for their own political ends to such an extent that their torture and murder of innocent people is recognisable only as the work of madmen. They have taken the Old Testament Wisdom literature and separated light from darkness into Wisdom and Folly. They accuse the latter of leading men from the path of wisdom, yet Sofia is to be found within the very blackness embodied by Folly. Here lies your dilemma. You worship Sofia as Christ's heavenly bride, but the Roman Church seeks to destroy the sacred marriage, to create disunity between men and women, darkness and light."

Padre Francesco slammed his cup of wine down on the table in an uncharacteristic outburst of frustration. "Then what am I do?"

"You must ask yourself a question," replied Rosa. "What do you think Christ would do in your situation? Would he sit back and allow a hypocrite such as Bishop Pazzini to wield his authority, or would he stand up to him?"

Padre Francesco smiled at Rosa's practical wisdom, which always simplified the most seemingly complicated of problems. Unlike the verbosity of ecclesiastical theology, which only succeeded in making Christ's teachings inaccessible to the layperson. "He would stand up to him," he answered.

"Then that is what you must do. Christ may have been gentle and kind but don't forget that he was also a powerful revolutionary. A true disciple of Sofia may nurture qualities of love, respect and compassion, but they are still driven by a sense of righteous anger to challenge the injustices they see in society."

"Thank you, Rosa," said Padre Francesco with a grateful smile. "You are right, as usual."

"Not always, but when I am it is because Sofia is guiding my words."

"Then I give thanks to Lady Wisdom," said Padre Francesco, gazing at Rosa with a warm light glowing in his watery eyes. Then he leant forward and took her hands in his. "Rosa, I haven't tried to hide my love and respect for you over these many years we have known each other. As your brother-in-law and a priest, I have always remained platonic in my affections for you, and I fear I am too old to change my ways now. But, perhaps, if I could just, that is to say..."

"Hold me?" asked Rosa, sparing Padre Francesco from saying that which was difficult to voice. He nodded and she stood up, leading him to her bedroom, where she sat him down on the bed and caressed his white hair and lined face. "Don't fear that your God will punish you for lying beside me tonight, Francesco, for Christ also lay with his priestess Mary Magdalene. It is only the Church Fathers, with their fear of the body and of women, who make restrictions on your natural desire to be intimate with another. The act of lovemaking between a woman and a man is the most sacred of rituals. Many years ago the high priestess and lord of the land would have been joined each year in the sacred marriage to ensure the regeneration of the earth. Although we have lost the energy of our youth, perhaps our mere embrace this night will help to replenish the courage of our people."

Padre Francesco gazed into her eyes and felt the strength of his love and respect for her deep inside of him. "Bless you, Rosa." Then he drew her down onto the bed beside him, cradling her head upon his shoulder and wrapping his arms around her. Entwined in their warm embrace, like the spent Goddess and Horned God, Rosa and Padre Francesco drifted off to sleep, smiles of contentment playing upon their aged faces.

In the Galletti farmhouse, a man was also consumed with physical desire, but of a violent and threatening kind. "Enrico! Stop!" Caterina screamed, struggling to free herself from his grasp. Enrico slapped her hard across the face, stunning her, and threw her over the kitchen table. "No! Get off me!" Caterina screamed again, trying to kick his body away from her and pulling at his hair to prevent him from biting her neck and chest. But Enrico was too strong and heavy for her slender frame. He ripped at her bodice, exposing her breasts, and bit down hard on her nipple, causing her to cry out. Grabbing her kicking legs, he forced her thighs apart and pawed at her tender flesh. "Bastard!" Caterina bellowed at him, fighting as hard as she could against his violent assault.

Just then, the silence of the night was filled with the chilling howl of a wolf. Enrico stilled and raised his head to listen, all thought of raping his wife disappearing. Panting from their fight, Caterina and Enrico both looked through the open window at the bright light of the full mother moon. Again, the howling lament sounded, but this time so loud it was as if the wolf was in the same room.

"That's it!" said Enrico, climbing off Caterina and grabbing his rifle. "This time I'm going to kill the beast."

"Enrico, no! He's your cousin, for pity's sake!" pleaded Caterina, presuming it to be Luca, whose illness caused him to howl like a wolf at the time of the full moon.

"Silence!" Enrico shouted, grabbing Caterina's arm and dragging her upstairs to their bedroom, where he threw her on the floor before slamming the door behind him and locking it from the outside. "You'll stay in this room until I decide when you can leave, and you can be sure that that will not be for a very long time. A whore like you needs to learn to obey her husband. Understand?" But before Caterina could reply, there was another howl. Enrico ran downstairs, stopping on the porch with his rifle cocked to listen for any sounds. Then, in the distance, he saw a movement among the trees marking his boundary line and fired his gun. "This time I'm going to get you, Wolf-man!"

Luca felt his heart begin to pound, but reminded himself of his ability to vanish into the shadows, which he'd developed over a lifetime of practice. Creeping along the low hedge encircling the farmstead, he waited until Enrico was looking in the other direction, then leapt over the hedge into the coastal road, but he had under-estimated Enrico's hunting prowess and was soon running as fast as he could towards the square. Enrico pursued him, firing his gun again and nearly hitting Luca as he sped past the opening to the track, but Enrico was forced to stop and reload his rifle, which was only capable of firing two shots before requiring further ammunition. Luca gained a further head start and pounded up the road towards Niccolo, watched by a woman from the vantage of her bedroom window. "Help! Enrico's shooting at me!"

Niccolo gestured for Luca to run into the orchard while he stood outside his consulting room waiting for Enrico. A few moments later, the overweight hunter appeared running up the road and stopped in front of Niccolo, gasping for breath. "Have you seen the wretched wolf-man?"

Niccolo glared at him. "I assume by wolf-man, you are referring to your cousin and my patient Luca?"

"Your patient?" cried Enrico, incredulous that a beast could be described in such terms.

Niccolo assumed the authoritative air of a medical professional. "Yes, my patient. Luca suffers from a rare disease, but he is harmless. If you shot him, you would be tried and hung for his murder. He is no more a wolf than I am. He is a sick man who needs help and understanding, above all from his family. Go and have a drink at the *taverna*, Enrico, and thank God that I have saved you from the gallows."

Enrico stared at the doctor in bewilderment, but nevertheless lowered his rifle. "I still say he's a werewolf and there are others who would agree with me." Then he headed off to join the group of men at the *taverna*, who were still discussing what course of action they should take the following day.

"There is no such thing as a werewolf!" Niccolo called out after Enrico, then waited until he had disappeared beneath the *pergola*, at which point he crept into the orchard.

Alessandro, Luca and Veronica emerged from the shadows and the four sat together among the trees. Luca's breath was still coming in short bursts. "Thank you for your protection, Niccolo."

"You're most welcome. Such ignorance makes my blood boil."

"How's Caterina?" asked Alessandro, who was restless for news.

"She's safe, for now," replied Luca.

"What happened?"

"The beast was upon her, clawing at her body," explained Luca, running his shaking hands through his long hair. "I felt powerless to help her until the clouds above me dispersed, allowing the full moon to shine down on my face. I knew then that I could turn the illness that has plagued my life into something positive. I howled like a wolf, knowing the hunter Enrico would not be able to resist the chase. Then I ran to you as fast as my legs could carry me. It was not an experience I would wish to repeat, I can tell you." Luca shivered, realising what it must be like for Mother Nature's animals when men hunt them down and slaughter them.

"You're a brave man, Luca," remarked Alessandro, ashamed of the part he had played in instigating the evening's events. "It's my fault. If I hadn't left the stage, none of this would have happened. Not only did I endanger Caterina's life but Padre Francesco has been stripped of his priesthood. The villagers are certain to obey the Bishop now out of fear of further punishment."

"Alessandro, you mustn't blame yourself. How were you to know what would happen?" asked Veronica.

Luca and Niccolo murmured in agreement and then fell silent, lost in their own fears and doubts until Niccolo gave a sigh. "I fear it will take a miracle to change their minds."

"Where's Caterina now?" Veronica asked Luca.

"I saw him taking her upstairs. He must have locked her in a bedroom."

"Then we must find a way to keep him away from the farmhouse," said Alessandro.

"I sent him to the *taverna*," said Niccolo. "Hopefully he will drink himself into a stupor and fall asleep at the table, but I could..." Niccolo's response was cut short by a woman's scream.

Alessandro leapt up, "Luca, stay with Veronica. Niccolo, come."

Alessandro and Niccolo rushed into the square to find a group of men running from the *taverna* to a small house two doors down from Emilia. Donata opened the door and burst into the square. "It's a miracle! A miracle, I tell you!" The doors of the neighbouring houses along *Via Principale* opened as more people came to find out what all the fuss was about. "Oh Doctor, come and see the miracle of our Blessed Mother for yourself," she exclaimed, leading Niccolo inside the house where her son, who had lain in bed unable to move for thirty-three years, now sat upright in a chair. "Show him, Rafaello. Show the doctor." Rafaello pushed against the arms of the chair with his bony hands until he stood up. Then he took a couple of hesitant steps on shaking legs towards Niccolo, a smile of inexplicable joy lighting up his pallid face. Niccolo stared at Rafaello, dumbfounded by the recovery of his patient, whom he knew to have been paralysed from the chest down since birth.

"What happened, Rafaello?" Niccolo asked, helping him to sit back down, for his newly cured limbs were still weak. Then Rafaello told him and the villagers who were peering in through the doorway and windows, the story of the miracle.

* * * * * * *

I was asleep in my bed when all at once my room was filled with a brilliant light. So bright were the rays from the light that I imagined the moon itself was in my room. Shielding my eyes, I looked towards the end of my bed and standing there was the most beautiful woman I have ever seen. Her face was as black as night and her turquoise robe sparkled in the light. Then she spoke to me. "Stand up and walk, Rafaello." I stared in awe, knowing that I was in the presence of the Black Madonna. My heart began to beat faster and faster, and tears of joy and wonder filled my eyes. "Stand up, Rafaello," she repeated, gesturing for me to climb out of bed. I shook my head, knowing that it was impossible for me to grant her request. All of a sudden, I felt a tingling sensation in my chest, which slowly worked its way down my legs to my toes, until my whole body was glowing and trembling. To my astonishment, my legs drew themselves up and swung around, until I was sitting on the edge of my bed. Step by step, my feet began to creep forward, carrying my body with them, until I stumbled across the room towards the Black Madonna and fell at her feet, kissing them and thanking her for healing my useless limbs.

"Pray tell me, Blessed Mother, how may I repay your kindness?" I asked.

"At my festival of prayers tomorrow," she replied, "you must bear my statue to the chapel." Then she disappeared in a dazzling array of light.

* * * * * * *

Word had spread and, on finishing his story, Rafaello looked up to find yet more villagers peering into the room. Niccolo stepped forward to examine Rafaello and test his reflexes, which all seemed to be functioning, and shook his head in wonder. It truly was a medical miracle. Never had he heard of a patient who had been paralysed since birth recovering the use of his limbs. Meanwhile, the villagers were waiting with anticipation for the doctor's diagnosis. Dionisio, who had been one of the first to arrive on the scene, voiced the question on everybody's lips. "Is it as he says, Doctor? Are my cousin's limbs healed? Is it a miracle?"

Niccolo struggled to find the words to describe what had taken place. Rafaello's recovery was at odds with his scientific understanding of the body. The idea that a divine power had healed his patient was contrary to Niccolo's rational perception of the world, but needless to say Rafaello's recovery was quite miraculous. "There is no doubt that Rafaello has made a full recovery from his paralysis," he said. "It would appear that something miraculous has indeed taken place."

The villagers gasped in amazement and fell to their knees in reverence of the divine Mother. Niccolo looked at Alessandro. There would be no better time to encourage the villagers to defy the Bishop and hold their prayers at the chapel. Alessandro didn't have to wait long for his opportunity, for the men with whom he had spent the previous evening now looked to him again for guidance.

"What do you think, Storyteller?" asked Giorgio. The villagers stood up and gathered around Alessandro.

"It's clear to me that the Black Madonna has performed another miraculous healing in the village. To show your gratitude, I believe you must fulfil her bidding. Rafaello must help to carry her statue in the procession to the chapel, where her prayers should be held as they have always been."

There was much nodding of heads in agreement and cheering from the villagers, until Donata piped up, for despite being overjoyed by her son's healing, she was still fearful of what the Bishop might do if he discovered Rafaello taking part in the procession to the chapel. "What of Bishop Pazzini? He's forbidden us to pray at the chapel and insists that we attend Mass in the church."

Again the villagers responded in unison, but this time with sighs of reservation. Alessandro would have to work hard to rouse their defiance and courage, which had been sapped of much of its strength since the news of the burnings on Tuesday. Thinking back to the previous night, he felt sure that Dionisio and Giorgio, along with their father Bartolomeo, would support his attempt to persuade the villagers. "Bartolomeo, only yesterday we were talking about your need to defy the Bishop's attempt to control your farming methods. Surely you agree that it is just as important not to let him dictate how and where you should pray?" All eyes turned to the old farmer, who was held in high regard by the villagers. Alessandro had chosen well, for Bartolomeo was already puffing out his chest in preparation for battle.

"What do you think, Papa?" asked Dionisio, who was also keen to hear his father's opinion before giving his support to Alessandro.

Bartolomeo drew himself up as straight as his crooked back would allow and faced the villagers. "It is as the storyteller says. The Black Madonna has once more bestowed her generous healing powers on our village and we must worship her as she desires, not as the Bishop decrees. Tomorrow evening, we must proceed to the chapel, as has been the custom of our ancestors for generations. If we fail to honour her in this way, then she may desert us once and for all into the hands of the Bishop, and then we shall be truly damned!"

Dionisio cheered his father's call to rebellion, followed by Giorgio and the others. Even Donata could not help but smile at the enthusiasm of the men, before turning to Niccolo for his opinion. "Doctor, what do you think?"

Niccolo knew that he alone possessed the power of a learned man to influence the remaining fearful villagers, despite his own lack of belief in the divine. "Donata, I must agree with Bartolomeo. On having examined Rafaello, I am certain that the healing hands of the Black Madonna have been at work. We must therefore acknowledge her desire to be worshipped at the chapel."

Before anyone else could step in and voice yet further doubt, Alessandro grasped the moment to consolidate their plan of action. "So, my friends, we are all agreed. Tomorrow, you will continue with your daily lives as usual so as not to arouse suspicion. Come dusk you will meet in the village square to start the procession down to the chapel garden. By starting earlier in the evening, you should avoid the arrival of the Bishop. By the time he realises where you are, he will be too late to stop the proceedings." Laughter and applause greeted Alessandro's words, for he was well versed in rousing excitement in a crowd.

"Until tomorrow, Storyteller," said Bartolomeo, clapping him on the back. "And my heartfelt congratulations to you both, Donata and Rafaello." Maria embraced her sister and nephew, before hobbling home with Bartolomeo and Giorgio, leaving Donata to guide her ecstatic son back to bed.

"Are you coming to the *taverna*, Alessandro?" asked Dionisio.

"I'll join you in a moment," replied Alessandro. "I must speak with Niccolo first." Alessandro and Niccolo watched as the villagers wandered back to their homes to relate the story of the miracle to their loved ones. Where fear and defeat had resided earlier, now joy and defiance reigned.

"Congratulations, Alessandro, you did well," said Niccolo.

"Only with your help, which I am grateful for."

"Don't mention it. I want nothing more than to prevent my mother from being arrested by the Bishop."

"Then let us pray that tomorrow night will bring about his downfall. Will you join me for a drink to toast our success?"

Niccolo shook his head. "I'll let Veronica and Luca know what's happened and then walk her home."

"Until tomorrow, then," Alessandro replied, before making his way to the *taverna*. Rather than venturing upstairs to his room, he sat in a chair beneath the *pergola* where he could watch the man in the corner sleeping. Having drunk himself into a stupor, Enrico had fallen asleep at the table and remained undisturbed by the miraculous events of the evening. Alessandro kept a vigil, ensuring that he did not wake and return to Caterina before sleeping off the poison that brought out the beast in him. It would be a long night, but Alessandro had much to think about. Tomorrow morning, he would find some more doves and hide them beside the chapel so that Paolo could set them free during the ceremony. But would Caterina also find the strength to fly? And would his sister's spirit be laid to rest? After twenty years, his day of justice was upon him, but only the stars knew the events that were destined to unfold the following night at the Festival of Santa Sofia.

Sunday

15 August 1583

The Festival of Santa Sofia

Niccolo awoke on hearing Paolo's whimpers and leant over to stroke his cousin's forehead. "It's all right, Paolo. I'm here."

Paolo rubbed the sleep from his eyes and stretched out his arms. Then he remembered the previous evening's events. "Mamma! Where's Mamma?" he cried, pushing Niccolo's hand aside and running downstairs into the kitchen. Niccolo followed, greeting his mother and Padre Francesco, who were having breakfast at the table. "Rosa, hurry! We must go and find Mamma."

Rosa lifted Paolo onto her knee. "All in good time, Paolo. Your mother is quite safe. Our friend Luca saw to that. First you must eat some breakfast, yes?" Paolo nodded, comforted by Rosa's calm voice, and drank the milk she offered him.

Rosa glanced at Niccolo, who nodded in confirmation of Caterina's safety before announcing, "I have good news." Rosa and Padre Francesco stilled. "Last night, after you left the square, something happened." Niccolo paused, unsure of how to describe what had occurred, for he was still struggling to understand Rafaello's miraculous recovery.

"Yes? What is it?" asked Rosa.

"Donata's son, Rafaello. He's gained the use of his limbs."

"A miracle?"

"So it would seem."

Rosa clapped her hands together. "I knew Sofia would not

desert us. Yet again she has bestowed her healing grace upon our village and we must give her thanks."

"To show their gratitude," Niccolo continued, "the villagers agreed to ignore the Bishop and to hold the festival of prayers at the chapel."

Rosa laughed out loud in. "It couldn't be better! Now the Bishop is sure to come to the chapel garden. We must warn Veronica."

"Are you sure that we won't be endangering her?" asked Niccolo.

"We've already discussed this, Niccolo. There is no other option than to force the Bishop to reveal his guilt. For Veronica's own sake, we must allow her the opportunity to bring her abuser to justice."

"Then I will go and help her to prepare." Bidding them farewell, Niccolo wandered through the olive grove towards a narrow path, which wound past a healing spring and up the hill to the shepherd's hut.

Rosa was swift to follow him out of the door with Paolo. "Come, Francesco, we have much to organise."

Taking Paolo by the hand, Rosa and Padre Francesco headed for the square, where they found a crowd of villagers outside Donata's house, eager to witness Rafaello's miraculous healing. The villagers parted to allow their priest and wisewoman to greet Donata and Rafaello. Rosa embraced them both, marvelling at his newfound ability to walk, before addressing the villagers. "How fortunate we are to once more witness the healing power of our Blessed Mother."

The villagers applauded as Bartolomeo stepped forward. "Padre Francesco, on behalf of us all, may I ask you to consider leading our festival of prayers at the chapel tonight? I know that we ask much of you, when the Bishop has robbed you of your powers, but we are lost without your leadership."

Padre Francesco smiled in appreciation. "It is with great pride that I accept your invitation. Tonight, as is our custom at the Festival of Santa Sofia, Rosa and I will lead you all in the procession to the chapel. There we will give thanks to the Madonna for her miracle."

His response was met with cheers of approval and several of the villagers approached Padre Francesco to kiss his hand. When the excitement had lulled, Rosa began to instruct the men and women in preparation for the festival. "Dionisio and Giorgio, find two others and carry the Black Madonna statue up from the chapel to the square. Elena, come with me to fetch the sacred veil. Bartolomeo, instruct the farmhands to gather grain from the fields and give it to the miller to grind. Women, you will need to make dough for the barley moon cakes from the ground grain, wine, honey and salt, and prepare the baskets of offerings. Tell your children to gather sticks for the fires and to make their garlands of vines and flowers. Men, kindle the fires to bake the barley cakes, fetch your drums and flutes, and prepare the torches for burning. We will meet in the square at dusk. Until then, remain strong in your decision to worship the Black Madonna in her sacred garden."

Excited and eager to follow their wisewoman's instructions, the villagers set about fulfilling their duties and Padre Francesco headed towards the church. Before going to the chapel with Elena, Rosa led Paolo to the Galletti farmhouse. Enrico and Caterina were nowhere to be seen, so Rosa let herself in, calling out until she heard Caterina's muffled voice from behind her bedroom door. Unlocking the bolt, Rosa pushed open the door to find Caterina with eyes red from crying, but she swallowed her tears to comfort Paolo. She could feel his slight body shaking with fear and relief, and she stroked his hair, whispering words of comfort. At last he grew calm and clambered off her knee, wandering into his bedroom to distract his anxious thoughts through play.

Caterina watched him go and then sat down on the bed.

"Oh Caterina, what has become of you?" asked Rosa.

Caterina's body began to convulse with heavy sobs. Rosa gathered her into her arms, stroking her hair and murmuring to her, in much the same way Caterina had comforted Paolo. "He... he tried...to rape me again."

"My poor girl," said Rosa, closing her eyes to stem the tears that threatened to fall and rocking Caterina like a babe until her sobs subsided. Then, settling her back against the pillows, Rosa took her hand. "Talk to me Caterina."

Caterina gave a moan of frustration. "I'm so angry. With Enrico for his violence. With the Bishop for encouraging it. With myself for accepting it. Why has it taken me so long to realise that Paolo deserves more than this? That I deserve more?"

"Don't be hard on yourself," said Rosa. "It isn't your fault. Remember when you were a child and the Church made you pray to a trinity of Father, Son and Holy Spirit? Tell me, where was the Mother? Where was the Daughter? How do you think that made you feel as a young girl?"

Caterina shrugged. "Worthless, I suppose. As if women didn't matter. Didn't even exist."

"Exactly. Then that feeling of worthlessness was reinforced by your father when he arranged your marriage to Enrico. And by society, which made you feel unable to leave Enrico, as if you deserved to be abused. Is it your fault that from an early age you were taught that you were weak and worthless?"

"I suppose not."

"And on top of all this, you lost your mother. Isn't it surprising that you put up with Enrico's violence for so long?"

Caterina nodded her head. "I accept now that I wasn't to blame for my mother's death. Listening to you and to Alessandro's story helped me to realise that there is no use harbouring guilt. We have no control over another soul's journey."

Rosa smiled. "You speak wisely. Like a priestess."

Caterina squeezed her hand. "I am ready to become one now."

"How did you find your strength?"

"I felt it stirring in me when Enrico killed the doves. Paolo was so upset. My need to protect my child drew on courage I never knew I had."

Rosa nodded. "Birthing and mothering challenge women, forcing us to delve deep within to find our inner resources. Our ancestors recognised the importance of these roles, which is why they worshipped a Mother Goddess for thousands of years before they created any statues of a male god. By suppressing the Goddess, the Church has belittled the role of the mother so that women no longer feel they are of any value."

"What about Mother Mary?" asked Caterina.

"The Church would have us believe she is a virgin, but the original meaning of a Virgin Goddess was that she was sexually free and independent. Now, women are expected to be frigid and obedient like the Virgin Mary. When we rejoice in the sexuality of our youth, we are whores. When we bleed and give birth, we are unclean. When we grow old and wise, we are witches. There is no other possible outcome but failure. No wonder so many women give up."

"Like Alessandro's mother."

"Like you."

Caterina looked at Rosa in defiance. "Not any more. Not now he tried to rape me again."

"Why is it different this time?"

"I thought about what you said. About defending the Goddess. I thought about Isabetta and Veronica. By accepting the rape of my body, I was also accepting the rape of my fellow women and of Mother Earth. I have to stand up to him now. For Paolo's sake. For Sofia. For every woman who's ever been abused. And for myself."

"What are you going to do?" asked Rosa.

"I'm going to leave him, but I just don't know how yet."

"Well, that's easy. You and Paolo can live with me."

"Yes, but he will follow."

"And when he does, he will find Niccolo, Alessandro, Luca and all the rest of your family and friends waiting for him."

"But what about the Bishop? He could still send me to a nunnery."

"If the Bishop ever tried to take you away from the village, he would have to fight the lot of us. Trust those who love you. Pray to Sofia for guidance and protection. And know that you have all that you need to cope with whatever life throws at you."

Rosa reached forward to embrace Caterina. "You are always free. Never forget that. You may not be able to control how other people behave towards you, but you always have the power to choose how you respond to them."

"Thank you, Rosa, for everything."

"What is the meaning of this?" shouted Enrico as he marched in, holding Paolo by the arm. "Get out, you old hag!" he growled, grabbing Rosa and dragging her to the door.

"No!" cried Caterina, lunging at Enrico, but he sent her flying onto the floor with a backhand across her face. Then he threw Rosa through the doorway and slammed the door shut behind them, bolting it. Caterina banged on the door, sobbing in anger and frustration.

As Enrico pushed Rosa down the stairs, she called up to Caterina, "Don't give up!" Paolo was crying hysterically, held fast by his father. "Look at your son, Enrico! Look what you are doing to him!" Rosa cried, but he just shoved her backwards out of the front door. "Don't be frightened, Paolo. Sofia is with you. All will be well, I promise." The door slammed in her face but she wasn't finished. "You are not your mother, Enrico! Do not repeat her mistakes!" Silence followed, punctuated by Paolo's muffled sobs, but there was nothing more Rosa could do to protect him. Glancing up at the bedroom window, she caught sight of Caterina gazing down at her. Rosa clenched her fist in the air and Caterina mimicked her warrior gesture, a brave smile breaking through her tears as she watched Rosa disappear up the track.

Back in the square, Rosa found Elena and they headed off to the chapel. There Rosa took the black veil from off the altar and they unfolded the sacred cloth, which was sewn with a thousand silver swastikas to symbolise the stars in the night sky.

"Where's Caterina?" asked Elena.

"Enrico's locked her up."

Elena looked aghast. "The brute!"

At that moment, Alessandro stepped inside the chapel carrying another birdcage containing three doves. "Any news of Caterina?"

Rosa went to greet Alessandro. "I went to the house this morning to find her locked in the bedroom. I managed to speak with her before Enrico threw me out, but he's locked her up again. It remains to be seen whether he will allow her to come to the festival." Alessandro scowled as Rosa pointed at the birdcage. "Are those for Paolo?"

"Yes. I'm going to leave them for him by the side of the chapel closest to the ravine, where they will be hidden from view. He can find them there during the festival."

"I'll let him know that you've kept your promise."

Elena watched Alessandro leave with a wistful look in her eye. "It would seem the storyteller is quite enamoured with Caterina."

"Yes he is, but have no fear Elena," said Rosa, "your time to be loved will come when it's meant to." As they finished unravelling the veil's folds and shook out the dust that had settled over the year, the silver crosses glistened in the light. Draping it over their shoulders, they climbed back up through the woods towards the square, passing Dionisio, Giorgio and their two friends as they made their way down to collect the statue of the Black Madonna.

By the time Rosa and Elena reached the square it was deserted. The ground was strewn with stem cuttings and leaves from the garlands of vines the children had been making, and the long wooden tables were covered in flour and dough from the barley moon cakes. On the stage was a pile of drums and flutes, but the musicians were nowhere to be seen, having left for Arunca that morning. In preparation for the late night vigil of prayers, the villagers had retired to their homes to escape the heat of the midday sun and rest. Placing the veil on the stage, Rosa and Elena headed to the church. They soon returned with the sacred oil paintings of the Madonna in their ornate gilded frames, which Maria, Donata and the other older women would carry in the procession.

Alessandro watched their progress from the orchard where he was finalising the evening's plan with Luca. "What about Veronica?"

"Niccolo went to see her this morning," said Luca.

"Why don't you go and tell them where to hide so that I can find them later. I'll fetch the pail of boar's blood from Giorgio and meet you back in the square."

Luca scampered off through the trees and up the hill to his father's hut. There he found Niccolo and Veronica sharing a bowl of vegetable soup with Piero, whose white beard and long, cotton robe created a vision from the biblical past. "I've come with word from Alessandro. Niccolo, it's time to take Veronica down to the chapel garden. To the right of the chapel, by the side of the ravine, is a thicket of trees. Hide in there and Alessandro will find you with the bucket of pig's blood." Then Luca turned to Veronica, who was already wearing the white cotton dress in preparation for her later apparition, and clutched her hands in his hirsute one. "Be strong, sister. Niccolo will take care of you." With that, he ran back to the square, leaving their father to embrace Veronica before she too left with Niccolo.

Veronica held fast to Niccolo's hand as he led her down the side of the hill that faced away from the village and towards the chapel. At the bottom of the hill they joined the second, unused path through the woods, which wound its way from opposite the back of Enrico's land down to the chapel. By following this path instead of the main one leading from *Via Principale*, they were able to keep their movements secret from the villagers.

On reaching the chapel garden, Niccolo soon realised which thicket of trees Luca was referring to and settled Veronica on a blanket, where she would be hidden from view until it was time to appear before the Bishop. A tense silence followed while the darkening shadows of the trees and the stillness of the garden took their toll on both their nerves. Veronica shivered, more from fear than the chill. Niccolo enfolded her in his arms, stroking her long hair. "Are you frightened?"

"A little," she replied.

"You don't have to do this. I could take you home now if you want."

Veronica shook her head against his chest. "No. I must do this. I owe it to myself, to Isabetta, and to all those other women who have suffered at the hands of Bishop Pazzini. I could never forgive myself if his recent victims died at the stakes on Tuesday. He must be stopped."

Niccolo nodded, knowing she spoke the truth but fearful for her safety. Lifting her chin up with his hand, he stared into her eyes. "I promise I will take care of you. As soon as the Bishop has seen you, I will help you back to your father's home. I won't leave you until I know you're safe." Veronica welcomed his lips as they brushed against hers, for it was a strange night and she sought comfort from their passion.

"Niccolo?" Within moments, Alessandro's face appeared between the branches. "I've brought you the boar's blood." Placing the pail on the ground, Alessandro glanced at Veronica as she lay cradled against Niccolo's chest. Devoid of her usual earthy vigour, her eyes gazed wide open like those of a startled rabbit, reminding Alessandro of his sister. "Are you sure you still want to go ahead with this, Veronica?"

"Yes, I'm sure."

Alessandro let out a long breath in an attempt to calm his nerves. "Right. At Luca's signal, Niccolo, throw the blood over Veronica before she stands in front of the Bishop."

"What will Luca's signal be?"

Alessandro smiled, distracted by the memory of Luca's eagerness to play his part in the night's drama. "No less than the howl of a wolf. We hope this will be sufficient to distract everyone so that it will seem as if Veronica has appeared from nowhere." The friends laughed with affection at how Luca was beginning to embrace his affliction rather than cowering in fear of it. Their laughter was a necessary release of tension, but it could only ever be temporary. Within moments, the enormity of the situation came back to haunt them and Alessandro reached out to touch Veronica's arm. "May Sofia guide and protect you."

As Alessandro ran along *Via Principale*, dusk was falling. The square was lit by the light of the full mother moon and by burning torches held high above the men's heads. Alessandro caught sight of Paolo standing amid a group of children by the stage. Enrico was over by the butchery with Giorgio and Dionisio, who were holding the statue of the Black Madonna. Caterina was nowhere to be seen. Alessandro cursed aloud, imagining her locked up all alone, but Luca called to him from the shadows beneath the consulting room balcony, "One more night, Alessandro. Then you will be free to help her." At that moment, Rosa and Padre Francesco came out of the church and walked towards the centre of the square. An owl glided overhead and Rosa watched its flight, wondering whether it portended a battle or a death.

"Tell me about this evening's ritual, Luca. What's Rosa wearing?"

Luca understood Alessandro's need for distraction and gladly shared his understanding of the festival with him. "That's the multi-coloured robe of the Harvest Mother woven with flowers and fruit. It's similar to the one worn by the Black Goddess Isis, Queen of Egypt. Rosa's hair is entwined with corn stalks and an owl mask covers her eyes. On her forehead she wears a silver band with the horn of the crescent moon. This symbol harks back to the cult of the Black Goddess Diana, who was revered throughout these lands for generations before the Madonna. A blue cord is tied around Rosa's waist, from which hangs a pouch containing the skin shed by a serpent. In her right hand she carries a wooden staff, the top of which is crafted in the head of a *gorgon*, the warrior priestess with snakes writhing in her hair. In her other hand, Rosa carries the *kernos*. This represents the womb of Mother Earth. It has different compartments in which seeds of grain from each field are placed. In the centre of the *kernos* is a candle that lights the path to the wisdom of Sofia. The candle is the symbol of the flame of life, which is produced by the union of female and male."

Alessandro nodded, intrigued by Luca's description. Behind Rosa and Padre Francesco, he could see Rafaello and his three uncles lifting up the large, black statue. "I understand Rafaello must carry the Black Madonna to give thanks for his healing."

"Yes, although followers of Sofia know the statue originates from when Isis and the Roman goddess Diana were honoured in our groves. When the Roman Church arrived, the priestesses hid it in the cave until a time when all of Christendom worshipped such statues as Black Madonnas."

As Rafaello staggered past on his trembling legs, Alessandro saw the group of children following behind. They were dressed in the white robes of angels with garlands of vines and flowers in their hair, and were carrying baskets containing offerings of fruit, grain sheaves and soil. Their mothers and grandmothers formed the next group of pilgrims. He recognised Donata and Maria, carrying paintings of the Madonna, while others carried baskets containing cakes shaped like crescent moons. "What's in the baskets, Luca?"

"Ritual barley cakes. There's an ancient belief that whoever eats cakes made from the first harvested grain will inherit the wisdom from the underworld where the seeds grew. Padre Francesco and Rosa will use these cakes for the communion meal, to represent the body of the Horned God, the son-lover of the Goddess. They will also give the villagers wine as the symbol of his blood, which is scattered on his death to fertilise the fields. These were the sacraments used by our ancestors before the Roman Church adopted the ritual. Through these acts of communion and the repetition of prayers, the villagers hope the Blessed Mother will turn aside storms until the fields have been harvested."

Next came Elena, Cristina and the younger women, carrying a black veil high above their heads, which twinkled like the night sky. "What's that the women are carrying? It's beautiful."

"That's the Veil of Wisdom, which protects the mysteries of the Goddess. It can only be lifted by those who seek true communion with Sofia. To render the veil is to rape the Goddess."

Behind the women and children, a group of men appeared carrying a straw effigy. "And that's Befana, the ancient Harvest Mother. She'll be burnt as the symbol of the sacrificed deity, ensuring the regeneration of the earth." The remaining men formed a protective arc around the villagers. Some beat their drums in the shamanic rhythm of old. Others held their flaming torches high above their heads, lighting the way and protecting the villagers. "Let's hope that their fire is strong enough to shield us from Bishop Pazzini," Luca continued. "For he encircles us ever more closely with his net, intent on entrapping us in servitude, so that in time we might forget our communion with Sofia and with our true selves. It's our duty tonight to rip the Bishop's net to shreds before he can rent asunder the veil of the Black Goddess."

Rosa and Padre Francesco reached the shrine on the corner of *Via Principale* and halted. Padre Francesco spoke the words of a peasant girl's prayer to the Madonna, calling on her as the patroness of all rustic and agricultural interests. The prayer was followed by a loud hum of *amens* and then the procession moved down the lane towards the chapel garden.

Alessandro and Luca emerged from beneath the consulting room balcony to follow the last row of men. Catching sight of two women clinging to each other outside the church, Alessandro called out to them. "Emilia, are you and Agnesa not joining the procession?"

"I would no sooner take part in such wickedness led by that witch than dance with the devil. My mother and I will stay here and await the arrival of the Bishop. He must be told of how the hag and her lover have conspired to lead this village into the arms of Satan. Tonight justice will be ours!"

Alessandro turned back to Luca. "For once, Emilia's scheming may work to our advantage, for she is sure to bring the Bishop down to the chapel."

Luca smiled. "The old fool would be aghast to know she is abetting our plan to overthrow Bishop Pazzini." And with a last glance at the women, they set off down *Via Principale*.

On reaching the chapel garden, Alessandro and Luca hid among the olive and fig trees. Rosa and Padre Francesco positioned themselves on the chapel steps, while the villagers gathered in a circle around the well and apple tree. The men used their torches to light a pile of oak branches and lowered the effigy of Befana into the flames. A chorus of voices rose up, singing a dedication to the Harvest Mother. Rafaello and his uncles set the statue of the Black Madonna down on the steps of the chapel, so that it was raised up for all to see. Then Padre Francesco recited from the heavy bible that lay open in his hands.

> I am very dark, but comely,
> > O daughters of Jerusalem,
> > like the tents of Kedar,
> > like the curtains of Solomon.
> Do not gaze at me because I am swarthy,
> > because the sun has scorched me.
> My mother's sons were angry with me,
> > they made me keeper of the vineyards;
> > but, my own vineyard I have not kept!
> Tell me, you whom my soul loves,
> > where you pasture your flock,
> > where you make it lie down at noon;
> For why should I be like one who wanders
> > beside the flocks of your companions?

"What's Padre Francesco saying?" asked Alessandro.

"He's reading from the Wisdom text of the Song of Songs, which the Church Fathers included in their bible," Luca replied. "They didn't realise that the voice speaking is that of Sofia, the Black Goddess of Wisdom, who is berating her people for abandoning her."

Rosa then approached the well where she cupped her hands

into the water to wet her head three times. "This is an ancient ritual used by the moon priestesses, who were believed to have magical control over the weather and the making of rain," explained Luca. "The Roman Church adopted the same ritual for its baptism ceremony. By cleaning out the water from the well and drawing fresh water to throw over herself, Rosa hopes to ensure that the rain will continue to fertilise the soil." Alessandro watched as Elena then draped the veil of the Black Goddess over Rosa's head and shoulders, creating a train behind her, as if she were a bride, standing beside her groom Padre Francesco. One by one, the children approached the Black Madonna to light their candles of devotion and lay their baskets of offerings at her feet. All the while, the men beat their drums and played their flutes. "The women are performing a spiral dance around the bonfire, drumming their feet in a fertility ritual to revitalize the waters of the underworld."

When all the offerings had been made, Rosa lifted the *kernos* high in the air and asked for the Harvest Mother's blessing on their fields. Padre Francesco motioned to Rafaello and laid his hand upon his head, blessing him. In return, Rafaello gave Padre Francesco his baptism gown, for it was his most prized vestment. It would be hung with all the other clothes belonging to those who had been recipients of divine healing. Next, Rosa recited a prayer of thanksgiving to the Black Madonna for her gift of healing, which was followed by a loud cheer from the crowd. Then Rafaello partook of the communion meal, while the villagers arranged themselves in a line behind him. One by one, they accepted the barley moon cake offered to them by their wisewoman and received the holy wine from Padre Francesco.

"Stop! I command you to stop!" Bishop Pazzini stormed into the garden, accompanied not only by Emilia and Agnesa, but by eight menacing guards from the Inquisition's court in Arunca. Excited by the prospect of what devilment he might discover, the

Bishop had come prepared to do battle in the name of the Roman Church. The guards accompanied him as he strode through the villagers, pushing them out of his way. Mothers ran to protect their children, while the men tried to form a shield around them. Amid the commotion, Paolo crept behind the chapel to find the doves Alessandro had promised to leave for him. Enrico watched his son's progress from afar and made his way through the crowd to see what Paolo was up to.

Meanwhile, Rosa and Padre Francesco stood their ground as the Bishop and guards approached them. An anxious silence stole through the garden in anticipation of the Bishop's reaction. It was not long in coming. Ripping the veil from Rosa's head, Bishop Pazzini struck the plate of barley cakes out of her hands. "Witch! How dare you defile our Lord's Supper with your venomous touch!"

Rosa felt a calm serenity flow through her, as if she had been preparing for this moment all her life. Despite knowing that if their plan failed she faced certain death, Rosa experienced no fear. Only a steadfast belief in the Black Goddess and a rejection of all that stood in her way. "I am no witch. I am a priestess of Sofia and it is she whom you must answer to." Padre Francesco turned to stare in horror at Rosa, for by her words she had signed her own death warrant. Rosa met his gaze with eyes that sparkled with defiance and Padre Francesco could only feel admiration for her courage.

"Guards, seize the witch!" ordered Bishop Pazzini.

The villagers erupted and Alessandro signalled to Luca. At once, the wolf-man threw back his head and let out an ear-piercing howl, which echoed off the mountainside, filling the garden with its lupine lament. All eyes, including those of Bishop Pazzini, turned to stare at the trees on the far left of the garden where Luca was cowering. Everyone, except for Enrico. On rounding the side of the chapel, he discovered Paolo holding a birdcage containing three doves. Guessing at once who had left the gift for his son, Enrico seized the cage, holding it above Paolo's head.

"No!" cried Paolo, climbing up onto the low wall running alongside the ravine in order to retrieve the birds from his father.

Recovering from the momentary distraction of Luca's howling, the Bishop turned his attention back to Rosa, intent on arresting her. He was brought to a sudden halt, however, by the ghastly apparition in the trees behind her. It was the spirit of a peasant girl he had been forced to punish, but here she stood before him in the same white dress, dripping with blood. Jacobo Pazzini knew at once that the devil had come to take his revenge, but just as his mouth opened wide in fear, a high-pitched scream rang out.

Alessandro looked from the Bishop towards Veronica, but she had already disappeared into the thicket of trees. His eyes drawn to the ravine, he then watched in horror as Paolo teetered on the wall, lost his balance and fell headlong into the river below. "Paolo!" screamed Rosa, who had witnessed the same scene and rushed over to the edge of the ravine, followed by the others. Leaning over the wall, they gazed down at Paolo's lifeless body lying in the water below.

Niccolo heard his mother's screams from the thicket of trees. "Veronica, Paolo's in trouble. Stay here and wait for me." Sliding out between the trees, he motioned to Alessandro hiding in the nearby shadows with Luca. "Quick, go and fetch Caterina." Alessandro nodded, his heart clamouring with fear, for he knew that it would take a miracle for Paolo to survive such a fall and the village had already been blessed with one. With a last look at the crowd over by the ravine, he turned and left through the gate.

Alessandro ran as fast as he could back to the square and to Enrico's farmhouse. All the while, he cursed his own stupidity for endangering Paolo with his gift of the doves. Throwing open the front door, he ran upstairs to find both bedrooms empty. One of the doors was hanging off its hinges with large sections of wood sliced out of it. An ornamental axe that had once hung on the bedroom wall now lay in the doorway. Alessandro shook his head in disbelief. Caterina must have taken the axe from the wall and knocked the door down. Then he smiled to himself. She'd done it. She'd at last found the courage to defy her husband. But there was no time now to contemplate Caterina's triumph. Where could she be? He hadn't passed her on his return so she couldn't have made her way to the chapel. Alessandro began to search for her in the orchard and fields, but he wouldn't find her, for she had already begun her descent to the chapel garden using the path that led from the back of Enrico's land.

As she neared the chapel garden, Caterina could hear raised voices and the cries of women. Assuming that the arrival of Bishop Pazzini was the cause of the villagers' anguish, Caterina crept with caution through the rose bushes into the garden. She was surprised to discover everyone, including Bishop Pazzini and his guards, peering into the ravine. Out of the corner of her eye, she spied the diminutive figure of Rosa standing on the wall. As if sensing her niece's presence, Rosa turned to stare at Caterina, her face contorted in agony. Caterina knew something dreadful had happened and her shutters of fatalism lowered their protective shield. As if in a dream, she walked towards Rosa through the crowd of sorrowful faces that parted before her. Rosa clambered off the wall and held out her arms. "Caterina." The old wisewoman faltered, at a loss for words. "Caterina. There was a struggle. Enrico...the doves. Paolo fell." Caterina clenched her jaw to swallow the scream that welled up from deep within. Stumbling forward, she grasped onto Rosa's outstretched arm for support. "Niccolo is with him," explained Rosa, pointing towards the rocks below, where Niccolo was trying to revive Paolo. Caterina leant over the wall and saw her son's body draped over the rocks. Niccolo was kneeling beside him, his head bent over Paolo's chest.

"Paolo!" Screaming his name again and again, Caterina began to climb down the foot and handholds carved into the rock face.

"Caterina, no!" cried Rosa, but she was left to watch along with the others as Caterina climbed down to the bottom and waded through the water towards her son. It was only then that she saw what Niccolo's torchlight had earlier revealed to the crowd. Paolo's pale head was crowned by a halo of red blood, fanning out over the bleached rock upon which he lay. Caterina looked at Niccolo, seeking his reassurance, but tears flowed down his stoic face.

"I'm so sorry, Caterina," he said, "so very sorry."

Caterina sank to her knees in the water, feeling an explosion of pain rushing up from her stomach, causing her to retch repeatedly. When her vomiting had subsided, she put her hands in the river to splash water over her face. But the river was awash with Paolo's blood, which streaked down her pale dress in red rivulets. Caterina turned to the body of her son and lifted him into her arms. She lay her face against his, nudging it this way and that, smelling his skin for the last remnants of life. Then she raised her head up towards the crowd of faces staring down at her from high above. Looking up from the depths of the ravine, with her blood-stained dress and tortured eyes illuminated by the burning flames of Niccolo's torch, she seemed to the onlookers like a vision from hell itself. Then her eyes stopped roaming and she focussed on a single face in the crowd. As she raised up the body of her son on outstretched arms, a scream tore up from the depths of her anguish. The coil that had been winding tighter and tighter in her chest snapped, unleashing a spiral of unspent rage. "Are you happy now? Was killing my unborn child not penance enough? Raping me? Beating me? Was all this not enough that you had to rob me of my only child? My only chance of being a mother? Murderer! You killed my baby! You killed Paolo!" she sobbed as she sank to her knees in the water, rocking her son's body against her breast. The villagers stared down at her aghast, then all eyes turned to look at the man accused of murdering his son. Enrico was slumped against the wall, his eyes staring at Paolo's inert body. Then he turned away, stumbling through the crowd towards the woods. Padre Francesco called out to him, but Enrico was beyond the reach of guidance now.

"Now do you see how God wreaks his vengeance on those who do not respect the authority of the Holy Mother Church?" declared Bishop Pazzini, his fears concerning the spectre now allayed by its disappearance. The villagers turned to stare at him, first in disbelief and then in anger.

Rosa pushed past her neighbours until she stood in front of him. Despite being dwarfed by his large frame, she raised her staff and punctuated each sentence with a sharp jab to his chest. "It is you and you alone who are responsible for this child's death. If you hadn't marched down here, terrorising us with your threats, then we wouldn't have been distracted from minding our children."

Initially stunned by her audacity, Bishop Pazzini grabbed the staff from out of her hand and beat her over the head with it. Rosa fell to the ground dazed. Padre Francesco tried to reach her but the eight guards formed a protective circle around the Bishop and his victim. The villagers were powerless to come to Rosa's aid as Bishop Pazzini stood over her. "You dare to accuse me, a bishop, when everyone here knows you to be a witch? It is you who has the devil's power to conjure a spirit at will. And it is you who already stands accused of murdering a woman and her babe. No doubt you caused the child to fall at the same time as distracting our attention by conjuring that ghastly apparition."

Rosa realised then that he had indeed seen Veronica but that their plan had failed. The distraction of Paolo's fall had given him enough time to control any emotion he may have been prompted to display. In the end, all they had succeeded in doing was providing the Bishop with yet more evidence to accuse her. There was nothing left but for Rosa to defend herself and the Black Goddess. "You can accuse me all you like, but I would never seek to conjure a spirit, let alone murder a child. I am not evil. I am a priestess of Sofia and your disruption of her thanksgiving prayers is a sacrilege."

Rosa's courageous words were met with another blow to her head. "In the name of God and the Roman Church, I arrest you on the charge of heresy and witchcraft. Guards, seize the hag!" Rosa struggled to raise her head as two Inquisition guards pulled her up to standing. The villagers, trapped behind the barrier of guards, uttered cries of outrage, calling for their wisewoman to be set free. Only Emilia and Agnesa smiled with triumph from their vantage point on the chapel steps.

"Mother?" Niccolo could hear the anxious voices of the villagers calling out Rosa's name, but could see nothing from the depths of the ravine. Just then, in the silence as he waited for Rosa's response, Niccolo heard a small noise emanate from Paolo. Turning his attention to the boy lying cradled in his mother's arms, Niccolo placed his cheek against Paolo's mouth and felt a shallow breath upon his skin. Then, reaching for his neck, Niccolo felt for a pulse and leapt back in surprised delight when the vein began to throb. "He's alive! Paolo's alive!" Caterina gasped and her whole body began to shake as she sobbed and laughed at the same time, feeling the rise and fall of her son's chest to reassure herself that he was indeed alive. "Quick, Caterina. We must get him to my room." Niccolo removed his shirt. "Put Paolo over my shoulders and tie the shirt like a harness around his back and my waist. Follow behind as I climb to make sure he doesn't fall."

Caterina did as she was asked, her anxiety returning in response to the urgency in Niccolo's voice. "Will he recover, Niccolo?"

"I can't be sure, Caterina, that's why we must hurry."

Step by step, they began the long climb back up the ravine, with Caterina holding her son onto Niccolo's back. The villagers heard his cries and rushed back towards the edge of the ravine, peering over the low wall to shout words of encouragement.

"It seems your plans for murder have been thwarted, Witch!" said Bishop Pazzini, scowling at Rosa, but she didn't care what he thought. Paolo was alive. That's all that mattered. Taking advantage of the distraction, Padre Francesco tried to push his way between the guards to reach Rosa, but the guards' weapons rendered him powerless to free his beloved and instead he found himself held by them. His actions had not gone unnoticed by Bishop Pazzini, who now marched over to Padre Francesco. Once more, the villagers turned away from the ravine to watch anxiously as their priest's fate was delivered. "As for you, Francesco. I will be calling you as a witness in the witch's trial. It's obvious that you have fallen under some magical spell of hers."

"Rosa is no witch and nothing could ever force me to say so," said Padre Francesco.

Bishop Pazzini laughed out loud. "We will see about that, Francesco." The Bishop's laughter unnerved the villagers and they watched him closely as he walked in a circle around their priest and wisewoman. At last he came to a halt and looked in turn from Rosa to Padre Francesco. "It seems you are rather enamoured with the hag, Francesco. I wonder if you will hold your tongue when you are forced to watch her tortured? Swearing that she is a witch would of course bring her torture to a swift end and ensure that she was given a quick death."

The crowd erupted once more in outrage at the Bishop's threats. Several of the men followed Dionisio and Giorgio as they charged at the guards in an attempt to free their aunt. However, the men were soon held at bay, helpless when confronted with the guards' swords and rifles. The Bishop smiled with triumph at the anxiety evident in Padre Francesco, whose mind was suddenly filled with a vision of Christ throwing tables aside in the Temple of the Pharisees, and his courage grew in defiance of the Bishop. "You disgust me! You represent everything Christ despised in a priest. I will not betray my Lord's name by bowing before your evil."

Bishop Pazzini glowered at Padre Francesco before bellowing at the guards, "Take them back to the square and chain them to the cart. Tonight they will discover the comfort of the Inquisition's cells in Arunca." With a final glare at the crowd, Bishop Pazzini led the procession out of the garden. Padre Francesco and Rosa staggered forward as the guards hauled them away. The villagers watched their retreating figures in despair and clung to each other for support, frightened by the seeming hopelessness of the situation.

As they neared the top of the ravine, Niccolo and Caterina could hear the anxious voices of the villagers. Niccolo was reminded of his mother's predicament and called out to her again. "Mother?" His raised voice attracted the villagers and they turned back to the edge of the ravine as Dionisio and Giorgio held out their arms to help Niccolo and Caterina with Paolo.

The smile of delight on Caterina's face was a bittersweet reminder of the joy amid such sorrow. "Paolo's alive! He's alive!" she cried. A huge cheer erupted through the crowd. Several of the villagers broke down in tears, their relief at Paolo's survival edged with anxiety over the fate of Rosa and Padre Francesco. As Dionisio helped to lower his nephew from Niccolo's back, Caterina looked about her. "Where are Rosa and Padre Francesco?" A hush fell on the crowd as Niccolo and Caterina waited for news. "Well?"

Bartolomeo stepped forward to break the news of his sister Rosa's demise. "Bishop Pazzini has arrested Rosa on a charge of heresy and witchcraft. He has taken her and Padre Francesco to the Inquisition's cells in Arunca."

Niccolo was silent for a moment as he digested the news. Then his anger erupted. "Did no one try to stop the Bishop from taking them?"

The men lowered their eyes in shame and Dionisio spoke up in defence of them. "Cousin, we did everything in our power, but the guards were armed with swords and rifles while we had nothing but our prayers."

Caterina gave a bitter sigh. "It was the weapons of war that first destroyed our ancestors' peaceful worship of the divine Mother so many years ago."

"Then we must find a way to make sure they do not succeed this time," said Niccolo, looking around at the villagers, willing them to find their courage and fight with him to free Rosa and Padre Francesco. Just then, Paolo coughed and the attention of the crowd turned to the young boy. Niccolo checked his breathing again and made sure that the blood from his head wound was congealing. Taking the sacred veil from where it lay ripped on the chapel steps, he draped its heavy folds over Paolo, whispering to Caterina, "Keep him warm while I speak with Veronica."

The villagers gathered around Caterina to marvel at her son's miraculous survival, while Niccolo ran off, disappearing between the trees. "Veronica? Luca?"

"Here." Luca stepped out from behind one of the trees, followed by Veronica. She'd draped the blanket over herself to cover the pig's blood, which was now drying in crusty welts upon her dress.

"I'm so sorry about your mother, Niccolo," she said.

Niccolo shook his head, unable to voice his anxiety and aware of the urgent need to dress Paolo's wound. "Luca, would you take Veronica home?"

"Of course, but where's Alessandro?"

Niccolo frowned. "I haven't seen him since Paolo fell, when I sent him to fetch Caterina."

"But Caterina arrived soon after he left."

Niccolo stared at Luca in confusion. "They must have missed each other in the woods. He must still be searching the village for her, which means that he doesn't know of my mother and Padre Francesco's fate. Luca, go and find him once you've taken Veronica home. Veronica, forgive me, but I must tend to Paolo."

Veronica reached up to stroke his cheek. "Of course. I will be quite safe. Go."

Niccolo headed out of the thicket towards the crowd surrounding Paolo, and gathered him in his arms, motioning to Caterina.

Caterina started to follow him but paused to seek out her aunt's face from the crowd. "Elena, the fire."

Elena understood and nodded. "I will see to it."

Caterina then followed Niccolo up the path, leaving the villagers to gather the scattered remains of their festival of prayers. The men carried the statue of the Black Madonna inside the chapel, while the women transferred the candles and offerings to the altar. One by one, they knelt before the statue and prayed for the Black Madonna's help in healing Paolo and protecting Rosa and Padre Francesco. Then they started their sorrowful procession back up through the woods to their homes.

Only Elena remained at the chapel once the last devotee had left. Drawing back the curtain in the corner, she made her way into the cave of the Black Goddess. The flames of her fire had all but died away but there were still some embers glowing. Elena blew on them, adding some dry straw to catch the heat, and it was not long before the flames were dancing once more, nurtured by the breath of her prayers.

Meanwhile, back in the square, Alessandro's search for Caterina had proven futile. He was just about to set off down *Via Principale* when he saw the torches rounding the corner by the shrine and heard Bishop Pazzini's booming voice. In that moment, Alessandro knew that their plan had failed and his heart sank.

Moving back into the shadows of the orchard, he waited as the Bishop and guards entered the square, dragging behind them the dishevelled figures of Rosa and Padre Francesco. He watched as the guards hoisted them up onto a cart and heard the clanking of chains as their feet and hands were shackled. Then, the Bishop climbed inside his litter and the guards mounted their horses to begin the journey back to Arunca. Alessandro's last image of the convoy was of Rosa's defiant features etched against the fullness of the mother moon.

Once the cart had rolled out of sight, Alessandro sank to his knees on the hard, scorched earth. He had failed to bring his sister's murderer to justice and now his actions had caused the death of Paolo and the arrest of Rosa and Padre Francesco. Caterina would never forgive him. There was nothing for it but to leave as soon as possible. His mind made up, Alessandro ran as fast as he could up the road that led in the opposite direction from Arunca.

Having led Veronica back to the safety of their father's hut, Luca continued along the path that led to the back of Enrico's land, intent on finding Alessandro. All at once, a gunshot blasted over his head. Luca's heart missed a beat as he swung round to see Enrico staggering through the trees. With a near empty bottle of wine in one hand and his rifle cocked in the other, Enrico charged towards Luca. "There's nowhere to run to now, Wolf-man!" Luca disagreed and began to run as fast as his legs could carry him across Enrico's barren land and into the forest that lay beyond. As he sought to flee the hunter, a chemical change seemed to take place in Luca's body, unleashing an unnatural strength and speed, as if the spirit of a wolf had indeed taken possession of his limbs. Galloping between the trees, he soon escaped from Enrico, whose mind and body were enfeebled by alcohol. Sinking to his knees, Enrico fell back on the forest floor, his gun letting off one final shot. Several pairs of close-set eyes appeared, glinting red in the light of the moon, as the pack of wolves began to circle ever closer to their prey.

Caterina flinched as she heard the shot and ran into the village square with Niccolo. Expecting to find the guards firing their weapons at Rosa and Padre Francesco, they were stunned to discover the square empty. "Where did that shot come from?" asked Caterina.

"I don't know, but it seems Rosa and Padre Francesco have been spared for now, at least. Come, we must get Paolo upstairs." Inside the consulting room, Niccolo laid Paolo on the bed. He was very pale and his pulse was faint, but the wound on his head was clotting well. Niccolo set about cleaning and dressing the wound before checking the rest of Paolo's body for any other signs of injury. When he had finished, he looked up at Caterina. "It truly is a miracle, Caterina. Apart from the wound on his head, which seems to be relatively superficial, the rest of Paolo's body appears to have survived intact. The impact of hitting the water has stunned his brain and he will most likely remain asleep for several hours, if not days, while his body heals itself. There is little more we can do now than to keep him warm and wait for him to awake." Caterina let out a deep exhalation of breath and sank to the floor, where she sat with her head hanging low between her knees. "You're faint. Quick, smell these."

Caterina shook her head, waving away the jar of salts. "I'll be fine, thank you. I just need a few moments." Feelings of extreme loss, succeeded by hope, but then compounded by fear for Rosa and Padre Francesco, had finally taken their toll on Caterina. Secure in the knowledge that Paolo was safe, she retreated into the void of meditation and prayer to listen to Sofia's words of wisdom.

In the stillness of her mind, Caterina felt herself falling from a great height through the multitudinous layers of life, symbolised in the row upon row of branches stemming from the Tree of Life. Eventually, she found herself standing in the depths of a cavern. Before her lay a path of burning coals, across which she needed to walk if she was to reach the Black Goddess on the other side. Deep inside her belly, Caterina could feel a ball of fire revolving, generating the strength and courage she needed to walk through the burning coals. Step by step, she strode across the coals and was surprised to feel no pain in her feet. On reaching the Goddess seated on the throne, Caterina knelt before her and awaited her words of wisdom.

"Now you are ready, my child. You have stepped into the cave of the Black Goddess, the Crone of death and destruction, and have experienced pain, loss and despair. You have walked through the burning coals of initiation and discovered my fire of passion and courage burning deep inside of you. It is time now for you to suckle my milk of divine love and wisdom to complete your transformation and to allow you to be reborn as the free spirit of the dove. Come, child."

Caterina felt herself being cradled in the arms of the Great Mother and turned her head to suckle at the abundant milk pouring forth from her pendulous breast. At once, Caterina was transformed into a brilliant white dove, and flew up through the branches of the Tree of Life until she burst forth into the night sky in a shower of shooting stars.

Caterina's dulled senses began to throb once more as she pulled herself out of the void of sacred knowledge. Allowing her eyes to become accustomed to the light, she stared at her son lying on the bed. Reflecting on her escape from the farmhouse and her tirade against Enrico, Caterina knew that she would never again bow to his authority or that of Bishop Pazzini. She would not return to her marital home and she would not allow the Bishop to wield his power over the village. She would stand up and fight. Just then, she saw a movement in the sky through the open casement. Silhouetted against the face of the mother moon, three birds fluttered past to freedom. "The doves!" exclaimed Caterina, watching as they flew towards the trees. Memories of the afternoon spent making tomato sauce with Alessandro prompted her to ask Niccolo his whereabouts.

"We don't know, Caterina," replied Niccolo. "When Paolo fell, I sent him to find you. No one has seen him since. Luca is out now searching for him."

"He would not abandon us. Not now."

Niccolo sought to reassure her, although he too was concerned about the storyteller's disappearance. "No, he wouldn't leave. I'm sure of it. He's probably out looking for you now. Come, let's take Paolo to the house and rest, for tomorrow we must find a way to free my mother and Padre Francesco."

Back at the Lorini farmhouse, Niccolo laid Paolo on his bed and cast his mind back to that morning, when he had awoken to find the young boy lying on the straw mattress. He'd kept strong throughout the evening's events, driven by his need to care for those he loved, but now he gave vent to his own emotions, allowing his tears to fall. Caterina stroked his back, urging him to lie down. Spreading a blanket over him, she then curled up on the bed beside Paolo, breathing in the sweet smell of his skin. Niccolo's thoughts returned to the young woman lying in the shepherd's hut and his heart swelled. Perhaps all was not lost, for the night would once more give birth to the dawn of a new beginning.

Monday

16 August 1583

Santa Sofia

"Caterina! Caterina!" Elena's cries reached Caterina as she sat on the bed tending to Paolo. She had had a restless night, aware of her son's every murmur, but she left him now in Niccolo's care to go and greet her aunt.

"What is it Elena?"

"Enrico. He's..." Elena faltered.

"What's happened?"

Elena took a deep breath, unsure of how Caterina would react to the news. "Giorgio was in the forest early this morning, checking his snares, when he found him," she said.

"And?"

"Enrico...he...he's dead."

Caterina gasped in shock. "How?"

"He must have wandered drunk into the forest. Giorgio found an empty wine bottle by his side."

Caterina frowned. "The wine poisoned him?"

"No one knows, but something terrible happened."

"What?"

Elena's hands were trembling in Caterina's grasp. "Wild animals...they...they savaged his body. The men are gathering his few remains for burial."

Caterina clasped a hand to her mouth and leant back against the balustrade for support. Then she gathered her wits about her.

"I must go and speak with Giorgio."

Caterina turned back to inform Niccolo, but he was standing at the top of the stairs and had heard everything. "Go, Caterina. I will stay and look after Paolo."

Caterina and Elena soon arrived in the square, where they found a group of villagers gathered outside the butchery. Caterina pushed past Emilia and Agnesa to reach her uncle. "Giorgio, what happened to Enrico? Tell me what you saw."

The strong man was shaking, shocked by the sight that had greeted him in the forest. As he was describing what he had seen, there was a commotion in front of the church. Bishop Pazzini arrived, accompanied by two guards and the court notary, a thin man with a hooked nose and beady eyes. On seeing the crowd, the Bishop sent the notary to gather evidence from Rosa's house, and then strode over to the butchery. "What's going on here?"

Emilia had watched the morning's events unfold in despair, for with Enrico dead she was now powerless to take revenge on Caterina. As she looked up at Bishop Pazzini, she caught sight of her nephew Luca beneath the consulting room balcony, and a plan took seed in her mind. "It is my poor cousin Enrico, the witch Caterina's husband. He has been killed, savaged by a wild beast, and I know which one." The villagers turned to stare at Emilia in confusion. Pointing over at Luca hovering in the shadows, Emilia began to gesticulate, "It was him! It was the wolf-man!"

The Bishop was quick to seize the moment and shouted at the two guards to fetch Luca. Before he had chance to run away, the guards were upon him and dragged him over to stand before Bishop Pazzini, who flinched in disgust at the sight of the hairy wolf-man. "What are you?"

Luca stammered in response. "I am Luca."

"He is a werewolf!" cried Emilia. "We all heard him last night howling to the full moon, no doubt scouring the forest for victims to devour. I saw him, after everyone had gone to bed, coming from the direction of Enrico's land, his jaws dripping with blood. It was him, I tell you!"

"Liar!" said Caterina. "Luca is a kind and gentle man who suffers from a misunderstood illness. It is ludicrous to suggest that he killed my husband."

"Well you would say that, Witch, because it was you who sent him to carry out the crime," continued Emilia. "I saw him on the night of the dance, trying to save you from your husband after he found you with the storyteller. You were powerless to kill Enrico yourself, so you asked your friend the wolf-man to do it for you."

"Enough!" Bishop Pazzini was growing impatient with the woman's ranting. It had been difficult enough to persuade the reticent Inquisitor to hurry through Rosa's case in time for the following day's public burnings, but there was ample evidence against her. To try to convict the beautiful, young woman Caterina alongside Rosa might jeopardise his case, and he was determined to watch her burn as soon as possible. However, Luca might serve him well if he could convince the court that the werewolf was Rosa's familiar and an accomplice to her crimes. His decision made, the Bishop ignored Emilia's accusations against Caterina and instead turned his attention to Luca. "I arrest you on the charge of being a werewolf, and of killing and devouring Enrico under instructions from the witch Rosa. You will come with me now to Arunca, where you will be tried later today as her accomplice."

The villagers let out cries of dismay, for they had grown to tolerate Luca, even to sympathise with his predicament. Although his appearance was frightening and his howling strange, they were certain that a man with such a musical ear could not be capable of murder, let alone of eating human flesh. Caterina was desperate to save Luca, but her thoughts were with her son. She knew how close she had come to being arrested herself, and for Paolo's sake, she would have to remain silent.

"Emilia, you and your mother will also accompany us to Arunca," continued the Bishop. "We will need to hear your testaments this afternoon at the trial."

"We are your humble servants, my Lord." Although disappointed by her inability to implicate Caterina, Emilia was nevertheless excited by the prospect of seeing Rosa brought to justice and her shameful nephew disposed of. Gathering up their baskets, Emilia and Agnesa followed the Bishop as the guards dragged Luca towards the cart.

Caterina watched until the convoy had disappeared from view, leaving only the notary's steed tied to the fence by the church. Offering up a prayer to Sofia for Luca and Rosa's safe deliverance, she grasped Elena's arm. "Quick, we must hurry back to Paolo."

Meanwhile, Niccolo was tending to Paolo when he heard a noise in the kitchen below. Leaving Paolo asleep, he went downstairs into the house to find a thin man rummaging through a chest. "Who are you?" he demanded.

The man straightened and turned, staring at Niccolo with a haughty expression on his tight-lipped face. "I am the notary from the court in Arunca. I have been sent here by the Inquisitor to gather evidence for Rosa Lorini's trail. Who are you?"

Niccolo sensed that it would be better if the notary did not know he was Rosa's son. "I am the village doctor, Niccolo. I am tending to a sick boy in the bedroom upstairs."

Brushing past Niccolo, the notary headed into Rosa's room and soon discovered her bottles of ointments and pouches of medicinal herbs stacked on the shelves.

"What do you need with those things?" asked Niccolo. "Rosa is no witch. She is a midwife and a healer. Those are just her medicines she uses to treat people." The notary ignored Niccolo, continuing to place the items in a sack as evidence of Rosa's malpractices. Desperate to help his mother, Niccolo had been pondering on how he could gain access to her trial and make a defence. His status as a doctor gave him an air of authority, which he now used to his advantage. "When is the trial of Rosa Lorini to be held?"

"This afternoon, but the Inquisition's trials are held in private."

"I'm the village physician. The court needs to hear my statement concerning the said victim Lora Cesi."

The notary stilled, for the doctor had a valid point. There was always a physician present at the trials to give his verdict regarding the cause of death. The Inquisitor would no doubt be pleased if he brought the doctor to the court. "Come, then. You can accompany me to the Dominican convent in Arunca where the trial is to be held, but you must be quick. Bishop Pazzini has instructed me to return as soon as possible."

Niccolo's heart shuddered but he tried to appear calm. "Why the urgency?"

"There are some public burnings organised for tomorrow morning. The Bishop is keen for the witch to be sentenced along with the others."

"Doesn't the Congregation of the Holy Office in Rome need to review her case before sentencing?"

The notary sneered. "The weight of evidence against this particular woman is so compelling that her trial will be quite straightforward. The Inquisitor will be able to pass judgement without needing to refer her case to the authorities in Rome."

Niccolo clenched his hands together. Where was Alessandro? They had but a day to free Rosa before she was sent to the most torturous of deaths. Knowing her obstinate nature and devotion to the Goddess, Niccolo was sure that Rosa would refuse to be converted to the Church, which would no doubt mean interrogation under torture and death by burning. The idea of his mother suffering such pain was intolerable. There had to be something he could do to ease her imminent suffering. As he watched the notary packing the last of Rosa's jars, an idea came to him.

"Right, let's be off," said the notary.

Niccolo sought to buy some time as the notary headed for the door. "We must wait for the boy's mother to return before I can leave. Why don't you have a cup of wine while I fetch my medical bag?" The notary was persuaded by the offer of wine, giving Niccolo the opportunity to go upstairs and prepare a tincture of pain relief. Just as he was finishing, Caterina and Elena arrived back at the house to find the notary seated beneath the *pergola*.

"Who are you?" demanded Caterina.

"I am the notary from the Inquisition, sent to gather evidence against the witch Rosa Lorini."

Descending the stairs, Niccolo gave Caterina a warning glance. "I am travelling with him to the court to give my physician's statement at the woman's trial." Having finished his wine, the notary gathered up his sack of evidence and headed back through the olive grove. In the few moments Niccolo had alone with Caterina, he handed her the bottle of pain relief. "Meet me at the Dominican convent in Arunca. Bring this pain relief for Rosa and some money to bribe the guards. The Bishop wants her sentenced at the burnings tomorrow morning."

Caterina gasped. "How are we going to free them with such little time? Where's Alessandro?"

Niccolo frowned. "I don't know. Have you seen Luca?"

"He's been arrested on account of Enrico's murder. Bishop Pazzini has taken him to Arunca to be tried this afternoon with Rosa."

"Doctor?" called the notary, who was waiting at the gate.

Niccolo bent down to pick up his bag. "Meet me this afternoon outside the court. Find a way to get inside the convent, and bring the money and pain relief."

When Niccolo had gone, Caterina and Elena went upstairs to see Paolo, who was still sound asleep. They redressed his wound and bathed his body, before covering him with a fresh, cotton sheet. "How much longer will it be before he wakes?" asked Elena.

"I don't know. Niccolo seems to think it should be soon. In the next couple of days perhaps. I hate seeing him like this. He seems so pale and still, almost as if..."

"Hush now, Caterina. Paolo's alive and that's all that matters. He will wake soon. Now, how are you going to smuggle yourself into the convent?"

Caterina shook her head, for it seemed like an impossible task. Then she sat in quiet contemplation, asking Sofia for guidance. In answer to her prayers, Caterina saw an image of her late great aunt Lucia, who had been a nun. Perhaps her grandmother Maria still had Lucia's habit and would lend it to her. Then she could disguise herself as a nun and avoid suspicion in the convent. Bribing a guard to let her see Rosa would be easy enough. All she needed was a pouch of coins, which she could collect from Enrico's store in the farmhouse. "Elena, can I entrust you to watch over Paolo while I'm gone?"

"Of course, but where are you going?"

"First to your house to borrow Aunt Lucia's habit, then onto Arunca to meet Niccolo."

"How will you get there?"

Caterina shrugged. "I will see which peddlers are selling their wares in the square. Perhaps Tomasso will take me on his cart."

Then, dropping a kiss on Paolo's brow, Caterina set off to her grandmother's house.

The Inquisition Trial

The Dominican Convent, Arunca

At the Dominican convent in Arunca, the trial of Rosa and Luca was underway. A large cell, approached by a steep, underground stairwell below the refectory, doubled as both a courtroom and a torture chamber. Its stonewalls gave off a damp smell that hung in the airless room. Daylight filtered in through a narrow, barred window near the vaulted ceiling, while flaming torches cast their light on a series of chains, ropes and pulleys hanging from the wooden beam overhead.

Present in the cell was the Inquisitor from the Commission of Cardinals, seated on a throne-like chair in the middle of the far wall. His colourful red robes and *biretta* were in stark contrast to the gloomy chamber. To his right was the notary, seated at a table with a quill poised over a piece of parchment. He was recording a list of items retrieved from Rosa's house. An expert had verified that the assortment of herbs and potions were those used for witchcraft, having merely glanced at them with disinterest. To the Inquisitor's left and behind him, as was customary for an inferior ecclesiastic, sat Bishop Pazzini. He was perched on a small, wooden chair, attempting to look dignified despite his rolls of flesh sagging over the sides of the seat. As the trials were held in private to ensure quick and successful convictions, the only other person present was the prosecution interrogator acting on behalf of the Inquisitor. Standing at the front, he cast an imposing stance, his head thrown back as he awaited the arrival of the witnesses.

The side door on the right opened and two guards led Padre Francesco in from the row of cells being used to house the prisoners and witnesses. Emilia and Agnesa followed, handkerchiefs pressed to their noses to ward off the stench from the cells, and sat beside Padre Francesco on the wooden bench running along the left wall. When everyone was seated, the Inquisitor nodded to the prosecutor, who called for the physician to deliver his testament.

As a guard ushered Niccolo into the cell, Bishop Pazzini flinched and leapt up in outrage. "This man cannot give evidence. He's the witch's son!"

Niccolo didn't falter, staring straight at the Inquisitor. "I am the doctor of Santa Sofia and I examined the said victim Lora Cesi in childbirth. I am therefore qualified to give a physician's statement."

The Inquisitor decided to overrule the Bishop for he was keen, like many of the cardinals, to give the accused as fair a trial as possible. Public opinion against the Inquisition was growing and he was wary of allowing anyone the opportunity to find fault with his judgement, especially in Arunca where the planned burnings on the morrow would be the first of their kind. "Let us hear what the doctor has to say." Bishop Pazzini glowered at the notary as he sat recording every word uttered during the trial.

Niccolo took his seat on the high-backed chair situated opposite the Inquisitor and swore an oath upon the bible. Then he began to make the defence he hoped would spare his mother's life. "Thank you, Your Eminence. Last Wednesday evening, Rosa Lorini was assisting Lora Cesi in childbirth. Lora had struggled for two days to deliver her child, but was unable to due to the overly large size of the babe. I was also in attendance and examined Lora myself. I found that the midwife Rosa was correct in her diagnosis. Lora would never have been able to deliver the child. It is indeed natural that she died due to the length and pain of her labour."

"Liar!" Emilia screeched, jumping up from the bench.

"Silence!" The Inquisitor ordered Emilia to sit down and indicated to the prosecution interrogator to proceed.

"What about the boy Paolo Galletti? What is your view on how he came to fall into the ravine on Sunday night?"

"I saw exactly what happened. Paolo climbed up onto the wall to try to fetch a cage of doves from his father, and in the struggle he fell."

"What of the spirit conjured by Rosa Lorini?"

An image of Veronica flickered into his mind, but Niccolo could not jeopardise her safety by revealing that she was still alive. His only option was to deny the apparition.

"I saw no spirit. Rosa is not a witch and she cannot conjure spirits."

"Do you also deny that Rosa Lorini was offering communion to the villagers at the Festival of the Assumption?"

Niccolo faltered, knowing that his mother had performed the rite in full view of the Bishop and his guards. To deny she had taken part would be a blatant lie, only serving to weaken his case. Instead, he chose to tell a half-truth. "Rosa simply came to Padre Francesco's aid as he was overwhelmed by the amount of worshippers partaking of communion."

The prosecution interrogator paused, as if to give weight to his final question. "Doctor, have you ever heard Rosa Lorini refer to herself as 'a priestess of Sofia'?"

Niccolo was at a loss for words. To reply in affirmation would be tantamount to an accusation of heresy. Neither could he deny it when Rosa had declared it twice to the Bishop. Niccolo glanced up at Padre Francesco, who shook his head in denial. Perhaps it was best to claim ignorance, for he had been hidden from view on both occasions. "Not that I am aware of."

"A simple yes or no will suffice, Doctor."

Niccolo felt a bead of perspiration trickle down the side of his face. There was nothing for it but to deny Rosa's claim and hope that he wasn't accused of being a false witness, for those found guilty of perjury had their testaments disregarded and were given harsh punishments of banishment, incarceration or imprisonment on the galleys of the Papal ships. "No, I have not."

"Thank you."

Believing himself dismissed, Niccolo stood up to leave when the Inquisitor called out, "Doctor!" Niccolo's heart leapt. "What about Luca Dini, the second accused? Is it your belief that he transmuted into a werewolf and killed Enrico Galletti under orders from Rosa Lorini?"

Niccolo sighed with relief at the Inquisitor's question and turned to face him. He was on firm ground now for he knew every word he uttered about Luca would be the truth. "Luca suffers from a medical condition called *lycanthropy*. We are still not sure what causes it, but it renders him sensitive to light. Living in the shadows generates excessive hair growth and discolouration of the skin and nails. Such symptoms often lead the sufferer to believe that they are part human and part wolf. However, I can assure you that Luca is not a werewolf. Neither do I believe that he killed Enrico Galletti, nor that Rosa Lorini ordered him to. Enrico was known for his heavy drinking and in my opinion died from alcohol poisoning, at which point wild animals in the forest fed on his corpse."

"Thank you, Doctor," said the Inquisitor. "You may sit down now."

Niccolo took his seat next to Padre Francesco, who gave him a small smile of encouragement. Next, the Inquisitor called for Emilia's testament. He had already deemed Agnesa an unreliable witness due to her age and failing eyesight. Leaving her mother to listen from the bench, Emilia sat down on the chair opposite the Inquisitor, smoothing the black veil she wore over her grey hair, which was swept back in a bun at the nape of her long, bony neck.

The prosecutor approached with the bible for Emilia to swear her oath, and then began to question her. "Emilia Cesi, you are the mother of the said victim Lora Cesi?"

"Yes."

"Could you please tell the court what happened on the night of your daughter's death?"

"Like every woman in childbirth, my daughter had struggled with the pain of labour, but she was just about to deliver her child when the witch Rosa sent her assistant Caterina to gather some potions from her house. A short while after her return, my mother and I went into the bedroom to find Lora dead, her babe still trapped inside her. I found these by her bedside, the potions used by the witch to kill my daughter!" Emilia waved her hands in the air, holding aloft the pouches of herbs that Rosa had used to lessen Lora's suffering.

The notary stepped forward to retrieve the pouches and compared them with those he had found at Rosa's house. "The witness is correct. These are the same herbs I discovered at the house of the accused."

"On the night of the festival, did you see the spirit conjured by the accused Rosa Lorini?" continued the prosecutor.

"Oh yes, it was terrifying. The ghost of a shepherd girl who vanished a few weeks ago appeared by the ravine, dripping with blood. The witch probably killed her too and conjured her spirit to cause my cousin Paolo Galletti to fall into the ravine. There is no doubt in my mind that Rosa tried to kill Paolo, the same way she killed Lora and her baby."

The interrogator paused for dramatic effect, allowing time for the witness's words to be appreciated by the occupants of the court. "Is it also your view that the accused Rosa Lorini is a witch and holds great sway over the villagers' religious rites?"

Emilia nodded her head with such vigour that her veil slipped backwards, causing her to grapple to retrieve it. "Without doubt. It is said she worships the goddess Diana in a secret cave and I have even seen her riding her broomstick through the night sky. She has cast her spell over Padre Francesco, for it is he who allows the witch to lead her heathen prayers at the festival." Emilia pointed with disgust at Padre Francesco who lowered his eyes.

"And of the accused Luca Dini, what is your opinion?"

"Everyone knows Luca is a werewolf. His only friends are the witch Rosa and her assistant Caterina, who he tried to save from Enrico's chastisement on the night of the dance. It is my belief that Rosa and Caterina sent the werewolf to kill Enrico because he had grown suspicious of their witchcraft. Why else would he have locked Caterina in the house on the night of the festival?"

"Thank you, Emilia. You may sit down now." The prosecutor gave a self-satisfied smile. The physician's statement had been a wearisome addition to the trial, but the Inquisitor was unlikely to give it much credence owing to the doctor's relationship with the accused. That aside, Emilia's testimony had substantiated Bishop Pazzini's prior submission of evidence and should ensure a straightforward conviction. As the prosecutor was contemplating his chances of victory, the Inquisitor looked along the bench and called Padre Francesco as the final witness. Padre Francesco offered up a silent prayer to Christ before assuming his position on the chair, where he too swore an oath on the bible. "Francesco Lorini, you were the village priest of Santa Sofia up until the evening of the fourteenth of August, is that correct?"

"Yes."

"Would you please tell us why Bishop Pazzini was forced to suspend you *a divinis* on that night?"

Padre Francesco glanced at the Bishop to find him smirking at him. "I believe the Bishop thought that I had lied to protect my niece Caterina."

"And had you?"

Padre Francesco squirmed with discomfort, unaccustomed to lying but resolute in the justness of his actions. "I knew Caterina's husband Enrico to be a violent man and I didn't want her to suffer at his hands."

"So you lied to your Bishop?"

"I did not think it necessary for Caterina to be punished."

Frustrated by his refusal to give a direct answer, the prosecutor nonetheless chose to move forward in his questioning. "If you were no longer granted the powers of the priesthood, could you please tell the court why you led the prayers at the Festival of the Assumption?"

Padre Francesco faltered, wary of incriminating his parishioners. "There was no one else to lead the villagers in their prayers."

"But Bishop Pazzini had already organised to hold midnight Mass in the church. Why did you defy his order?"

Padre Francesco's mind went blank and, before he could restrain himself, he declared, "Because it is what Christ would have wanted me to do."

A collective gasp filled the courtroom. Again the prosecutor paused to allow the severity of the witness's words to take their toll. "Francesco, did you or did you not allow the accused Rosa Lorini to lead the prayers with you?"

The evidence against Rosa was strong and Padre Francesco felt powerless to protect her. "I asked Rosa to help me to distribute communion because there were many communicants and I was growing tired."

"So, in your opinion, the accused is not a witch? You know of no cave in which she worships the devil? You saw no spirit conjured by her? The boy Paolo's fall was an accident? And Lora died of natural causes?"

"No...yes..."

"Which is it to be, yes or no?"

The speed and force of the interrogation was unnerving and Padre Francesco raised his voice in distress, "Rosa is not a witch!"

Emilia leapt up again. "Liar! You're only defending Rosa because the witch has you in her claws. I saw you leaving for her house after the dance, where you no doubt spent the night fornicating in her devilish arms."

The Inquisitor sat up straighter on his throne and frowned down at Padre Francesco. "Is this true, Francesco? Did you, a priest and the accused's own brother-in-law, lie with her?"

Padre Francesco's resolve gave way under the weight of the questioning. "Yes, Your Eminence, I did. I love Rosa because she is wise and kind, and she understands more about the true nature of Christ's teachings than many of the Church's own priests."

"You see! You see! He is under the witch's spell!" shrieked Emilia, as chaos erupted in the small courtroom.

"Silence in court!" shouted the Inquisitor. "That will be all, Prosecutor. Guards, take the witnesses behind the screen." Bishop Pazzini and the prosecutor exchanged triumphant smiles. Padre Francesco had played right into their hands. With his confession, he had succeeded in providing strong evidence of Rosa's bewitching abilities, for only the devil could cause a priest to criticise his Church and fellow ecclesiastics.

The guards led Padre Francesco, Niccolo and the two women to the far right corner of the courtroom where a wooden screen had been erected, instructing them to sit down on a bench behind the screen so that they were hidden from view. It was time now for the accused to be brought into the courtroom and they were not allowed to see the identity of the witnesses. From behind the screen, Padre Francesco and Niccolo were left to listen as Rosa and Luca were dragged into the room and made to stand in front of the Inquisitor. "Rosa Lorini, you stand accused of the murder of Lora Cesi and of her unborn child, and of the attempted murder of Paolo Galletti, both through the means of witchcraft. You also stand accused of bewitching the village priest Francesco Lorini, conjuring a spirit, defiling the sacrament, instructing your familiar werewolf to kill Enrico Galletti, and claiming heretically to be a priestess of a pagan goddess by the name of Sofia. How do you plead?"

"Not guilty."

A heavy silence hung in the air while the Inquisitor referred to his notes and then turned to address Luca. "Luca Dini, you stand accused of being Rosa Lorini's animal familiar, and of murdering Enrico Galletti when you transmuted into a werewolf on her instruction. How do you plead?"

"Not guilty."

The Inquisitor looked across at the notary to verify that he was recording the accused's responses, before continuing. "Under the laws of the Inquisition, it is your right to give the court the names of your enemies, to make a defence and to bring forth your own witnesses. Please proceed."

Rosa pulled herself up as straight as possible. "No."

The Inquisitor looked down at her in confusion. "I beg your pardon?"

"Luca and I are not going to make a defence."

From behind the screen came gasps of joy from Emilia and Agnesa, mingled with sighs of despair from Niccolo and Padre Francesco.

"You do realise that in choosing not to provide your own defence, the court will assume that you accept the prosecution's testimony, which I have to say is compelling?" asked the Inquisitor.

"Luca and I refuse to make a defence because we do not acknowledge the authority of the Roman Church nor of this court," Rosa explained. The Inquisitor's eyes nearly sprung out of their sockets. Rosa returned his stare without flinching, but her legs were beginning to shake. She glanced across at Luca, who nodded, confident in her ability to speak on his behalf.

Meanwhile, the Inquisitor sought to determine the extent of the accused's heretical beliefs. "Rosa Lorini, do you believe in the Virgin Birth?"

"Do I believe that Mother Mary was a virgin when she gave birth to Christ? No, I do not. A child cannot be conceived without a man spilling his seed inside a woman's womb. As I see it, Christ's mother Mary became pregnant and Joseph married her so that her child would not be a bastard."

"Silence! Enough of your lies!" The Inquisitor was now beside himself. Even Bishop Pazzini could not hide his shock at the deeply heretical nature of Rosa's words. He had suspected her of being a witch, but to hear her implicate herself in such an absolute way was astonishing. His anger tempered, the Inquisitor then questioned her about the second central doctrine of the Church. "Do you believe in the true divinity of Jesus Christ?"

"I believe that Christ was one of us and that the myth of the Mother Goddess's divine Son, who has existed since time immemorial, was placed upon him. As I understand it, Christ was the son of a woman and the lover of another woman, his priestess Mary Magdalene, both of whom would have been judged by the Church to be 'fallen' women. Yet Christ loved and respected them, and all other women, regardless of whether or not they had sinned in the eyes of the priests. Now Christ's own Church is torturing and killing thousands upon thousands of women because we're not deemed to be obedient and pure like the Virgin Mary, but she was in fact strong and sexual, just like the Mother Goddess she embodies. How can the Church believe it is carrying out the work of Christ when it seeks to destroy the true nature of his mother and priestesses?" Rosa paused to catch her breath and felt the glow from the fire raging in her belly.

The court was silent as the Inquisitor took a deep breath to calm himself before questioning Rosa further. "You call yourself a priestess of Sofia. Who is Sofia?"

"Sofia is the Black Goddess of Wisdom. She has existed since the beginning of time under many names such as Isis, Athena, Diana."

The Inquisitor nodded in comprehension. "So you are one of the witches of the Society of Diana that still worships at the site of the walnut tree in Benevento?"

Rosa shook her head. "No, I am not, although I share many of their beliefs. I belong to a long line of priestesses who have served the Black Goddess in my village."

"Are there any more of you?"

"No, I am the last." Rosa had no qualms about lying to protect Caterina and Elena.

"What is your opinion of the Black Madonna?"

"She embodies the Black Goddess within the Roman Church. In the same way that Lady Wisdom of the Old Testament embodies Sofia as the Christian Goddess."

"There is no goddess in Christian theology!" bellowed the Inquisitor.

In contrast, Rosa remained quietly defiant in her response. "I beg to differ. The Early Church did in fact worship Sophia as the Christian Goddess. It was only when the literalist priests took control, with their dogma and pursuit of power through violence, that they forced the feminine divine underground. In so doing, the Roman Church committed its gravest error, for it is in this very darkness that the Black Goddess finds her strength, and soon she will rise up again as the Virgin Warrior to challenge those who stand in the way of her path to wisdom!"

In the Inquisitor's opinion, Rosa was quite clearly married to the devil. There would be no need to consult the opinion of the *consultori*, the six lawyers and theologians who formed an advisory committee to the court, or to refer the case to the special tribunal in Rome. The accused had been given the opportunity to respond to the charges and her declaration of heretical beliefs was ample evidence in itself. All that was left was to try to convert her back into the bosom of the Church through the only means left open to him. "Rosa Lorini, the burden of evidence indicates your guilt, which you deny but are unable to disprove. This, combined with your heretical repudiation of the central doctrines of the Church, leads me to find you guilty of all aforementioned charges including that of formal heresy. You will be sentenced to death by burning in the morning. In the meantime, the court will proceed to interrogation under torture to attempt to reconcile you to the Church and save your soul for eternal life." Rosa glared at the Inquisitor in defiance. "Luca Dini, do you have nothing to add?" The wolf-man shook his head in denial. "So you are in agreement with everything Rosa said?" Luca nodded his head. "Speak up, man!"

"Yes," Luca stuttered.

The Inquisitor could not hide his astonishment. The witch and her familiar seemed to take delight in signing their own death warrants. "Then I also find you, Luca Dini, guilty of all charges and sentence you to interrogation under torture. Guards, take the witnesses out of the courtroom." Two guards picked up either end of the screen and marched towards the side door, ushering the witnesses back into the corridor so that they remained hidden at all times from the accused. Niccolo hung back, desperate to catch a glimpse of his mother. The proceedings were unfurling so fast and there was now no opportunity for Rosa to be given the pain relief before her torture began.

"Not you, Francesco." Padre Francesco looked up to find the Bishop bearing down on him. Seizing him by the scruff of his neck, Bishop Pazzini dragged Padre Francesco out from behind the screen. "The Inquisitor and I are keen for you to watch the witch being tortured. Only then will you be freed from the power of the devil's bewitchment." Padre Francesco gazed at Rosa. He knew that the Bishop only desired him to suffer, but at least he would be present to offer her support.

"Mother!"

Rosa heard Niccolo's anxious cry. "Have no fear, Niccolo. Sofia is with me."

"Take him out!" ordered the Inquisitor.

Peering around the side of the screen, Niccolo's last image was of two guards taking hold of Rosa's arms as the torture instruments were carried past him into the chamber and laid on the bench.

The guards threw Niccolo up the stone stairs and out of the door into the cloisters. The glare of the sun forced him to shield his eyes until they grew accustomed to the light, whereupon he could make out a group of nuns leading Emilia and Agnesa to Vespers in the chapel. There they would kneel in the choir stalls to listen to the bells ring evensong, before lodging in the convent after evening meditation. A figure stepped out from the cloisters beside him and touched his arm. "My son." Niccolo recognised the woman's gentle tones and gazed down at Caterina. Her face was shrouded beneath a heavy black veil, which flowed over a rough, brown habit tied at the waist with a knotted cord belt. "Come with me." Emilia and Agnesa had disappeared from view and the guards had returned to the torture chamber, so Niccolo followed Caterina into the walled garden in the centre of the quadrant where they sat down on a stone bench in front of a statue of the Madonna. Without glancing at each other, they assumed the position of devotees in prayer and conversed through whispered words.

"What's happening?" asked Caterina.

"Rosa refused to make a defence. They've been committed to interrogation under torture."

Caterina stifled a gasp. "What about the pain relief?"

"It's too late now but you must get it to Rosa before the burnings."

"Is there no escape for her?"

"It would appear not," said Niccolo, his voice wooden.

Caterina fought back tears. "And Luca?"

"The same."

"How shall we get the pain relief to him?"

"You must tell Rosa to give him some tomorrow on the way to the burnings."

The hopelessness of their predicament struck Caterina and she cried out in frustration. "Where is Alessandro?"

"Hush. I don't know, but he won't fail us. I'm sure of it."

"Perhaps running away is all he knows," replied Caterina. "What can we do to help Rosa and Luca?"

Niccolo glanced sideways at her with tears in his eyes. "There is nothing we can do but pray."

Caterina clutched her shaking hands together, while Niccolo crossed his chest for the first time since he had trained as a doctor. Looking up at the statue of the Madonna, they began to pray in earnest for Rosa and Luca to be spared the pain of torture.

The cell had now been converted into a torture chamber. The prosecution interrogator had departed, leaving the Inquisitor, Bishop Pazzini, the notary and eight guards. The wooden screen had been removed and a collection of terrifying torture instruments now lay in full view on the witness bench. In the middle of the room was a table with some ropes, beside which the Inquisitor and Bishop were standing. Rosa was seated on the high-backed chair, her eyes averted from the torture instruments as she muttered prayers under her breath to Sofia. For all her spiritual belief and courage, she still feared whatever pain her body was about to endure. For his part, Luca had been forced to sit down next to Padre Francesco to await his own torture, but he too could not still the trembling in his legs.

Bishop Pazzini paced up and down the length of the bench, surveying the torture instruments. Keen to worsen Rosa's fear, he feigned ignorance and asked the Inquisitor to explain how the various torture techniques worked. This was a known way of inducing more terror in the victim. "What is this, Your Eminence?"

The Inquisitor looked at the instrument and grimaced. "That is 'the pear'."

"How does it work on a woman?" asked the Bishop, giving Rosa a snide smile.

"When inserted into the vagina, it is expanded by force of the screw to its maximum aperture. The inside of the vagina is ruptured and the spikes on the end rip through the woman's cervix." Rosa flinched and the blood drained from her face.

"Will you be using it on the accused?"

The Inquisitor glanced at Rosa but shook his head. "I think not. The pear is only used on those women found guilty of fornication with the devil. Although I believe the accused is in his power, there is no evidence to suspect that she has actually bedded him." Rosa thought she was about to faint but then caught sight of Padre Francesco, and his loving gaze gave her the strength to calm her breathing.

The Bishop looked rather disappointed, but his eyes soon fell upon another instrument. "What of the knife, Your Eminence?"

"It is used in a similar way to the red-hot pincers that tear flesh off the accused. The knife, however, is used with women in mind, to cut off their breasts." Rosa shuddered again, feeling a pain in her breasts. She was reminded of the story she had heard of a woman who had been sentenced to death by burning. Before the Inquisitor had lit the fire beneath her, he had sliced off her breasts and forced them into the mouths of her watching sons. It was beyond Rosa's comprehension how children could grow into adults capable of devising such heinous ways of torturing other human beings. Not only that, but how religious authorities could condone such torture in the names of their various gods. And how communities could stand back and allow it to take place. Such acts were so far removed from any sense of divine love and compassion that their roots could only grow where weakness and evil dwelt in the hearts of men.

"Do you intend to slice off the accused's breasts?" Bishop Pazzini's feverish question brought Rosa's musing to an abrupt end, forcing her thoughts back into the terrifying abyss of the torture chamber.

The Inquisitor paused as he thought how best to set about torturing the woman. "No, I do not. There are some other more appropriate and, dare I say, more acceptable forms of torture I would like to try first of all."

Bishop Pazzini struggled to control his impatience, for the Inquisitor seemed to be far too concerned with upholding the restrictive laws governing the torture of heretics. What did it matter which torture they inflicted on the hag? She was going to die anyway. Only Padre Francesco would be their witness and the Bishop would make sure that as soon as he had been forced to watch Rosa burn alive, he too would be sentenced to death. "What do you have in mind, Your Eminence?"

The Inquisitor ignored the Bishop and turned to address the guards. "Strip the accused and tie her to the table. You, over there, boil some water over the fire." Rosa swallowed a scream, still unsure as to what they were going to do to her. Two guards approached the chair and pulled Rosa up by the arms. Another two seized her dress and ripped it over her head to reveal her plump, wrinkled arms and legs poking out from beneath a sleeveless, cotton slip. "That's enough." Feeling a blush on her cheeks, Rosa sighed with relief that the Inquisitor was at least merciless enough to spare her the humiliation of being bared for all to see.

Her relief was short-lived though when the four guards grasped her legs and arms, hoisting her onto the table. There they placed her on her back, binding her with three ropes drawn across her chest, thighs and ankles, which they tightened with sticks to form tourniquets that cut into her bare flesh. Between the figures of the guards surrounding the table, Rosa's eyes searched for Padre Francesco and Luca. They, too, were being held by guards and could only look on in sorrow and fear.

The Inquisitor approached the table and studied Rosa's body to determine whether or not she was fit for torture. Despite her advanced years, he was satisfied that she was in good enough health to withstand the pain, and decided to proceed. "Hold her head and tip it backwards." Someone drew up a chair and sat behind Rosa, seizing her head and forcing it backwards, so that her throat was exposed. As Rosa smelt the foulness of Bishop Pazzini's breath upon her face, she imagined he was going to slit her throat. Then the Inquisitor's next words drifted through the haze of her mind. "We will begin by trying to wash away the stench of Rosa Lorini's heretical proclamations, thereby cleansing her soul of the devil's influence." Rosa's breath was coming in short bursts of fear now as a guard inserted an iron prong and funnel into her mouth, forcing her jaw wide open. Rosa closed her eyes and tried to focus her mind on retreating to the abyss of meditation and prayer, where the pain would be lessened. She heard Padre Francesco and Luca's gasps of horror only moments before the boiling water struck her throat, scalding her. Unbeknown to Rosa, another guard had fetched a jug of boiling water and was pouring it down the funnel into her mouth. Rosa tried to wrench her head from side to side to escape the pain, but the Bishop held her head still in his grasp, forcing her to gulp down the burning water. At last, she succeeded in freeing herself, when her writhing jogged the guard holding the jug and some drops of boiling water fell on the Bishop, who swore loudly much to the Inquisitor's disapproval.

"Enough!" The disruption provoked the Inquisitor to stop the torment, although the Bishop was eager to vent his revenge on Rosa by grabbing her head again, ripping at her hair. "I said that is enough, Bishop Pazzini. It is not your place to inflict torture upon the accused. However, your actions have given me an idea for our next course of action if the accused still refuses to repent." As the guard withdrew the iron prong and funnel, blood poured from Rosa's scalded mouth and throat. She spluttered and retched, gagging on the blood. Tears welled up in response to the pain but she closed her eyes to stem their flow. She would not give Bishop Pazzini the satisfaction of seeing her cry. "Rosa Lorini, by washing your mouth out with boiling water, I have attempted to cleanse your soul of the devil. Do you repent of your crimes? Will you be reconciled to the Holy Mother Church?"

Rosa could have laughed out loud at the sanctimonious way in which the Inquisitor spoke, as if he were a father trying to teach his child better manners. However, her voice box was temporarily paralysed and she flinched as she swallowed another mouthful of blood. Instead, she raised her head up and shook it in defiance. The Inquisitor raised his eyebrows at Bishop Pazzini, incredulous at the stubbornness of the witch. "Well, then, we must proceed to the next stage of torture."

"What now?" asked the Bishop, who couldn't hide his excitement.

The Inquisitor glared at him. They were not supposed to enjoy inflicting pain on the accused, only act as God's mediators in reconverting the heretic back into his loving arms. This bishop seemed all too eager to torture women and send them to their deaths. In fact, since his arrival in Arunca, Bishop Pazzini had forced the Inquisitor into an impossible position, providing evidence against seven people whom the Inquisitor would otherwise have left alone. This was not the way of the south, where the Church held only a tenuous position. Then the Inquisitor picked up a stick to continue with the torture that he himself found distasteful. "Hold the accused's head still again."

The Bishop needed no further encouragement to seize Rosa's head, while the Inquisitor walked around the table until he too was standing behind her. Rosa's eyes searched about her, wondering what they were going to do next, but all she could see were the chains and pulleys hanging from the beam overhead. The Inquisitor took hold of her long plait of white hair and tied it around the stick. Then he began to twist the stick tighter and tighter. Rosa closed her eyes in agony as her hair was wrenched strand by strand from her scalp, until the skin itself tore open to expose her skullcap, sending rivulets of blood cascading down her back.

"Enough!" Padre Francesco struggled to free himself from the guards' hold, but he was too frail. With tears flowing down his lined cheeks, he pleaded with the Inquisitor. "Please, no more! Have mercy!"

The Inquisitor let go of the stick and stared with sadness at Padre Francesco. "It seems, Francesco, that the power wielded over you by the witch is still strong. Only when her pain no longer affects you will we know that you have been freed from her bewitchment." Padre Francesco gazed at Rosa with eyes full of guilt, for his outcry had only succeeded in lengthening her torture, but she just smiled at him through the streams of blood flowing from her scalp and mouth. Padre Francesco felt that his own heart would bleed and prayed to Christ to relieve Rosa's suffering. Luca, for his part, remained transfixed by the pool of blood forming on the floor beneath the table. All of a sudden, he was jolted from his reverie by the Inquisitor calling his name. "Luca! It is my belief that as Rosa's familiar you must be tortured alongside the witch if her power is to be weakened. Guards, set up the two *strappados*."

Bishop Pazzini smirked in triumph. Now the hag would discover what real pain felt like, and before long she'd be singing his praises. Two of the guards reached up to pull down the long ropes, which were threaded through pulleys attached to the beam overhead. Having released Rosa's bonds and pulled her off the table, a guard tied her wrists behind her back with one of the ropes. Another guard holding onto Luca did the same to him with the other rope. Once their hands were bound, three guards positioned themselves behind each of the accused. Then they pulled down hard on the free ends of the ropes, dragging Rosa and Luca up into the air by their bound wrists. Rosa cried out from the pain in her arms and shoulders as the joints were forced to carry her full body weight. Once the guards had lifted both of them to a great height, the Inquisitor gave the order. "Drop them!" The guards allowed the ropes to run free so that Rosa and Luca fell through the air, only to be dragged back up again just before they hit the floor. Each time, the Inquisitor asked them if they were ready to repent. Each time they shook their heads, their obstinate silence incomprehensible to him. This procedure was repeated again and again in quick succession until their shoulder, elbow and wrist joints dislocated from the strain. Rosa could not bite back the screams that tore up from her wrenched limbs while Luca moaned in agony. All the while the notary recorded their cries of pain on the parchment. Padre Francesco couldn't bear to watch Rosa suffer such pain, but he prayed for strength to hide his emotions and shorten the length of her torture. "Enough! Lower them down."

An hour had passed since Rosa's torture had begun, which was the maximum amount of time deemed appropriate. The Inquisitor felt sure that the accused would now be converted back into the sanctity of the Church. As the ropes were lowered, Rosa and Luca fell onto the floor in a heap, shuddering with each jolt to their limbs. Their arms hung useless by their sides and a searing pain swept from their necks down through their shoulders and arms.

"Stand up!" ordered the Inquisitor. Unable to lean on their

arms for support, Rosa and Luca rolled onto their knees and struggled to push themselves up to standing. Swaying on their trembling legs they stood side by side, their heads bowed. Rosa's mouth had swollen to a great size and her scalp still oozed blood from the constant reopening of her wounds. She tried to focus on the flagstones beneath her, but everything appeared cloudy and confused to her retreating mind. "Do you, Rosa Lorini, now admit to being a heretic and a witch? Do you beg for God's forgiveness and to be reconciled to the Holy Mother Roman Church?"

Rosa heard the Inquisitor's questions as if from a great distance. She blinked in an attempt to shake off the veil that was shrouding her ability to respond, but there was a light in her third eye that was growing stronger and stronger. It grew nearer until she could distinguish the leaping flames of a raging fire and there, wrapped around the fire, was the serpent. Rosa's eyes looked upwards to find the majestic statue of the Black Goddess staring down at her, tears of blood flowing down her stone cheeks. Come, she whispered, come brave warrior priestess. Rosa curled her burnt lips up in a smile and inclined her head. It was nearly time now. Soon her spirit would leave this earth to join those other departed souls who dwelt in the starry realm. Only a few more hours and her pain would be no more. The Black Goddess of Death would come and Rosa's spirit would be reborn from the fertile depths of her womb.

"Rosa? Can you here me?" asked the Inquisitor.

With one last look at the vision of Sofia, Rosa drew herself out of her meditative state and stared for a few moments at the Inquisitor. Then she turned to the leering Bishop and spat out a mouthful of blood. "No." Her answer was barely audible from the injuries her throat had sustained, but her eyes were fiery with defiance.

The Inquisitor expelled a sigh of disbelief. Usually after suffering the agony of the *strappado*, the accused would admit to their crimes and sing psalms in praise of the Lord. "Luca, do you still support Rosa?"

The wolf-man was trembling from the pain but struggled to hold his head up and respond. "Yes."

The Inquisitor turned to face the Bishop. "It seems you were right after all, Bishop Pazzini. The devil has a powerful hold on the witch. Even her familiar still worships her."

Bishop Pazzini nodded, unable to contain his excitement at the overwhelming victory. Now he would watch the hag scream his name out in agony as the flames licked her body on the funeral pyre. Then he would seize ownership of her farmstead and reap the profits of her labour.

The Inquisitor noted the Bishop's evident pleasure and frowned. He could only feel sadness that he had failed to save them from the devil's grasp. "Rosa Lorini and Luca Dini, you have been found guilty of formal heresy by attempting to overthrow the central doctrines of the Church, including the Virgin Birth and the full divinity of our Lord Jesus Christ, as well as by professing to worship a pagan goddess. Despite interrogation under torture, you remain unrepentant and refuse to be reconciled to the Church. You will meet your fate tomorrow morning, when you will be given one last chance to save your souls before the fires are lit beneath you. Guards, take them to their cells."

As the guards dragged Rosa and Luca towards the cells, Padre Francesco leapt up from the bench. He'd tried to remain silent so as not to jeopardise Rosa's life but there was little to lose now. "No, please, I beg you. Rosa and Luca don't know what they're saying. They are both suffering from religious delirium and deserve nothing more than to be sent to an insane asylum for safekeeping. Ask the doctor. He will support me in this."

The Inquisitor looked at Padre Francesco with pity in his eyes. It was clear that he was still bewitched by the accused, which stood to reason seeing as the witch's powers had not been lessened by her torture. They would wait to see if he changed his mind after the witch had been burnt, but if she still managed to wield her powers over him from hell, then Padre Francesco would have to suffer the same fate. "Francesco, it is clear to me that you are still enamoured with the witch. You will come with us to witness the burnings tomorrow where we will see if her death brings about your release."

"Otherwise, we will watch you burn too," threatened Bishop Pazzini.

The Inquisitor glared at him. "Guards, take Francesco to his cell." With that, he instructed the remaining guards to clear away the torture instruments and mop up the pool of blood, the sight of which made the Inquisitor quick to depart from the chamber, leaving Bishop Pazzini to delight in the spoils of his triumph.

From his vantage point in the walled garden, Niccolo watched the Inquisitor and then Bishop Pazzini emerge from below the refectory. At last his mother's hour of torture must be over. "Quick, Caterina. Go and speak with the guard at the entrance to the cells. I'll wait for you here."

Taking a breath to still her trembling limbs, Caterina adopted the pose of a nun in quiet meditation and left the garden. As she crossed the quadrant, now shrouded in the gloomy light of dusk, she glanced up and down the cloisters. It was early evening and the bells were ringing once more, calling the nuns to Compline in the chapel. There they would sing hymns together as each one prepared to meet her holy bridegroom or her death in the silence of the forthcoming night. Caterina crept into the shadows and peered at the heavy wooden door guarding the entrance to the cells. There was one guard on duty, lolling on a stool in front of the door. Caterina clenched her hand around the purse of coins and asked Sofia for her protection, before approaching the guard. "Forgive me, my son."

The guard looked up at the nun with disinterest and a certain lack of respect. He had no time for these women who dressed themselves up like the Virgin Mary. "What do you want?"

Caterina offered the guard her most beguiling smile. "I have been sent to tend to the prisoner Rosa Lorini."

The guard frowned, confused by the nun's strange request. "No one told me about this."

"Perhaps this will remind you." Caterina held her breath as she handed over the purse weighted with coins. On opening the purse, the guard smiled and reflected on how fortunate he was to have a job that brought such opportunities. He could impress the women at the *taverna* that night with his wealth. Chuckling to himself, the guard drew back the heavy wrought-iron bolts on the door behind him and glanced into the distance to assure himself that no one was watching before ushering Caterina inside. Seizing a flaming torch from a bracket on the wall, he led her down a narrow flight of uneven steps into a dank and airless corridor. There were cells on either side housing the prisoners. Caterina covered her nose and mouth with her arm to fend off the stench, while the guard let her to the farthest door on the right.

"Here we are. Be quick. Knock on the outer door when you've finished." Caterina nodded as he opened the door to Rosa's cell and placed the flaming torch high up in a wall bracket to illuminate the room. "Stand up, prisoner. You've got a visitor." The guard closed the door behind him, leaving Caterina to search the shadows for Rosa. As she grew accustomed to the flames dancing across the cell walls, Caterina saw a movement in the far corner.

"Rosa? It's me, Caterina." A low moan of entreaty reached her and she rushed over to find Rosa propped up against the wall, sitting on the cold, damp flagstones. Her head hung low and in the flickering light Caterina could see that her hair was matted with blood. "Oh, Rosa." Choking back the tears, Caterina placed her finger under Rosa's chin and raised her head up. The old wisewoman's lips were swollen and blistered, her face streaked with blood. "What have they done to you?"

Rosa tried to smile but her lips were so sore and burnt that she could only manage a grimace. With great effort, she opened her mouth to try to comfort Caterina. "Sofia was...with me."

Caterina gazed down at Rosa, her heart swelling with love and pride. She knew that whatever pain Rosa had endured, she had remained faithful to the Black Goddess. "You didn't repent, did you?" Rosa shook her head. "You stubborn old warrior!" Caterina gave a gentle laugh and watched as Rosa's eyes lit up with her old flicker of defiance before closing once more in pain. Feeling for the vial in the folds of her habit, Caterina brought the bottle up to Rosa's lips. "This is some pain relief Niccolo prepared for you. Some of it is for Luca. It's a narcotic and should last until morning to numb the pain of the fires." Caterina's voice cracked on remembering the ghastly fate that awaited Rosa.

The wisewoman drank the liquid, wincing as it struck her burnt mouth and throat. Through half-open eyes, Rosa saw the tears on Caterina's cheeks. She tried to lift up her hand to wipe them away, but was unable to due to her dislocated shoulder. Taking a deep breath, she forced the air out over her vocal chords, which crackled in protest. "The fire."

Caterina stared into Rosa's deep, limpid eyes, assuming she spoke of the fire that would be lit beneath her the following day. "I know, but the pain relief will help, I promise."

Rosa shook her head and tried once more. "Sofia."

Then Caterina understood what Rosa was trying to say. "The fire beneath the statue of Sofia?"

Rosa nodded and summoned her strength to withstand the pain of uttering her next few words. "You are...her priestess... now. Keep...her fire...alight." Rosa sank back against the wall, exhausted by her pain.

Caterina bit down hard on her lip to stop herself from crying out. Why did Rosa have to suffer? Why did she have to die? Where was the Black Goddess now? As if in response, the clouds dispersed, allowing the moon to shine her light down on Rosa's face through the barred window. She gazed up at the now waning moon, which would soon disappear, only to be reborn three days later from the night skies. Rosa drew comfort from the lunar cycle, which spoke to her of rebirth and regeneration, for soon her spirit would be reborn out of the void of death. All that was left for her in this lifetime was to love those she would soon leave. Gazing back at Caterina, Rosa searched her eyes. "Paolo?"

"He's stable. Niccolo says his body is sleeping to recover from the shock of the fall, but he should wake soon."

Rosa's eyes filled with tears for the little boy who had come so close to death. He was too young to join her fading spirit. Then, the image of another boy replaced that of Paolo. Niccolo, her son, walking with her through the forest as a young child, collecting flowers and herbs for her tinctures. Niccolo, the doctor, caring for the sick and dying. The tears streamed down her aged face in the knowledge that never again would she see her son's smile or hear his laughter. The salt in her tears stung as they seeped into the blisters around her mouth and she flinched in discomfort. "Tell Niccolo... I love him."

Caterina sobbed and reached out to embrace Rosa, but there was nowhere on her body she could touch without hurting her. Instead, she pressed a gentle kiss on Rosa's forehead. "I love you, Rosa."

"And I you."

Someone pounded on the door. "Come on!" The guard was anxious and Caterina knew she had to go if she was not to jeopardise their secret meeting. With a last, long look into Rosa's moonlit eyes, Caterina strode towards the door.

"The fire," Rosa rasped.

Caterina smiled through her tears. "You have my word that I

will never let it go out. Not now it is roaring in my belly."

Rosa nodded, her eyes brimming with tears of joy for Caterina's rebirth. As the two women stared at each other, the moment seemed to become suspended in an eternal vortex of loss and love, pain and joy. Then it was gone and Caterina fled down the corridor, hearing the bang of Rosa's cell door as the guard slammed it shut and turned the key.

"Caterina!" Niccolo's hushed cry came to her from the shadows of the cloisters as she exited the door to the cells. Seeing the tears upon her face, Niccolo reached out to take her hands. "You saw her?"

"Yes."

"How is she?"

Caterina shrugged, not knowing how to tell Niccolo that his mother was in so much pain she could barely speak. "Courageous and wise, as always."

"Is she in pain?"

"Yes, but I gave her the pain relief so she should feel better soon."

Niccolo squeezed her hands. "Thank you, Caterina. You risked much."

"Not nearly as much as she has risked for us."

The clanging of the bells began, signalling the end of Compline. "We must be quick. They'll close the gates soon," said Niccolo. Caterina once more adopted the slow pace of a nun and edged towards the gates, soon followed by Niccolo. With no one in sight, they crept into the street and disappeared into the shadows of a nearby doorway.

Caterina removed the nun's habit from over her dress. "What now? Shall we return to Santa Sofia?"

"There's nothing more we can do here. Let's go back and tell the villagers what we know. Perhaps between us we can think of a way to help Rosa and Luca."

Caterina stared at him in surprise. "Are you still hopeful?"

"We cannot give up yet. Not when my mother still lives."

Caterina saw the defiance in Niccolo's eyes and recognised it as that of his mother, but he hadn't seen Rosa. He didn't realise how close she was to death. Caterina didn't want him to nurture false hope, for then her death would be even harder to bear. "Niccolo, it would take a miracle to save her now."

"Then let's start praying."

"You are as stubborn as her." Caterina gave a gentle laugh in an attempt to lighten his mood and linked her arm through his. "Come, Tommaso said he would wait for us in the square. Let's find him and return home."

They were soon settled in the back of Tommaso's cart, wedged between the empty milk churns. As they set off along the winding road that led back to Santa Sofia, Caterina leant back to gaze up at the glittering heavens. Not even the stars could have forecasted the dramatic unfolding of recent events in her life. Six days ago she had still been at the mercy of Enrico's bullying, Paolo remained unharmed, Rosa was defiant in opposing the Bishop, and she hadn't even met Alessandro. Now everything had changed. She had at last found her courage to stand up to Enrico, Paolo lay wounded, Rosa had been sentenced to death, and Alessandro had stolen her heart and disappeared. What had become of her life? Of those people she had loved and feared, but who nonetheless had seemed permanent features of her existence? How quickly Fate could twirl her spindle this way and that, until the past seemed but a distant dream. What did tomorrow hold for them all? Would Rosa and Luca die? Would Paolo awake? Would Alessandro return? With her mind twisting and turning down different pathways, Caterina soon succumbed to the numbing balm of sleep.

Santa Sofia

Caterina was still sleeping when Tommaso's cart rolled into Santa Sofia. A man ran over from the *taverna* and leapt up onto the back of the cart, clasping Niccolo's hand before sinking down onto his knees beside Caterina's sleeping body. Awoken by a pressure against her lips, Caterina opened her eyes. "Alessandro!" Caterina moved into his arms, but within moments she pulled free to give him an accusing stare. "Where have you been?"

Alessandro stroked a tendril of hair from her forehead. "I'm sorry I left so quickly but there was little time."

"Time for what?"

Alessandro's face broke into a wide smile. "Come, there are some friends of mine I want you to meet."

As he helped her down from the cart, she became aware of the huge throng of people filling the square, most of whom were strangers. "Who are all these people?"

Alessandro draped his arm around her shoulders and ushered her over to a group standing outside the *taverna*. Caterina could make out Dionisio and Giorgio, but she didn't recognise the other two men. One of them rivalled even Giorgio in size, while the other was younger with a full head of curls. "These are my friends from San Martino who I lived with for a year before coming here."

Caterina was still confused. "What are they doing here?"

253

Alessandro stopped, turning her in his arms so that she was facing him, and looked at her with eyes glowing with excitement and hope. "They have come to help us, Caterina."

"To help us?"

"To save Rosa and Luca, and to overthrow Bishop Pazzini once and for all."

"How?"

Alessandro paused, knowing that Caterina would be frightened by his words. "We're going to storm the burnings tomorrow."

Caterina gasped. "What about the guards? It isn't safe!"

"There are at least two hundred of us, including all the men and boys of fighting age from San Martino and Santa Sofia. The news of our revolt has spread to neighbouring villages in the diocese, thanks to Matteo the fish-seller. We have word that many more men are keen to join our fight. This will give us enough power to overthrow the guards and force the Commission of Cardinals to meet our demands."

Niccolo wandered up. "To free Rosa and Luca is one thing, for we can achieve that by manpower alone. To force the Church to sentence one of its own is another matter altogether. In doing so, the Church would weaken its presence in the south, which is already precarious in the current climate of peasant revolts."

"I am confident that we have enough evidence to force the Inquisitor to convict Bishop Pazzini. The cardinals will be placed in an impossible position. They would be betraying their own Inquisition if they did not punish him."

"What strong evidence do we have?"

Alessandro paused, knowing that Niccolo would not approve, but there was no other option and the young woman was adamant that she wanted to help. Searching the shadows of the orchard, Alessandro caught sight of her leaning against a tree and beckoned to her. Niccolo turned and his pulse quickened in response to the woman walking towards him. "Veronica!" Then it dawned on him that Veronica was standing out in the open for all to see. And that Alessandro had been the one to call her, which meant that she was implicated in his plan. A wave of protectiveness washed over him. "Veronica has risked too much already, Alessandro."

Veronica placed a finger across Niccolo's mouth. "Hush, Niccolo. It is not only Alessandro who desires to see the Bishop punished for his crimes. Don't forget that it was I who suffered at his hands, and no doubt my brother Luca today."

Niccolo stilled, knowing that he had no right to try to control her. "What are you planning to do?"

"I will accompany you tomorrow to the burnings and prove to the cardinals that I am no spirit conjured by Rosa, but alive and well. I will tell them what the Bishop did to me and show them my scars if that is what it takes to free my brother and Rosa."

Niccolo turned to Alessandro. "What makes you think that the Inquisition will listen to Veronica now, any more than they would have done before?"

"Because she will have an army of men standing behind her this time. Isn't that right, my friends?" shouted Alessandro, leaping up onto one of Dionisio's wooden tables to deliver his speech to the assembled villagers.

* * * * * * *

Bishop Pazzini sits in judgement over this village and those of your neighbours, demanding that you give up your farming and religious traditions. He believes in only one path. The path of personal gain. And he wreaks vengeance upon those who dare to stand in his way. Tomorrow, he will seek the death of the wisewoman Rosa, who showed such courage in defending your right to worship at the chapel. And of Luca, who is an innocent victim of an unfortunate disease. And of five other people whom he intends to watch with pleasure as they writhe in the flames.

This young woman who stands beside me is the most recent victim of the Bishop's evil. A few weeks ago, he raped her and threw her into the ravine. By chance, Veronica survived and she has sworn to accompany us to tell the cardinals of the crimes committed against her by the Bishop. With the force of our army behind her, the cardinals will have no other choice but to arrest Bishop Pazzini and charge him with attempted murder and apostasy to the devil. Not to mention spouting false accusations leading to the unjust prosecution of innocent women and men. These are serious crimes against the Roman Church and the courts of the Inquisition are renowned for giving out heavy sentences to bishops against whom there is weighty evidence.

Such a show of courage from this young woman Veronica should be an inspiration to all of us men. So I now call upon each and every one of you to gather your weapons and prepare to follow us into battle. Only let me give you a warning. There must be no killing tomorrow. Our force in numbers alone will be enough to overpower the guards and make our demands heard. There is to be no bloodshed. Otherwise we will only succeed in lowering ourselves to the same depths as our enemy. Instead we will show the Church that justice can be served without torture and without death.

And so, my friends, I leave you now to your beds. People of Santa Sofia, offer your homes to our friends from San Martino and rest a while. Tomorrow we meet at dawn and our fight begins!

* * * * * * *

A deafening uproar followed the storyteller's words. The men roared their approval, brandishing their weapons in the air, while Alessandro remained on the table, punching his fist in the air to further excite the crowd. The tension in the air was explosive and Niccolo pushed his way forward to congratulate Alessandro.

Helping him down off the table, Niccolo clapped him on the back. "You certainly know how to rouse a crowd. You even managed to dispel my fears."

"Then I must have succeeded, my reticent friend." Niccolo laughed and joined in with the crowd's raucous applause. The wave of support caused a lump of emotion to gather in Alessandro's throat. On spying Veronica standing with Caterina, he nudged Niccolo. "Go to her. I will see you at dawn."

"Until then. Thank you, Alessandro."

Niccolo turned to leave, but the images of two scheming women came to Alessandro's mind. "What about Emilia and Agnesa? If they're here, we must stop them from warning the Bishop."

"Rest assured that they are staying in the nun's cells at Arunca. The Bishop has offered them lodgings in the convent so that they can watch the burnings tomorrow."

Alessandro's eyes glowed with hostility. "It would be preferable if they never left those cells. Perhaps I'll remind the Inquisitor that they made false accusations in court."

"That would be appreciated, my friend," said Niccolo. "Goodnight." Leaving Alessandro to survey the square as it slowly emptied, Niccolo approached Veronica. "Would you like me to accompany you to your father's home?"

"My father is away in the fields, pasturing his sheep, but you are welcome to come home with me."

Niccolo recognised the invitation in Veronica's eyes and nodded. "Come, then."

As they turned to leave, Caterina called out to her. "Veronica, wait." Removing the red ribbon that was tied in her hair, Caterina handed it to her. "Take this and wear it tomorrow. It will help to protect you."

"Thank you, Caterina, and for getting the pain relief to my brother. Niccolo just told me of your bravery." Veronica embraced her cousin and then took Niccolo's hand, disappearing into the shadows of the orchard. But as Niccolo moved towards the steep path leading up the hill, Veronica hung back, pulling at his hand.

"What is it?"

Veronica gazed up at him from beneath her long eyelashes and gave him a mysterious smile. "Come. You will see." Niccolo followed her around the base of the hill until they came to the lane leading down to the chapel. There, Veronica took the overgrown path through the trees, which led towards the sacred spring. Guided by the light of the now waning moon, they climbed over the grey rocks until they came to a pool nestling at the bottom of the steep wooded hillside. Crude walls of pink bricks enclosed the spring water, laid by the Romans who had once used the pool as a healing spa. On the overhanging rocks, images of a mermaid and serpent had been carved. Niccolo glanced in confusion at Veronica, but she just smiled and stepped backwards. Then she pulled her cotton dress up over her head to stand before him in all her naked beauty. Niccolo's breath caught in his throat, but then his gaze fell to her bruises and he reached out to stroke one of her scars.

"Is it not too soon, Veronica?"

She understood his concern, but she knew what she needed. "I will not let the Bishop affect my life for another moment. This is my body and I will reclaim it. Heal me, Niccolo." Then she turned towards the pool and stepped into the warm water. Leaning back to wet her hair, her glistening breasts upturned to the moon, she whispered to him, "Come. Join me." Niccolo needed no further invitation. Mesmerised as he was by her raw sensuality, he stripped off his clothes and stepped into the pool. Then gathering Veronica into his arms, he began to kiss her scars and bruises, reclaiming her body through his loving touch.

Meanwhile, Alessandro watched impatiently as the last villagers left, aware that Caterina was waiting for him at the *taverna*. Once he felt sure everyone had a bed for the night, he went to join her. She was anxious to leave and stood up as he approached. "I must see Paolo. Elena is with him but she will need relieving."

At the mention of Paolo, Alessandro's eyes fell downcast. "I went to visit him earlier."

Caterina wondered why he seemed so hesitant but was touched by his kindness. "How is he?"

"Stable, Elena said, but still sleeping."

Caterina gave a sigh. "When will he wake? I cannot bear to be separated any longer from him."

Once again Alessandro lowered his eyes, hiding the pain he felt on hearing her distress, for his shame at causing Paolo's fall weighed heavily on him. "It won't be long now. Paolo is strong and you will soon hear his laughter again. Come, let's go and see him." Then they bid goodnight to Dionisio and Federico, the innkeeper from San Martino, who sat sharing a flask of wine together. Alessandro was reminded of the courage the men of San Martino had shown. They had shared a good year of laughter, song and storytelling, and their lack of hesitation in answering his call to arms that morning had moved him. "My thanks to you Federico and to all the men of San Martino. I will never be able to repay your kindness in joining our fight."

Federico smiled at Alessandro with the affection of a brother. "It is nothing, my friend. Perhaps now your trust in people may be somewhat restored." Alessandro nodded, touched that Federico should have such an understanding of his sense of betrayal, before leading Caterina back to Rosa's farmhouse.

On their arrival, Caterina went upstairs into Niccolo's bedroom. Elena was curled up beside Paolo, pressing a damp cloth to his flushed forehead. "Is something wrong?"

"No, he's just warm from the summer's night."

"Is there any change?"

Elena sat up and stretched her aching limbs. "He has stirred at times and murmured in his sleep. I think he will wake soon."

"I hope so." Caterina stroked Paolo's cheek, before noticing the shadows beneath her aunt's eyes. "You're exhausted. Go home and rest."

Elena shrugged. "I'm fine. You need your rest more than me. How's Rosa?"

Caterina's eyes clouded over. "In pain. They tortured her well. I gave her the pain relief so she should be feeling more comfortable now."

Elena watched as Caterina struggled to remain calm amid the chaos surrounding her. "You're so strong, Caterina. I always knew you had it in you."

Alessandro stepped inside the room. "So did I."

Caterina blushed at his blatant display of familiarity in front of Elena, for she was aware of her aunt's attraction to Alessandro, but Elena was not one to hold a grudge. "Why don't you two go downstairs and get some rest. I'll stay here tonight with Paolo."

Caterina embraced Elena. "I can't thank you enough for all you have done for us."

"It's nothing, Caterina. You would do the same for me. That's what families are for. Now go, before you faint with exhaustion."

Caterina smiled in gratitude and left the room, climbing down the stone steps until she reached the *pergola*. There she stopped to wait for Alessandro. She could sense his presence behind her, but she was unaware that his confidence was faltering as he wondered whether she could ever forgive him for endangering Paolo's life. Hindered by his fears, Alessandro stood rooted to the spot behind Caterina, willing her to turn around and walk into his arms. Moments passed until Caterina could no longer justify looking into the distance. Taking a deep breath, she turned around to find Alessandro standing there, watching her. His uncertainty was endearing and Caterina's confidence grew in her knowledge that he too was unsure of the situation they now found themselves in. "You must also be tired from your long hike to and from San Martino."

Relieved that Caterina had broken the silence, Alessandro responded in kind. "I am a little weary."

"You can sleep in Rosa's room. I'm sure she wouldn't mind." Caterina led the way into the back room, where she lit a couple of candles. Alessandro's presence filled the small room and Caterina edged towards the door. "Good night."

Alessandro watched as Caterina walked through the doorway. "Caterina, wait!" Caterina turned and gazed up at Alessandro's troubled features. "I just wondered… I know it is much to ask… but could you ever forgive me?"

"Forgive you for what?"

"For the doves. For the part I played in causing Paolo's fall."

Caterina let out a sigh. Now she understood why he had been acting strangely whenever Paolo's name was mentioned. "Alessandro, I don't blame you. Your gift of the doves brought Paolo much happiness. It was Enrico alone who caused his fall."

Alessandro sighed with relief, but her mention of Enrico reminded him of her escape. "Tell me, how did you find the strength to break down your bedroom door?"

"I thought about Paolo. He deserved so much more. As did I. In the end it was an easy choice. Freedom and love over imprisonment and hate." Alessandro smiled. "And what about you, Alessandro? You didn't run away this time. Have you also discovered how to be free?"

He nodded. "I realised that I didn't need to keep searching anymore. Everything that I need is here in my heart where my soul dwells and my love for you burns." Caterina stilled and looked deep into his eyes. They had known each other for only a week, but in those few days he had shown such kindness to her and the villagers of Santa Sofia. Compassion and courage were two of the characteristics she most admired in a man and Alessandro embodied them both. It was not a difficult decision for Caterina to make that night. She felt no sorrow at her husband's death. Only the gentle stretching of her wings. With a smile, Caterina leant forwards and kissed Alessandro, who held her tightly against him, before lowering her onto the bed. While her body pulsated beneath his touch, Caterina's spirit learnt how it felt to soar high enough to touch the stars, before settling like the first blanket of snow upon the peaks.

Tuesday

17 August 1583

The *Auto-da-fé*

At dawn, Niccolo and Alessandro surveyed the expectant crowd gathered in the square. Climbing up onto a table, Alessandro raised his voice above the noise. "Gather up your weapons, men, and march with us! Our fight for freedom begins!" His cry to arms was met with shouts of support from the villagers. During the night, more groups of men had arrived in carts from the other villages in the diocese. Encouraged by Matteo's news of the revolt, they were eager to join the fight and free their fellow villagers from the fires. The army of men now brandished their weapons high in the air, spades and pitchforks jostling between rifles and axes. Huntsmen, butchers, foresters and farmers moved forward together in one mass of angry intent, following Alessandro down the road that led to Arunca.

The womenfolk stood in their doorways as they passed by, calling out words of encouragement and offering up prayers for the men's safe return. Alone amid the sea of men, Veronica sat high upon a white mare led by Niccolo. Her deep red dress rippled in the gentle breeze, matching the ribbon tied in her hair for protection. Caterina waved at her cousin and wished that she too could go to Arunca, but her place was in the cave of the Black Goddess, keeping her fire alight. Alessandro glanced over his shoulder to seek her out and hold her gaze, before disappearing out of view. Caterina was reminded of their night of passion and smiled to herself, but her happiness was tinged with anxiety over the day's potential outcome.

"Caterina, what should we do?" As the last men rounded the corner, Donata approached her great-niece. She was at a loss like many of the women who now gathered around their wisewoman's assistant. Caterina was touched by the women's need to turn to her in Rosa's wake and assumed her role of wise counsellor with humility and devotion, praying to Sofia to guide her words.

* * * * * * *

Today, the Church Fathers will try to silence Rosa's belief in the divine Mother's strength and passion, because it threatens their ability to control women. If our Blessed Mother were to grow as powerful as she once was through public worship by people like Rosa, the Church would lose much of its power and wealth. The priests are too frightened to follow the true teachings of Christ because then they would have to accept us as their equals. Instead, they burn our wisewomen in their fires to destroy the ancient wisdom of the divine Mother and to keep us women in chains.

We may not have the physical strength to go into battle, but we have the power of our minds, hearts and voices. Bring your children, for we will spend the day in prayer at the Chapel of the Black Madonna. Join me in praying to her for the safe deliverance of Rosa and Luca, and of all our courageous men who are now marching on Arunca in defiance of the Church's corruption and hypocrisy. With each of our prayers, the power of the divine Mother will grow stronger until one day we will no longer have to fight for justice and we will know the true meaning of freedom.

* * * * * * *

The women threw their arms in the air with cries of defiance.

Many reached out to touch Caterina and give thanks for her inspiring words. Then they rushed home to gather their sleepy children and make provisions for the day.

Cristina approached Caterina with a broad smile. "You truly are a she-wolf." Caterina blushed, unaccustomed to her new role. "How's Paolo?"

"He still hasn't woken. Elena is with him, but I would like to take him with us to the chapel. Perhaps if we place him within the circle, our prayers may help to heal him."

"You seem so strong despite everything that's happening. I can't imagine how I would cope if one of my children were so ill."

"I never thought I would," replied Caterina, "but my maternal instinct has summoned up strength I never knew I had."

Cristina nodded. "I'll come back with you. Between us, we can carry Paolo to the chapel and lay him on some blankets." Caterina smiled in gratitude, wondering how she would have coped without the love and support of her family and friends. Together they wandered back to collect Elena from Rosa's house. Wrapping Paolo in a blanket, the three of them then took it in turns to carry him through the woods to Sofia's garden. Maria and Donata followed them, leading the long line of women and children on their pilgrimage to the chapel. There they would spend the day in prayer, nurturing the power of the divine Mother to overthrow the tyranny of the Church, while the men used their physical force to achieve the same end.

Marching along the road that carved its way through the mountainside, Alessandro and his army of men arrived at the last hamlet before the city of Arunca. Their numbers had swollen as they progressed, gathering men from the many small and scattered communities that had fallen victim to Bishop Pazzini's despotism. Some knew the prisoners who were to be burned and were eager to free them. Most simply desired the Bishop to be overthrown so that they could go back to their traditional ways of life.

Alessandro jumped up onto a large boulder, waiting until all the men had gathered in the hamlet's thoroughfare before addressing the now sizeable army. "Friends, it is not long before we'll arrive in Arunca. As we approach the outskirts of the city, disperse into smaller groups and join the crowds of travellers who will have come to watch the spectacle. Once inside the city walls, assume your positions in the streets leading into the main square. By forming a circle around the cardinals and their guards, we will trap them on all sides. Await my signal and then storm the square with all the courage that I know dwells within each of you. May the blessings of the Black Madonna be with us all."

The men responded with a barrage of battle cries, before beginning the last stretch of their march to freedom.

In the Dominican convent in Arunca, Rosa's cell door was pushed open to reveal Bishop Pazzini standing on the threshold. Rosa glanced at him and then looked away in disgust. The narcotic had numbed her pain and although her body was weak, her mind and voice had grown strong once more. "Stand up and look at me, Witch!"

Rosa cast her eyes back at the Bishop. "Why?"

"Because that is my order and you will obey me."

Rosa gave a disdainful snort, her voice rasping. "I don't acknowledge your authority."

Bishop Pazzini turned puce with rage. Never had he encountered such a hag who refused, even after torture, to show him the respect he deserved. Then he remembered that it was he who would triumph in a few hours as she burnt on the stake. "We will see if you beg for mercy when the flames start to lick your feet."

Rosa glared at him. "Never."

"Why?" the Bishop asked with a mocking laugh. "Do you think your goddess will flutter down to save you?"

"She won't rest until she sends her avenging crone to strike you down," Rosa said, her scalded vocal chords crackling.

"This crone you speak of. That's you, I presume?"

"Perhaps."

"And I suppose you have a legion of witches waiting to go into battle with you against the powers of the Holy Mother Church?" asked the Bishop. Rosa smiled to herself, remembering her dream. Niccolo and Alessandro had stormed the burnings with an army of warring countrymen. She had experienced the prophetic nature of her dreams many times and was filled with anticipation. Turning to look out of the high window, she dismissed the Bishop with her silence. Barely able to contain himself from striking the life out of her, Bishop Pazzini forced himself to leave, slamming the door behind him. "Guards! Bring the prisoners to the square." Then, with a flurry of his robes, he marched back to the square to convene with the Inquisitor.

The guards began to open the cell doors, dragging the chained occupants up the stairs. Out in the quadrant, they threw them onto the back of an open cart. Rosa found herself crouched beside Luca, who was unable to prevent his legs from shaking in fear. "Sofia will protect you, Luca."

"Will she? Perhaps this is what I deserve."

Rosa looked at him in surprise, saddened by the loss of his newfound confidence. "Why, Luca?"

"My cousin tried to kill me. My grandmother and aunt handed me over to the Inquisition. If my own family believes that I deserve to die, who am I to disagree?"

Rosa could see the tears of rejection welling up in Luca's eyes and swallowed to soothe her throat before comforting him. "The only reason your mother's relatives are so cruel to you is because they're ashamed of her affair with your father. They need to believe that they are better than other people because they themselves feel worthless. Pity them for their weakness but don't give their opinion of you any credence. Those of us who know you well love you for your kindness, humility and wisdom. Draw strength from our love."

Luca's fear was such that Rosa's words were of little consolation. "Look at me, Rosa. The Black Goddess has cursed me since birth with my affliction. Why would she protect me now?"

"You see your illness as a curse, but I see it as a blessing," Rosa replied, wincing as she coughed. "Those of you born with disabilities are known as star children, keepers of the ancient wisdom who dwell in the Great Star Nation. Your wise, old souls are reborn into the bodies of babies who suffer pain and fear in their first years of life, to ensure that they develop the strength, wisdom and compassion at an early age to become great healers."

"How can I heal others when I'm a wolf?" asked Luca.

"The wolf is the ancient protector of the Black Goddess. Hecate, Artemis and Diana were all accompanied by wolves, who protected the untameable powers they embodied."

"What of my relation to the moon? Doesn't that make me a werewolf?"

"The idea that the full moon causes 'lunacy' was invented by the Church to stop us from holding lunar rites at night. Your response to the moon demonstrates your close relationship with the Black Goddess. If you survive the fires today, you must protect her mysteries, which teach us the true meaning of freedom. Don't be afraid of your wild nature, Luca, embrace it and run with the wolves!"

Luca's eyes shone with the light of hope and rebellion. Then, as the cart drew near to the square, he was reminded of their looming fate. "If only Sofia would give me a second chance, I would serve her all the days of my life, but I fear there is no way of surviving the fires."

Rosa remembered the flask of pain relief Caterina had placed in her dress pocket. Nudging Luca, she gestured to the bottle. As the cart swung round a corner she leant sideways, allowing the bottle to fall into Luca's hands. Grimacing from the pain of his ruptured joints, he hid the bottle beneath the folds of his shirt. "Drink it, Luca. It will numb the pain of the fires. Perhaps it will help to keep you alive, for there is always hope. If your purpose in this lifetime has not been fulfilled, then you will not die today. Pray to Sofia and she will comfort you." Luca nodded and when the guards' eyes were averted, he swallowed the tincture. Within moments he felt his fears drift away and the pain in his body lessen. Then he smiled at Rosa in gratitude for her healing.

As the cart rolled into the main square, Rosa was taken aback by the festive gaiety of the scene. Crowds of people flanked three sides of the square, with the cathedral and a stage seating the assembled dignitaries from the Church and State making up the fourth side. In the centre were the pyres, and a shiver ran through Rosa's body as she surveyed the stakes reaching up high into the blue sky. There was an air of excitement in the crowd, as if it were a festival day of fun and frivolity. Rosa wondered what drove people to enjoy watching their fellow men and women die in such an agonising way. Jugglers and acrobats mingled through the crowd, entertaining the awaiting audience. Peddlers hawked their goods with loud cries, selling flasks of wine and baskets of figs. And children ran about in play, oblivious to the reason for the gathering. Rosa could only wonder sadly at the extent of the Church's power of oration. For it had succeeded not only in persuading many to believe in the existence of witches and in its need to rid society of their evil, but to actually take delight in watching them burn to death. Or perhaps here in the south, where people were more accepting of wisewomen and healers, the assembled spectators were motivated by simple voyeurism.

On the arrival of the cart of prisoners, the crowd became frenzied as people jostled to throw rotten eggs and fruit at them.

Luca ducked as an egg splattered over the woman sitting next to him. He'd grown accustomed to the villagers' increasing acceptance of him, but once more found himself the object of ridicule. "Remember, Luca, Sofia loves you," Rosa said and Luca attempted a smile before lowering his head beneath the barrage of rotten fruit.

At last, the cart pulled to a stop in front of the cathedral. The Inquisitor was seated on a throne high upon a wooden stage. It had been constructed on the steps of the cathedral with a canopy overhead to stave off the heat of the morning sun. On either side of him, the Commission of Cardinals were seated upon similar gilded thrones in their flowing red robes. A selection of minor ecclesiastics and dignitaries of State sat on the step below them. The guards dragged the prisoners out of the cart to stand in front of the high stage. The Inquisitor stood up and raised his hand until silence fell across the square. The moment of abjuration for the accused had arrived. He would use this opportunity to defend the machinations of the Inquisition, and to exhort the assembled crowd to reject the devil and follow the path of the Lord.

* * * * * * *

We are gathered here today to witness our Lord Jesus Christ triumph over the evil forces that have been plaguing our communities. These seven sinners have been found guilty of devil-worship, witchcraft and heresy. By delivering them into the flames, the Holy Office of the Inquisition will drive the devil out of them. However, the Almighty is a merciful father, and like the father of the prodigal son in The Gospel According to Luke, he will forgive those who truly repent.

'I will arise and go to my father, and I will say to him, "Father, I have sinned against heaven and before you; I am no longer worthy

to be called your son; treat me as one of your hired servants.'"
And he arose and came to his father. But while he was yet at a
distance, his father saw him and had compassion, and ran and
embraced him and kissed him. And the son said to him, 'Father, I
have sinned against heaven and before you; I am no longer worthy
to be called your son.' But the father said to his servants, 'Bring
quickly the best robe, and put it on him; and put a ring on his
hand, and shoes on his feet; and bring the fatted calf and kill it,
and let us eat and make merry; for this my son was dead, and is
alive again; he was lost, and is found.'

With the powers of His Holiness the Pope invested in me, I
stand before you sinners a loving father. I willingly embrace your
lost souls so that they may be saved from the torture of hell and
enter the garden of eternal life. The time has now come for you
to recant and to be reconciled to the Church before your bodies
are committed to the flames.

* * * * * * *

The Inquisitor turned to the first accused and listed the charges
against her. Then he gave her the opportunity to admit to the
crimes and beg his forgiveness. Rosa and Luca were last in line. As
they listened to the Inquisitor address each of the other five victims
in turn, Rosa sensed someone watching her. Out of the corner of
her eye, she caught sight of Padre Francesco and her heart leapt.
He was seated on the far right alongside Bishop Pazzini, Emilia and
Agnesa. His face was ashen and his hands trembled as they moved
over his rosary beads. Rosa felt a lump of emotion rising in her
throat but swallowed hard. She would not allow Bishop Pazzini the
satisfaction of seeing her tears. Instead, she averted her eyes from
Padre Francesco and prayed to Sofia for strength and courage.
  "Rosa Lorini?"

The Inquisitor's voice jolted her out of her reverie. It was only Luca and Rosa left now. All the others had been sentenced and led away to be tied to the stakes. Rosa could hear their cries of anguish and protest, and offered up a prayer for them before responding. "Yes?"

"It is my duty under the laws of the Inquisition to offer you one final chance to repent and be reconciled to the Holy Mother Church, so that your departed soul can be delivered up into eternal life. Do you, Rosa Lorini, repent of all your sins and embrace the Roman Church?"

Rosa glared at Bishop Pazzini. "No! I have committed no crime other than to believe in the freedom of women and to defend my role as a priestess of Sofia. I do not acknowledge the authority of the Roman Church owing to its corruption of the true teachings of Christ."

The Inquisitor flinched, before turning to Luca. "Luca Dini, do you repent of your sins and embrace the Roman Church?" Luca faltered, for his recent consumption of the narcotic had begun to enfeeble his mind and numb his limbs. Rosa nudged him, wary that the Inquisitor might discover he had taken some pain relief and delay the time of his burning. Blinking to clear his clouded vision, Luca shook his head. "Answer the question!"

Luca jumped and cried out, "No!"

The Inquisitor shook his head with regret, for in being unable to convert the last two prisoners, he had failed his God. Satan's hold on them was too great. At least through the burning of their flesh, his evil power would be dissolved and the Lord would vanquish once more. "Guards, tie them to the stakes!"

Rosa and Luca were dragged over to the two remaining stakes and lifted up onto the unlit pyres. Rosa glanced down and sighed in relief to see that the faggots were of wood and not the bodies of homosexuals, who were sometimes burned alive as fuel. Two guards held them against the stakes, while others wound ropes around their chests and legs. Then they each collected a flaming torch from their comrades and stood beside the pyres. Sobs of fear from the victims mingled with hysterical cries from the frenzied crowd. None were more vicious than Agnesa and Emilia, who shrieked loudest of all, "Burn them! Burn them!"

Rosa felt her heart begin to pound and her breath to quicken. Looking up at the stage, she searched for Padre Francesco. He was watching her, his face wet with streaming tears. She tried to smile but her lips were trembling too much. The drums began to roll and time seemed to stand still as everyone waited for the Inquisitor to give the signal. Holding a bell up high above his head, he had just begun to lower it when a single gunshot echoed through the square. A pause followed as everyone froze in suspended motion, and then a deafening roar filled the silence. Men poured into the square from every street and alleyway, their faces snarling with aggression. Wielding their weapons high above their heads, they charged through the onlookers who scattered with screams of fear.

Realising they were under attack, Bishop Pazzini was quick to react. In his desperation to see Rosa burn, he ran bellowing towards the guards next to her and Luca's pyres. "Light the fires! Light the fires!" The guards kindled the stacks of dry wood with their torches, sending flames shooting upwards to lick at Rosa and Luca's feet. The wolf-man tried to raise his legs up away from the heat, but Rosa had no strength left to move. Instead, she closed her eyes in agony as the pain of her burning legs seared through her body.

Led by Giorgio and Federico, the army of men reached the inner circle of pyres and began battling with the guards, snatching the burning torches to prevent them from lighting the other fires and untying the victims.

Three men ran through the chaos of fighting, smoke and clashing metal. Each coming from a different direction, they were all focussed on reaching the same point in the middle of the circle. "Mother!" Rosa heard Niccolo's cry only moments before he reached her burning pyre. Leaping through the flames, he began kicking the burning logs from underneath her, soon aided by Alessandro.

As they struggled to untie her bonds, Rosa cried out, "Leave me! Free Luca!"

Alessandro hesitated, catching sight of Luca screaming, and looked to Niccolo. "Go, Alessandro. I am nearly done here." Alessandro nodded and ran over to Luca's pyre, passing Padre Francesco as he rushed towards Rosa.

A man watched Alessandro's progress from the stage and memories of a young man carrying his sister's corpse up the aisle flooded his mind. Bishop Pazzini blinked, unable to believe his eyes, for there before him, leading the rabble lot of revolutionaries, was Isabetta's brother Alessandro. Just at that moment, Giorgio and Federico leapt onto the stage and seized the Bishop by his arms. "Take your hands off me, infidels!" he demanded, but his captors ignored him. The Bishop looked around for help only to find that the stage was surrounded by a large group of angry men imprisoning the Inquisitor and fellow dignitaries. All the guards now sat chained together in various wooden carts, while another wall of men held the braying crowd of onlookers at bay. Glancing back towards Alessandro, the Bishop watched as he succeeded in loosening the rope from the werewolf's legs and carried him down from the pyre.

Alessandro laid Luca on the ground and held his furry hand. Luca opened his eyes and stared at the man who had saved his life a second time, once from loneliness and now from death. "Thank you." His voice was barely audible from fear and shock, but the narcotic had numbed some of the pain in his charred feet and legs.

Alessandro looked down at Luca's bleeding legs, choking on the putrid smell of his burnt flesh. He needed urgent medical care. "I'll fetch Niccolo," said Alessandro, rushing back to where Rosa was lying in Padre Francesco's arms, being tended to by her son.

Niccolo looked up as he approached. "How is he?"

"His feet and legs are badly burnt."

Niccolo was torn, knowing there was little more he could do to save his mother, whose old and tortured body lay dying, and yet unable to leave her. As usual, Rosa solved his dilemma. Reaching out to grasp his arm, she whispered, "Go to Luca. Tell him to run with the wolves and to tell our story." Niccolo looked into the deep, wise pools of his mother's eyes and his own filled with tears. Rosa reached up to caress his cheek and smiled through her tears. "Do this as your mother's last wish."

Niccolo nodded and pulled her into his arms, rocking her against his chest like a child. Then he kissed her forehead. "I love you, Mother."

"And I you." Rosa clasped her son's face against her own and breathed in the smell of his skin for the last time, before resting back in Padre Francesco's arms.

Alessandro looked down with sadness at the old wisewoman. "Thank you for showing me the path to freedom."

Struggling to keep her eyes from closing, Rosa looked up at him. "Take care of Caterina and Paolo for me."

Alessandro smiled, picturing their faces. "I will."

Padre Francesco could see Niccolo battling with the pain of losing his mother and sought to reassure him. "Have no fear. I will take care of her."

With a last look at the face of his dying mother, Niccolo followed Alessandro to where Luca was lying and bent down to take a look at his injuries. "Alessandro, help me to carry him to Tommaso's cart." Between them, they hauled Luca's body to the cart, which was surrounded by a group of men guarding Veronica. Alessandro shouted out and they rushed forward to help lower Luca onto some blankets in the back of the cart. Niccolo rummaged around in his bag to find the medicines he needed. "Veronica, I need your help administering these." Veronica sat beside her brother, holding his hand and murmuring words of encouragement.

Meanwhile, Alessandro surveyed the scene and nodded his head in satisfaction. Everything was in place. The time had at last come to bring his sister's murderer to justice. An image of his grandfather came to mind and he called to his spirit to be with him. As he looked towards the stage, his eyes were drawn to the shrine of the Black Madonna on the distant mountain peak. It reminded him of her superior power in comparison with the weakness of the priests and the Church, and filled him with courage. He prayed to Sofia for guidance and offered himself as her vessel, trusting that whatever was about to happen was meant to be. "Niccolo, I must speak with the Inquisitor now. Can you listen for when Veronica needs to give her evidence?"

Niccolo gave a nod, distracted by tending to Luca, but then it dawned on him what Alessandro was about to do and he called out, "Good luck, my friend."

As Alessandro walked towards the Commission of Cardinals seated upon their thrones, Padre Francesco cradled Rosa in his arms. Her pulse had slowed to a faint beat now and as Padre Francesco stroked her brow, her eyes opened to search his face. With a gentle smile, she murmured in the silence that engulfed them, "You're a good man, Francesco. A true disciple of Christ."

He returned her smile, tears of sadness and loss falling from his eyes. "And you, Rosa, are a beautiful, stubborn wisewoman."

Rosa gave a small chuckle and then coughed, struggling for breath. There was a humming in her ears and her vision began to cloud. Then out of the darkness shone a brilliant light and she felt her spirit rising up towards it, where the Black Goddess Sofia was waiting, arms outstretched in welcome. Rosa smiled and greeted her with reverence. "My Lady".

Padre Francesco heard her words and knew that Rosa's spirit had at last found peace in the arms of Sofia. Laying a gentle kiss on her lips, he gathered her body up in his arms and carried her over to the cart, where a tearful Niccolo laid her next to Luca, and stroked her cheek before pulling a blanket over her face.

Meanwhile, Caterina and Elena had left the women and children of Santa Sofia praying in the chapel garden, to tend to the fire in the cave of the Black Goddess. With Paolo lying on a blanket close by, they added more wood to the fire, stoking the embers until flames began to soar. Then, at the same moment that Rosa's spirit left her body, a gust of wind tore through the cave and blew out the flames. Caterina gasped in dismay and leant forward to blow on the fading embers. Glancing up at the statue, she stilled at the sight of its face, for teardrops of blood were dripping down from Sofia's eyes over her stone cheeks. It was then that Caterina knew that the Black Goddess was in mourning for her priestess Rosa and she cried out in anguish. "No! Rosa! Rosa!"

Elena grasped her by the arms. "Caterina! Stop! What is it?" But Caterina was beside herself now and Elena could only hold her close and rock her, while she gave vent to her pain of losing Rosa and her fears for Paolo.

Time passed until all but a few of the fire's embers had burnt out. Then, in a moment of quiet between Caterina's ragged sobs, a cough was heard, a murmur and then a little voice whispered, "Mamma?"

Caterina's head swung back to Paolo. He was sitting up, rubbing his eyes as if waking from a deep sleep. "Paolo!" she cried and ran over to cradle him in her arms, touching her hands to his face and body, patting him as if to convince herself that he was alive. "How do you feel? Does anything hurt?"

The little boy rubbed the back of his head. "My head's a bit sore. Did I knock it?" Caterina laughed with relief.

"Caterina, look!" Elena pointed to the foot of the statue. "Look, Caterina, the fire!"

Caterina gazed at the flames now dancing within the serpent's body. Looking down at Paolo and then back at Elena, she nodded her head in much the same way that Rosa used to. "Rosa's soul lives on through Paolo. With her spirit guiding him, my son will open pathways for the Black Goddess to walk down." Elena recognised the voice of prophecy, for she had heard Rosa speak it often, and she watched Caterina with pride as she rained kisses on her saviour son's face, while the fire of Sofia burned brightly.

In the main square of Arunca, a hush fell over the crowd of onlookers as they watched the leader of the rebels approach the stage. His men parted, allowing him to climb the steps, but instead of addressing the Inquisitor, the man veered off to the right where Bishop Pazzini was being held. Alessandro stepped with slow deliberation towards his sister's murderer, holding Jacobo's gaze as he had done twenty years before. The Bishop glared back undeterred, prepared to wreak God's vengeance once and for all on the devilish cur. Alessandro came to a halt in front of him. "We meet again, Jacobo. Do you remember me?"

Bishop Pazzini raised his head up high in a condescending manner. "You are the brother of that whore Isabetta I was forced to chastise."

Alessandro swung at the Bishop, striking him in the face with his fist and causing blood to spurt from his broken nose. The Bishop staggered back but was held upright by Giorgio and Federico. Alessandro's breath was coming in short bursts as he struggled to control his temper. "I told you that one day I would find you and I would have my revenge. Now that day is upon us. Before the sun has set, I will see you punished for the crimes you committed against my sister and against all your other victims."

The Bishop let out a harsh laugh, any fear he may have felt

being engulfed by a tide of arrogance. "You will never succeed against the power of the Roman Church."

Alessandro gave a nonchalant shrug. "We will see." Then he walked back to the centre of the stage to stand in front of the Inquisitor, and began to deliver the most important speech of his life, employing all his powers of persuasion and rhetoric.

* * * * * * *

I am Alessandro Bellini and my men come from the villages of Santa Sofia, San Martino and others in the diocese. We are not here to spill blood but to demand justice.

There is a devil in your midst who must be brought before your courts and punished for his crimes. This man is a murderer and an abuser of women. He hides his evil lechery beneath the pious robes of a bishop and is held in high regard by the Roman Church. However, I have heard your priests say that the Inquisition is judicious in all its judgements. Thus I have every faith that once I have presented you with the evidence, you will punish him with the harshest of sentences.

The man whom I speak of raped and murdered my sister Isabetta twenty years ago. There are many here who will vouch that they have heard my story, but alas I can bring you no evidence.

Instead, I have brought you living proof of the severity of this bishop's crimes. Allow me to present Veronica Dini, who suffered a similar fate to that of my sister, but who by chance survived. She will tell you what crimes the bishop committed against her and show you her scars as physical evidence, if you so desire. And by her presence it will become clear that the bishop in question gave false evidence in yesterday's trial, wrongly accusing Rosa Lorini of conjuring a spirit, and thereby causing an innocent woman to die at the stake today.

No doubt you have by now guessed the identity of the priest,

Bishop Pazzini. I ask you to listen to Veronica's story before passing judgement and sending him straight to the galleys.

* * * * * * *

Niccolo led Veronica up the steps and onto the stage. Her legs were trembling, but she lifted her head up high to face the cardinals. The Inquisitor's expression had grown more and more stupefied with Alessandro's every word. On being told the identity of the priest, he had turned to glare at Bishop Pazzini. Whatever this girl had to say, the Inquisitor knew that the peasants would not have staged a revolt without there being a grain of truth in Alessandro's accusations. Something had to have upset them and their leader was an eloquent man. Perhaps it should not surprise him that such charges were being levelled at Bishop Pazzini. He already despised the man for his ready desire to watch people suffer under torture. Turning back to face the young woman standing before him, he nodded for her to commence. Veronica took a shaky breath before telling him about the crimes Bishop Pazzini had committed against her. When she came to the end of her story, she lifted her arms up. "My body still bears the scars and bruises, if you would like to see."

The Inquisitor shook his head. "That won't be necessary. Tell me about the festival night."

"After the attack, I was too scared to go out in case Bishop Pazzini tried to kill me again. The only time I went back to the chapel grounds was on the night of the festival. I wanted to watch the prayers. The Bishop saw me and accused Rosa of conjuring a spirit, but as you can see, I'm no spirit and Rosa was no witch. Bishop Pazzini was lying, Your Eminence, and I beg of you to punish him well. I don't want him to ever hurt me or another woman again." Veronica looked up at the row of listening cardinals. Their faces were filled with horror. Despite the vulgarity of the peasant girl, they could only feel pity for what she had endured. It was bad enough when one of their flock succumbed to the devil, but they were ignorant people on the whole. When one of their own bishops, an educated man given powers of religious authority, was found guilty of such crimes, the Inquisition judged him with much greater severity.

The Inquisitor wiped his trembling hand across his brow, for he had never faced such a difficult decision. Although intimidated by the mob surrounding the stage, he was also aware of his duty to uphold the laws of the Inquisition. He was not in a position to find Bishop Pazzini guilty of the said crimes without more substantial evidence, especially in the presence of the cardinals. If he delivered a false sentence, he could find himself punished for misuse of power. He would have to be seen to follow the correct legal process before capitulating to the men's demands if they became overly aggressive. His decision made, the Inquisitor stood up. The men standing beside him moved to push him down, but Alessandro held up his hand to stay them. "Alessandro and Veronica, I have listened to your grievances and you have my sympathy for the crimes that have been committed against you and your own. However, you must understand that I need more evidence before I can find Bishop Pazzini guilty. I have only your word and you bring no witnesses to testify to the truth of your accusations. Perhaps if you were to return with more evidence, I would be in a better position to bring Bishop Pazzini to justice."

"Lies! They're all lies!" Bishop Pazzini could no longer contain his rage and struggled to break free from Giorgio and Federico's grasp. For the Inquisitor to even contemplate punishing him, a bishop, for doing God's work and ridding the world of whores and witches, was intolerable. As he raged, blood spurted from his broken nose. "That woman Veronica is a concubine of the devil, like all the others were, sent by him to corrupt me. I am guilty of nothing but trying to strike the devil out of her and ridding my diocese of her evil. Clearly my initial attempt did not succeed, but there is still time to light the fires. Guards, seize the whore! Light the fires! Burn her! Burn the witch!"

There was a sharp intake of breath from the cardinals. The Inquisitor glowered in disbelief at Bishop Pazzini, for he had as good as admitted to the crimes but appeared to show no remorse. And he was even trying to govern the proceedings, regardless of the fact that he was the Inquisitor in charge. "What in the name of God are you doing?"

"My Lord Jesus Christ's work, of course. I am a bishop and it is my responsibility to rid the world of any devil-worshipping whore who tempts me from the sanctity of the priesthood."

The Inquisitor turned puce and shook with rage. "The Roman Church does not give you, or any other priest, the authority to make your own judgements and carry out your own punishments. His Holiness the Pope created the Bull Licet ab initio in 1542, to ensure that all those suspected of heresy and witchcraft were given a fair trial by the courts of the Inquisition. Nearly forty years have passed since bishops lost the right to uproot heresy themselves. Still you have taken it upon yourself to vilify a cardinal dogma of the Roman Church. Jacobo Pazzini, do you or do you not accept the authority of the Holy Office of the Inquisition over and above your role as bishop?"

Unable to tolerate the patronising manner in which the Inquisitor was reprimanding him, Bishop Pazzini turned on him. "You dare to criticise me for carrying on God's work, when you are but a snivelling lover of heretics? Before I came to Arunca, you hadn't found a single witch guilty of devil-worship. It was also clear you found torturing them abhorrent. I wonder why? Perhaps because you yourself are in the devil's grasp?"

Cries of disbelief filled the stage. Everyone turned from listening to the Bishop to watch how the Inquisitor would respond to his accusation. A long silence followed as the Inquisitor struggled to control his fury. Then, through gritted teeth, he addressed the Bishop. "As Inquisitor, my authority comes straight from His Holiness the Pope. Thus, in accusing me of devil-worship, you also accuse His Holiness." The Inquisitor paused to allow the severity of his words to take their toll. "Jacobo Pazzini, with these Lord Cardinals here present as witnesses to your confession and foul accusations, I find you guilty of formal apostasy to the devil and formal heresy against the Roman Church and His Holiness the Pope. You will be sentenced anon."

"Never!" cried the Bishop.

"Silence!" The roar of the Inquisitor's voice was sufficient to quieten even the Bishop, who glared at him in response. The Inquisitor then turned to Alessandro, who was having difficulty hiding his satisfaction. "Alessandro, it would seem that you need bring me no further evidence. By his own admission, Bishop Pazzini took it upon himself to castigate Veronica and, no doubt, your sister Isabetta. Abuse of religious authority is a very serious crime. You can rest assured that Bishop Pazzini will be dealt with most severely. Before I consult with the Commission of Cardinals, perhaps you would care to make explicit your demands?"

Alessandro glanced over at Niccolo, who nodded, granting him the freedom to speak for them.

* * * * * * *

I speak on behalf of all the men and women of Santa Sofia, San Martino and the surrounding villages, when I urge you to mete out the harshest of sentences to Bishop Pazzini.

On account of his use of false evidence and witnesses during the trials of the accused, we desire you also to pardon all those who were sentenced here today, especially Rosa Lorini and Luca Dini.

Thirdly, the villagers of Santa Sofia request that Francesco

Lorini be reinstated as their village priest. He has committed no crime other than to challenge Bishop Pazzini's tyranny.

We also desire Emilia Cesi and Agnesa Gamba to be punished for their false accusations and witness statements against Rosa Lorini and Luca Dini. Perhaps a long stay in the Dominican convent's cells would be appropriate.

Lastly, we ask that the Church respects our right to maintain our traditional ways of life and worship, without fear of arrest or torture or death. We are peaceful folk by nature and seek only justice and the freedom to live our lives as we choose.

* * * * * * *

Alessandro came to the end of his list of demands and stood waiting for the Inquisitor's reaction. The villagers had risked much storming the burnings. All his hopes were founded on the knowledge that the Church was aware of losing favour with people in the wayward south, and should therefore seek to appease rather than challenge dissent.

The Inquisitor inclined his head in response to Alessandro's requests. Then he turned to speak with the cardinals, who gathered around him to confer. A tense silence followed as the expectant crowd awaited their decision, trying to divine their opinions from the grim set of their faces and the nodding of their heads. When the Inquisitor was satisfied that there was a consensus among the Commission, he raised his voice for all to hear. "Countrymen of Arunca. On behalf of His Holiness the Pope and the Roman Church, the Commission of Cardinals and I accept your demands. Upon God's holy book, I hereby reinstate Francesco Lorini as priest of Santa Sofia."

On the back of Tommaso's cart, Luca grasped Padre Francesco's hand and held it up high in triumph, while the men of Santa Sofia roared their approval. Padre Francesco gave a sad smile, his joy at being able to continue to share Christ's true teachings marred by his knowledge that Rosa would no longer accompany him in leading the festival of prayers.

With a nod of his head in recognition of Padre Francesco, the Inquisitor continued. "With the power vested in me, I pardon all those found guilty of witchcraft and heresy today, owing to the false evidence given by Bishop Pazzini at their trials."

"No!" Bishop Pazzini cried, his eyes bulging from their sockets and his mouth foaming with spittle.

The Inquisitor glared at him then stepped forward to speak in private with Alessandro. "With my guards somewhat indisposed, could I ask some of your men to accompany the prisoners to their cells?"

Alessandro nodded, wondering how a man of such a gentlemanly disposition could commit such atrocities in the name of God. "Be my guest."

"Thank you." The Inquisitor addressed the men guarding the stage. "Take Bishop Pazzini, Emilia Cesi and Agnesa Gamba to the convent and lock them in the cells. They will be sentenced tomorrow." A pause followed the Inquisitor's words, then the square erupted as the men threw their fists in the air with triumph, roaring their approval. Niccolo pulled Veronica into his arms as she wept in relief, before leading her back to the safety of Tommaso's cart, where they found Luca smiling in delight, despite his wounds.

As the men began to gather for their victorious march home and the cardinals staggered down from the stage to free the guards, a lone figure stood in the middle of the square. With his face and palms turned towards the sky, Alessandro gave thanks to the spirit of his grandfather and to the Black Goddess Sofia for guiding his words and actions, at last bringing him to victory. Lowering his eyes from the heavens, he stared over at Jacobo Pazzini as Giorgio and Federico dragged him away to his prison cell, and gave a deep sigh. It was done. Justice had at last been served. After twenty years, he could now lay Isabetta's troubled spirit to rest. With a final nod of satisfaction, Alessandro walked back to the cart where the men were gathering. A cheer went up as he approached, the men reaching out to clap him on the back and give him thanks.

Alessandro leapt up onto the back of the cart to face them. "Today we stand victorious. Every one of you has made that triumph possible. Go home to your families and feel proud of the courage you have displayed here today. But let us not forget the bravery of one woman in particular. Rosa Lorini, the wisewoman of Santa Sofia, gave her life here today in defiance of the hypocrisy and abuse that hides in the name of religion. Let us be jubilant in our triumph, but let us show Rosa the respect she deserves and carry our wisewoman home for burial." Alessandro's words were met with a collective hailing of Rosa's name, and he looked behind him to see Niccolo and Padre Francesco sitting in the cart beside Rosa's covered body, tears of pain and pride flowing down their cheeks. Alessandro embraced them both in turn, thanked Veronica for her courage and clasped Luca's hand with affection, before leading the long march home.

In the chapel garden, the women and children were offering up prayers of thanksgiving for Paolo's safe deliverance. Lying in his mother's lap, Paolo seemed quite bemused by the events that had befallen him, but he was relieved to hear about his father's death. At least his mother would now be safe.

In the silence of prayer, a cry rang out from the trees as Giorgio burst through the garden gate, followed by Dionisio and the rest of the triumphant warriors. The women ran to greet their men folk, relieved to find them all accounted for and eager to hear their news. Cries of delight filled the garden as they learned of the men's success in storming the burnings and bringing Bishop Pazzini to justice.

Alessandro was one of the last to arrive. Standing on the raised path, he surveyed the scene, searching for Caterina, and smiled with a lover's joy on seeing her seated on the chapel steps with Paolo in her lap. As he drew near, Paolo turned his head to smile up at his mother and Alessandro felt his eyes well with relief. He was awake. Paolo was awake. Rushing forward, Alessandro swept them both up in his arms, planting kisses on their foreheads and causing Paolo to squeal. Caterina laughed with joy and reached up to caress Alessandro's cheek as he set them back down on the step. "We did it, Caterina! We did it!"

"No, you did it, Alessandro. Without you, the villagers would never have found the courage to revolt."

"And without them, I would never have been able to bring my sister's murderer to justice." Planting a gentle kiss on Caterina's lips, he then turned his attention to Paolo. "How are you feeling?"

"My head is a little sore."

"I'm not surprised. Only a soldier could have fallen that far and lived to tell the tale." Alessandro smiled down at Paolo, who reached out to grasp his hand. Touched by the gesture, Alessandro scooped him up in his arms and turned to survey the crowd of elated villagers.

"Where's Luca?" asked Caterina.

"We left him resting in the consulting room. His legs are badly burnt, but Niccolo thinks he will walk again."

Veronica arrived at the gate, followed by Padre Francesco and Niccolo. High on their shoulders they carried Rosa's body wrapped in white sheets. The sight reminded Alessandro that he still hadn't told Caterina of Rosa's tragic death. "Caterina, there's something I must tell you."

Caterina looked into the distance, her eyes welling with grief. "I know. Rosa is dead."

Only four days had passed since the wisewoman had taught

Alessandro the true meaning of freedom, but it felt to him like a lifetime lay between then and now. Cradling Caterina in the arc of his arm, Alessandro watched with her as the crowd before them parted, allowing Rosa's body to be carried to the chapel. The villagers fell to their knees in prayer, asking the Black Madonna to accept the departed soul of their wisewoman into her garden of paradise. Veronica led Padre Francesco and Niccolo to the steps of the chapel, where Caterina motioned for them to follow her. "Come. Elena and I have prepared the funeral pyre." Padre Francesco and Niccolo glanced at each other. They knew Caterina meant the fire in the sacred cave. Rosa had devoted her life to tending Sofia's fire and it seemed only fitting that her body be returned to the divine light that had given birth to her wisdom and compassion. Nodding their heads in assent, they carried her body down the tunnel and into the cave of the Black Goddess. The flames of the fire at the foot of the statue burned brightly as Rosa's body was lowered onto the pyre. Caterina stepped forward, flanked on either side by Padre Francesco and Niccolo. "Blessed Mother, Sofia, Black Goddess of Wisdom, we offer the body of your priestess Rosa into your sacred fire and pray that her soul will be reborn once more from your fertile womb. Blessed be."

Reappearing on the chapel steps, Caterina found the villagers still kneeling in prayer, many in tears. "Come, don't be sad for there is much to celebrate. In giving of her life, Rosa achieved that to which we should all aspire. She remained true to herself and to our Blessed Mother. Today we have witnessed how the love of the divine Mother will ultimately vanquish over the violence carried out in the name of God. Let us return to the village square to celebrate Rosa's life and the divine Mother whom she loved." Encouraged by Caterina's words, the villagers started to climb back through the woods to the square. There, Dionisio and

Federico set about preparing the funereal *fava* bean soup and wine for them to feast on. Veronica and Niccolo followed behind the others, while Padre Francesco and Paolo brought up the rear at the slow pace of an old man and a young boy.

Only Alessandro and Caterina were left in the chapel garden, and he stared into the depths of her blue eyes. "I'm so proud of you. What courage you have shown."

"Only with your help, for which I am grateful."

Alessandro shook his head. "I think you would have stretched your wings without my encouragement."

"Perhaps. But I am glad to have met you." Caterina smiled up at Alessandro as he gathered her into his arms.

Just then, there was a fluttering in the sky and Alessandro glanced over Caterina's shoulder to see the blackest of ravens perched upon the chapel bell tower. The raven stared down at him for several moments before flying off into the distance, her liberated soul silhouetted against the light of the waning moon.

The Nurse's Tale

15 August 1999

The Festival of the Assumption

London, England

When the old man finished his story, he stared into the flames of the fire. All around him, my ancestors waited with countless questions to ask him when he at last looked up.

"Tell us, what of the Bishop?"

"And Alessandro?"

"Were Emilia and Agnesa punished?"

"What of the boy Paolo?"

The old storyteller chuckled, holding up his hands to quieten their excited questioning. "If I could have another cup of wine to warm my aching legs, then I will tell you what happened to the people of Santa Sofia and the Bishop." When the old man had finished his drink, he told them the fate of his friends.

* * * * * * *

The Inquisitor upheld the oath he had sworn on the day of the burnings. He sentenced Bishop Jacobo Pazzini to life imprisonment on the galleys of a Papal ship. This was the harshest of punishments, for life in the galleys was a living hell. Chained to the oars without respite, the convicts were given little water and food. They often died from exhaustion with the oar still in their hands. Such was the fate of the priest who had taken delight in torturing Isabetta, Veronica, Rosa and the many others we will never know about.

His conspirators to perjury, Emilia and Agnesa, were sentenced to life imprisonment in the cells of the Dominican convent. There they spent their last years and to all accounts went quite mad. It is said that on the nights when the maiden moon shines her light, their screams can still be heard echoing through the cloisters.

Padre Francesco was reinstated as priest of Santa Sofia and continued to lead the villagers in their prayers. Caterina joined him each year on the night of the Festival of Santa Sofia, assuming Rosa's role as priestess of the Black Goddess, assisted by Elena and Veronica.

Padre Francesco asked Caterina's permission to train Paolo for the priesthood. Caterina was reticent until Padre Francesco reminded her of the significance of Paolo reawakening on the third day. Like the divine Son in religious myth who was sacrificed and reborn on the third day to ensure the regeneration of life, Padre Francesco believed Paolo's fall and reawakening on the third day was linked to the villagers' safe deliverance. Caterina agreed to his request, understanding how Rosa's spirit would live on through her son, for Paolo would become a priest like Padre Francesco, continuing the tradition of worshipping Sofia as the Christian Goddess and promoting the true teachings of Christ from within the Church. Although the role of priestess outside the confines of the Church was essential if change was to be brought about, Caterina had to accept the prevailing existence of the Church and therefore the necessity of nurturing priests who recognised the value of the feminine divine. And so Paolo was ordained, and on Padre Francesco's death took his place as priest of Santa Sofia. There were several years when mother and son led the villagers' prayers together on the night of the Festival of Santa Sofia, until Caterina's body fell silent and was offered into the fire of the Black Goddess.

Veronica took Caterina's place as priestess of the Black Goddess, when the bloodline came to a halt with the passing of Elena, leaving the responsibility with Niccolo's wife and their daughters. Niccolo thought it poignant that his wife should dedicate her life to serving Sofia just like his mother Rosa had done, but he was old by then and soon left Veronica on her own, a widowed wisewoman. She was so proud of him and delighted in telling their daughters about all his achievements. He had become a well-known doctor, often employed by the central tribunal of the Holy Inquisition in Rome to give a physician's statement regarding the accused. Through his evidence, he succeeded in saving many a poor victim from suffering torture and death by burning.

What can I tell you of Alessandro? Only that he no longer felt a need to wander the mountains in search of some elusive fulfilment. Having discovered the true meaning of freedom, he settled in Santa Sofia where he lived the rest of his days with Caterina and Paolo, entertaining the villagers with stories and songs on cold winter evenings like tonight. And this was the song he sang in homage to Sofia, Black Goddess of Wisdom.

> Sofia, sweet bride,
> Maiden of mine,
> I can hear your bells
> Heralding springtime,
> May your fires that burn brightly
> Inspire my words,
> Bringing forth your wisdom
> Into this world.
>
> Sofia, sweet bride,
> Lady of springs,
> I can feel your breath
> Upon the swan's wings,
> May your waters of healing
> Purify my soul,

And your serpent and wolf
Protect us all.

Sofia, sweet bride
Of the sun and moon,
I can see your white dawn
Shining through,
As the darkness of winter
Gives way to your light,
May your blessings be upon us
This day and this night.

* * * * * * *

On finishing his song, the storyteller pushed himself up from his chair and bowed in acknowledgement as the villagers stood to applaud him. Then he donned his coat, pulling his fur hat down over his long, white hair. "My thanks for your warm hospitality on this cold winter's night."

With his sack and guitar upon his back, he hobbled over to the door to continue his journey, but just as he was reaching for the latch, the innkeeper called out. "Storyteller, you forgot to tell us of Luca. What became of the wolf-man?"

The old man paused for a moment. "Once he had recovered from his injuries, Luca did as the dying priestess Rosa had bade him. In praise of the Black Goddess who had spared his life, he ran with the wolves, travelling far and wide, and protecting her mysteries by telling their story to those he met along the way. Alessandro was proved right for with every rendition of the songs of old, Luca found welcome wherever his path led him."

Then the old man was gone, shutting the door of the *taverna* behind him. The villagers settled down to discuss the story when, all of a sudden, the lamenting howl of a wolf filled the room as the full moon shone her light through the open casement.

They found his body a week later, nestled among the rocks on top of the mountain peak. There were paw prints of a large wolf in the snow around him, but Luca's body had not been touched. He is still remembered on the night of the full moon, when they say you can hear the howl of a wolf on the wind. And every second of February, his story of the Black Goddess and the people of Santa Sofia is retold, to remind us that however dark the cave may seem, there is always a flicker of light waiting to guide you to freedom.

The Mother's Tale

15 August 2008

The Festival of the Assumption

The Island of Gozo, Malta

I awoke the following morning beside my daughter's incubator, and went out into the corridor to find the nurse who had entertained me with her story of Santa Sofia. "Excuse me, where is the night nurse? Rosetta?"

"Rosetta? You must be mistaken, dear. There is no nurse by that name here anymore."

"Anymore?"

"A nurse called Rosetta used to work here. An old Italian lady, but she died last August. That's her over there." The nurse pointed to a photograph on the wall, from where the face of my storyteller gazed down at me.

I felt a shiver run through my body and whispered my gratitude to the soul of the wisewoman who had spoken to me in my dreams. I have never forgotten her story. In fact, my attempt to write it down became my salvation over the ensuing nine years. Nine more operations, countless invasive tests and pain on a daily basis. Not only did my daughter Sophia have to endure all of this, but in my role as her carer I had to inflict pain on her at an age when she couldn't understand. When she could only look at me with eyes full of betrayal.

And now we are here at the ancient Gozitan temple dedicated to the divine Mother and Daughter, to celebrate our nine years of journeying together. As we scatter the corn from our harvest dolls onto the bleached, white stones, I ask Sophia what it is that she is grateful for. "My pain because it has helped me to understand other people's pain. My operations because they have made me strong. My family and friends for taking care of me. And the Goddess, for teaching me that I'm never alone."

I hold her in my arms and we sob together from the depths of our souls. It is an unspoken acknowledgement of the journey we have shared and a letting go of the pain so that we can both be reborn today. Then she turns and reaches for the Flame of Avalon, a flame of peace created from many sacred world flames, including a burning torch from the fires of Hiroshima. "Mummy, the candle. We must say a prayer for peace." I smile with humility at the child who understands what it means to suffer, and light the candle as we pray together for union. For it is only when each person aspires to unite their feminine and masculine psyche as a whole; when women and men meet as equals in society; when Goddess is revered as highly as God, that the world has any hope of peace.

Sophia blows out the candle and we make our way towards the entrance of the temple. We have been journeying with the Black Harvest Goddess Demeter and her daughter Persephone since my daughter's birth at their festival time nine years ago, and now it is time to be reborn from their most ancient temple into a new stage of our lives. One in which my daughter wants to let go of her fear and I want to find the courage to tell our story.

We hold hands and look deep into each others' blue eyes. "I love you, Sophia. Thank you for shining your light into the dark corners of my soul and teaching me the true meaning of freedom."

She smiles her beautiful, enchanted smile. "I love you, too, Mummy. Come on, let's go." And she pulls me through the temple gateway, birthing me, releasing me. And we run with the wolves. We run to freedom.

Annabel Du Boulay, Gozo, Malta, August 2008